CONCEALED CARGO

FBI-K9 Series - Book 3

JODI BURNETT

"Let it not be said that I was silent when they needed me." - William Wilberforce

This book is dedicated to all victims of human trafficking. I hope to bring exposure to your plight. The more people are aware, the more we all can help with prevention along with healing and recovery. We see you, and we care.

Human Trafficking Definition:
Human trafficking is the use of force, fraud or coercion to exploit individuals for financial gain against their will. At the time of this writing, they estimate there are over 40.3 million victims of trafficking around the world today. There are two main types: sex trafficking and labor trafficking.

Concealed Cargo
CHILDREN FOR SALE

Jodi Burnett

Chapter One

✿❧❀

The familiar surge of adrenaline sprinted up Clay's spinal column as he and his partner waved down a low-rider El Camino towing a small, orange and white rental trailer. He took a deep breath and his shoulders stretched the fabric of his dark blue T-shirt emblazoned with FBI-K9 in bright yellow letters across his chest. All night, he and his K9 partner Ranger, an all-black Belgian Malinois, along with a group of Colorado State Troopers, had been operating a sobriety check-point for vehicles driving into Denver on I-70 from the eastern side of the state. In truth, he worked as a member of a joint FBI, state, and metropolitan police task-force, and they had an ulterior motive. Though, getting drunks off the road was a valid use of time, their true mission was looking for vehicles used for human trafficking.

A warm breeze blew dust across the dark highway that cut a straight east-to-west path through the Colorado farm lands between the Kansas border and Limon. The driver they flagged over rolled down his window using an old-fashioned turn crank, dating the car. "What the hell, man? Why did you stop me? I wasn't speeding."

Clay approached the driver's side, one hand on the butt of his gun and his other on the lead attached to Ranger's vest. "License and registration, please."

"What for? You assholes can't just pull me over for no reason. I got rights."

So he was playing the rights card, was he? Clay refrained from laughing. "License and registration, please."

"Why'd you pull me over, officer? You gotta tell me that. That's the law."

"Is it?"

"Shit." The man reached for the glove compartment and riffled through some papers. "I must have forgot to put it back after I cleaned out my car."

"Do you have a driver's license?" Clay remembered this old routine from his years as a police officer before becoming an FBI agent.

"I left my wallet at home."

"Where's home?"

"Kansas."

"What is your name?"

"Bob Smith."

"Right. Well, Bob Smith, have you been drinking tonight?"

"No, man. I'm driving."

A trooper approached the El Camino from the passenger's side and shined his flashlight into the car. The driver jumped when he noticed the beam.

Clay proceeded. "Mr. Smith, will you please step out of your vehicle?"

"You got no reason to harass me. I'm not getting out. I know what happens to a brother when he gets out."

Clay sighed. "I smell alcohol. I'd like you to perform a field sobriety test. Please, step out of your vehicle, sir."

"Oh, here we go. No officer, I told you, I haven't been drinking."

"Step out of your car, sir."

"Shit." The man clicked his door latch open and stuck one foot out. He glanced at the state cop with the flashlight standing on the other side.

Clay stepped back to give the man some room. "Thank you, sir. Please stand with your feet together." He drew a pen from the side pocket of his utility pants and held it in front of the man's face. "Keeping your head still, follow the movement of this pen with your eyes."

Not surprisingly, the driver's eyes jerked to track the motion.

"Now, I'd like you to take nine steps toward the rear of your car, turn and take nine steps back. Watch your feet and count your steps out loud."

Ranger watched the man's every move, and a low growl rumbled in his chest as the man neared the end of the El Camino, approaching the trailer. With each step, the driver swayed, but he completed the walk, and he returned to his spot in front of Clay. Ranger ignored the man then, and pressed his weight against the lead.

"Now, please stand with your feet together and your arms down at your sides, then raise one foot and count to ten."

"This is such bullshit." The driver clapped his hands to his thighs dramatically and raised one boot. "One, two, three—"

Ranger's growl built into a fierce bark. The man jumped backward. "Hey, that doesn't count! Your attack dog scared the shit out of me."

Whatever agitated Ranger about the trailer drew Clay's attention. He returned his gaze to the driver. "Please, face your vehicle and place your hands on the roof."

"Like hell." The man reached behind his back, shoved his baggy shirt aside, and whipped out a handgun.

"Gun!" Clay yelled. Adrenaline filled his nerves and shot through his brain. As the word formed in Clay's mouth, his Malinois lunged at the man's arm. Snarling, he clamped down into his flesh with vice-like fangs. The driver screamed as the dog pulled him off his feet. Clay tore the gun from the man's hand.

"*Pust,*" he ordered Ranger, as a calm professionalism replaced his racing pulse. Ranger released the man's arm, but remained on guard, growling with menace. Clay flipped the guy over and pressed his knee into the small of his back, pinning him to the ground until he could get his wrists cuffed together. Lifting him to his feet, Clay pushed the driver's chest against the side of his car, and frisked him for other weapons. The state trooper stood by, his weapon drawn and ready.

"Mr. Bob Smith, or whoever you are, you are under arrest for assault with a deadly weapon against an officer of the law, for resisting arrest, and driving while under the influence of alcohol." He handed the man off to the state cop. "Read him his rights and get him outta here. I'll check his car." Clay pointed his flashlight into the cab of the El Camino, searching the floor, seats, and compartments for more weapons, drugs, or any other incriminating evidence.

Ranger sat down next to the trailer and barked.

"Good boy, Ranger. Good dog."

Ranger barked twice more, then he lay down and whined.

"What is it, boy? We've got something in that trailer, don't we?" Clay followed the beam of his mag-light. He checked the hitch and the tires on his way to the back opening. He called out to the trooper. "Hey, you got any bolt cutters in your squad car?"

"Yes, sir. Hold on." The trooper secured the man in the

back seat of his silver-and-black Charger, then hurried to his trunk. He jogged over to Clay with the requested tool.

"Snap that lock." Clay pointed to a padlock holding the door closed.

The trooper cut through the lock and removed it. Clay undid the hinge and pulled the trailer door open. A putrid odor oozed out from the compartment. He took a step backward, wrinkling his nose against the offensive smell. Bile burned the back of his esophagus, and her eyes watered. He coughed as he flashed his beam inside the trailer. Five pairs of startled eyes stared out at him from the dark. Clay's gut tightened as if someone punched him, and his throat thickened. "Oh my, God."

The cop next to him covered his nose and mouth with his hand and took two steps back. Ranger sat down next to Clay's left boot.

"Okay, all of you, come on out of there."

No one moved.

"Come on. One at a time." Clay passed his light to his partner and held his hand out to the nearest, smallest child. A little girl. "Hey, you're going to be okay. I'm Agent Jennings with the FBI. You're safe now. Come on out."

Tears spilled over her dirty cheeks and a slightly older girl sitting next to the little one nudged her with her elbow. "May as well do as he says. He's a cop with a gun. He'll shoot you if you don't do what you're told."

Clay scrunched his brows together. "I'm not shooting anyone. I'm here to help you."

A hardened female voice rolled out from deep inside. "Oh, sure. You're no different from any other man. Pretend to be nice and then take what you want. It don't matter, 'cuz no one will believe what we say, anyhow."

Clay glanced at his partner who shrugged in return. He

tried again. "We want to help you. How long have you been locked in this trailer?"

"Since last night." A small hand slid into Clay's large outstretched one. He wrapped his fingers around the fragile bones. The thin girl stepped out of the compartment, knocking over a coffee can full of human waste. It fell onto the ground splashing the girl's bare feet and Clay's boots. She peered up at him, her eyes huge with fear.

"Hey, it's okay." Clay's heart wrenched. "The spill was just an accident. Is that where all of you have had to go to the bathroom this whole time?"

The small girl chewed her bottom lip and nodded.

"My God. Come on everyone, get out of there. You've gotta get some fresh air." He turned to the cop. "Call this in. We need to get these kids to safety. Call a bus."

With his gun still in his hand, the state trooper pressed the radio on his shoulder and called in for back-up and an ambulance.

Clay lined the five girls up by the side of the trailer. The oldest couldn't have been more than fourteen. They wore a smattering of cast-off clothing, only three of them had shoes. They all reeked of human excrement and body odor. "We're going to take you somewhere safe and get you cleaned up. But, while we're waiting, can you tell me about the man who drove you here?"

None of the girls spoke. The littlest one looked up at the tallest, who glared back. An obvious warning to keep her mouth shut.

"Where did you come from?"

Nothing.

Ranger left Clay's side and approached the small barefoot girl. He bumped her hand with his nose and then ran his tongue across her skin. The girl stared at the dog as he licked her fingers and she glanced up at Clay. He nodded his approval, and she rubbed Ranger's head. Ranger reached up and nuzzled her cheek. A slight laugh escaped her mouth before she threw her thin arms around the dog's neck and squeezed tight. The little girl burst into sobs and she fell to her knees, leaning into Ranger who seemed to have forgotten his identity as fierce attack dog. He apparently understood the child's vulnerability as instinctively as he perceived imminent threats.

Sirens cut into the quiet night as two more police cars and an ambulance pulled up, lights flashing. The arriving officers spoke with Clay's counterpart. They set up floodlights to brighten the scene and aid in the investigation. Clay helped the paramedics with the girls who treated them for minor cuts and bruises. Fortunately, none had injuries that merited a lights and sirens trip to the hospital.

A large ten-passenger van with several bench seats in back arrived next. A slender woman of average height climbed out and spoke to the state trooper in charge of securing the scene. She shoved a handful of long, unruly auburn curls behind her ear as she flashed him her ID. He nodded, and allowed her to pass. The woman made her way directly to the ambulance, first talking with the paramedic, and then the oldest girl.

Clay approached the cop he'd been working with. "Who's the redhead?"

"That's Eloise Clark—social worker extraordinaire—and don't even think about going there."

"What do you mean?"

"Don't get me wrong. She's an amazing advocate for kids like these, but she can be a pain in the ass, and she's a cold fish."

Clay chuckled. "I know the type. Social justice—hates men—and all that?"

"Yeah." The cop chuckled. "She has an enormous heart

for street kids though, so we put up with her sticking her nose in more places than she should."

"Will she take the girls?"

"Yeah, she'll go with them to the hospital to get them fully checked out, but this late at night, she'll have to bring them to the station for processing. In the morning she'll try to place them in homes until she can find their parents, or whatever."

"What a nightmare—poor kids."

"At least we found them before they were forced to sell themselves to the creeps coming into town for the pre-season Bronco game."

"Football's a big draw?"

"Yeah. All professional sports events bring the sicko's and perverts out. The Stock Show in January is one of the worst though. Rich cattlemen in Denver for weeks, holding parties and ordering prostitutes."

"But the littlest girl—she must only be ten or eleven."

"Welcome to the disgusting underbelly of vice, Agent Jennings."

Clay clenched his jaw. "We need to shut this shit down."

Chapter Two

R anger leapt into his kennel in the back of Clay's SUV. They drove to the police department to meet up with the arresting officer and process the dirt-bag trafficker that had pulled a gun on them. Clay hated paperwork, but he'd pitch in and do his part. After that, he and Ranger could call it a night. He didn't know how much rest he'd get though, because the thought of that small girl being manhandled by some pervert refused to leave his conscience alone. *How many more girls like her are out there on the streets tonight?*

They drove to the sub-station and went inside to wait for the cop to bring in the perp. Various riff-raff crowded the intake area, from the drunk and disorderly to petty criminals, pimps and prostitutes. All cussed and complained that they were innocent of their numerous crimes. Body odor and stale smoke made it hard to breathe as Clay walked with the officer past the crowd and heard the telltale deep rumble coming from Ranger's throat. Clay held the same distrusting opinion as his K9 partner of the menagerie of low-lifes.

The cop guided the suspect to the holding cell before

finding his way to a computer to file his report. Clay noticed the social worker he'd seen at tonight's bust. She bent over one of the girls, and wiped her face with gentle strokes of a washcloth. The youngest one who'd held his hand at the scene, saw him and perked up. She sent him a tentative wave. Something sharp deep inside pierced his heart and made his eyes sting. Clay hadn't spent much time around children. His kid sister had a couple, but they lived in Michigan and he never saw them. This little girl stirred a primal protective urge inside him. He smiled at her through the processing room's window, but Ranger trotted inside.

The social worker looked up. Her brow furrowed at the dog sniffing the child. One dark-red brow rose as her gaze moved up to study Clay.

"Hi." Clay followed his dog. "Don't worry, these two are old friends."

"Who are you? I've never seen you around here before."

"Agent Jennings, FBI." He offered her his best charming smile and held out his hand, but she turned back to her task of washing the girl's face. "I don't usually work from this PD, I'm a part of a joint task-force." He winked at the child petting his dog's silky ears, but spoke to the woman. "And you are?"

She glanced at him. "My name is Eloise Clark. I'm a social worker with Denver County Social Services."

"Nice to meet you. I hear you do an impressive job with kids like these."

"Like these? What do you mean by that, Agent Jennings?" She stood to face him.

Suddenly unsure, he rocked back on his heels. Obviously he'd insulted her somehow, but he couldn't figure out why. *Something I said?* "I'm not sure what I did to piss you off, Ms. Clark, but I just wanted to say 'good work'." He clipped his lead to Ranger's vest. "I'll leave you to it." He nodded to the girl. "Ranger, *kemne*." With a last lick to the girl's chin, Ranger obeyed Clay's command, and together they turned to go.

"Hey—wait, I'm sorry, Agent Jennings." The fluorescent lighting gave Eloise's pale skin a ghostly glow. Faint freckles dusted the bridge of her nose, spilling onto her cheeks. "I shouldn't have been short with you. I'm frustrated because I can't find housing for these girls tonight which means they'll have to stay here, in a jail cell."

"Isn't there a home, or something?" Clay was woefully uninformed about this side of crime.

"Nothing's available right now." Her hazel eyes grew earnest, and she tucked an errant strand of curls behind her ear. "They did nothing wrong and they've already been treated worse than animals, and now they have to be caged up again."

Clay stepped back into the room. "I agree it doesn't seem right, but at least here they'll be safe." He looked into the youthful faces. "Have you girls had something to eat?"

The older girl crossed her arms over her chest and jerked her head back and forth when she spoke. "Look, mister. We don't need your help. Just give us some cab fare and we'll be outta here. Me and my sisters have a home to go to. You can't put us in jail, we didn't do nothing."

Clay stared at the adolescent pretending to be tough. "Why were you girls in the trailer?"

"We were just hitching a ride. That's all. We don't even know the man who was driving us. And you can't lock us in jail unless you're arresting us."

"We want to help you."

"Oh sure, you do. I know what you want. What every man wants. Leave us alone unless you've got cash."

Clay cocked his head. What a sad way for a fourteen-year-old girl to view men.

Eloise moved to his side, and pressing his arm, turned him

toward the door. Quietly, she murmured. "Don't take it personally. That comment comes from her life experience. Thanks for rescuing these girls, Agent Jennings. I've got it from here."

"Clay."

Eloise's russet brows scrunched together, and she cocked her head to the side.

"My name—it's Clay."

"Oh." She offered him a brief smile. "You can call me El. I prefer it to Eloise. Have a good night, Clay." El turned back to the girls as she closed the door behind him.

Clay returned to the desk of the cop processing the scum-bag who had drawn his gun on them. *Bob Smith's* arm sported a bandage where Ranger apprehended him. The way the guy held himself, hunched over his arm, demonstrated his pain. It wasn't bad enough to curb his mouth, though. His complaints of injustice and abuse carried above the din of voices filling the room.

"I want my phone call. I know my rights. I get a phone call," the man yelled.

"Yeah, yeah." The intake officer led the perp to stand against the wall for his mug-shots and then rolled his fingers across an ink-pad before recording his fingerprints on paper.

Clay smirked to himself. *Go ahead and make your call. Lead us right to your accomplice in Denver.* Clay waited around until the scum-bag could make his call. He went in search of a cup of coffee and settled for what looked and smelled like burnt tar. Clay added two packets of sugar.

The arresting officer gave Clay the smirk of a co-conspira-tor, the side of his mouth twitching as he approached the suspect. "Don't worry. You'll get your call."

Clay shook his head. The falsities that Hollywood portrayed about legal procedures usually irritated him, but this particular misrepresentation frequently played into their hands. In truth, criminals didn't have the right to any phone calls. Phone calls were a privilege—one happily granted to the detainees because the police recorded the conversations, and they were admissible as evidence in the case against them. This call might lead them to the next link in the chain. Clay wanted to hunt down the local guy who waited to take ownership of the trailer full of girls.

The cop led the suspect to a phone mounted on the wall. Privacy was not an option, and Clay sat down in a hard-plastic chair eight feet away. He leaned it back on two legs, and sipping his bitter, scorched brew, he listened to the one-sided conversation.

"Hey, man. It's me." The guy's dark gaze shifted furtively around the room. "Wanted to let you know the ah... the entertainment won't be there in time for the party." The man listened and closed his eyes.

During the pause, Clay heard a male voice yelling on the other end of the phone, but he couldn't make out any words. That didn't concern him since they taped everything, but he was curious.

"I got pulled over, man. What did you want me to do?"

More distant screaming.

"I'm in jail—some bullshit about assault. Can you bail me out?"

Clay laughed aloud and patted Ranger's shoulder. "Let's go home, boy. That idiot's not going anywhere for a long time." On their way out, he stopped by the arresting officer's desk. "Catch any of that?"

"Sounds to me like he called the purchaser, probably a local pimp who expected the shipment of girls. They didn't give up much, but he called the guy he was talking to 'Jonny'".

"Can they get a location on the call?"

The cop shook his head. "The number he called belongs to a cell phone. We have the number, but most likely the guy will dump the phone. The best we can do is get a general location at the time of the call. I'll have that information soon."

"Thanks. It might not give us much, but it's something. See you tomorrow night?"

"I'll be here." The cop ran his fingers over Ranger's fur as they left.

El's gaze followed them as they walked toward the exit, so he flashed her another panty-melting smile, but she turned away. He wasn't used to such an uninterested reaction. Most women seemed happy with his attention, and usually flirted back. But not Eloise Clark. If anything, she came across as suspicious—but of what? All he did was help get those girls to a safe place.

Chapter Three

Candie turned down the volume on the TV show she watched with one of the other girls, while Jonny yelled on the phone in the other room. She listened intently, having learned early it was best to have an idea what was coming before it hit her in the form of a slap across the face or a punch in her gut. Jonny sounded furious, and it was only a matter of time before he took his anger out on one or more of his girls. So far the new kid, a little boy, had avoided a beating. But he wouldn't escape it forever.

"Where's Fancy?" The black girl sprawled next to her on the couch looked at Candie with round eyes.

She pasted a bored expression on her face and shrugged. "Not sure. I'll go downstairs and see if she's still sleeping." Candie used the excuse to leave the room before Jonny got off the phone. The clock said it was time to get ready to work the track, anyway. Candie tossed the remote to the girl and walked to the basement door.

The girls and the boy, whom Jonny called Steven, all slept downstairs in the basement of the run-down, one-bedroom ranch house on the outskirts of Denver. Dirty mattresses lay on the cement floor, some of which still held sleeping girls. They all had to share a single bathroom. No one was in there at the moment, so it was the perfect time to get her make-up on for the night. Briefly, Candie wondered where Jonny's head girl, his "bottom bitch" was. Fancy ran the girls' schedule and enforced the rules. Maybe Jonny sent her on a special date request.

Jonny and his stable of whores had been crashing in this house for several weeks, and if all went well, they'd probably stay through the football season. After that, Jonny would move them somewhere else, to another city. Candie had been with Jonny for about three years, she figured. She squeezed her eyes shut against the memories of her life before. That life disappeared, and there was nothing she could do about it now, but survive.

She heard doors slam upstairs, and she shuddered. Glass shattered, and Jonny swore.

"Candie? Where the hell are you?" He yelled from above.

"Coming." She answered, though she wished she could hide. In reality, it would be better to face him now than to let his anger grow. Candie set down her bottle of foundation and ran up the steep steps. "What's the matter, Daddy?" He forced all the girls to call him Daddy.

Jonny paced from the picture window to the front door and back. He clenched his hands and glared at a girl cowering in the corner. Jonny was a light-skinned half black, half Hispanic man, not much bigger than Candie, but he was mean and struck with his fists as fast as a rattlesnake. She did her best to stay out of arm's length when he was mad. And at the moment, he seethed.

"What happened? Is it Fancy?"

"No. She's working." He stopped pacing, jammed his hands onto his skinny hips, and stared at the floor before he answered. "The shipment of new hos isn't coming. The asshole driver got pulled over, and the cops confiscated all the bitches."

Blood drained from Candie's head. She swayed and reached out to steady herself by gripping the back of the couch. This was awful news. Jonny had a contract to provide girls for several pre-season football parties in penthouses downtown. He'd keep all the jobs anyway, fully expecting her and the others to work them all.

Steven peeked out from the kitchen at that moment. His large blue eyes stark in his pale face, darted from Jonny to Candie. Her stomach hardened and pushed acid up her throat. Little Stevie would learn the ropes the hard way. Not that there was an easy way. Jonny had already started grooming the kid, showing him porn and forcing him to practice some of what he saw. Still, he wasn't ready to endure what Jonny expected of him. Not that their pimp cared. He was only interested in the money such a prized choice would bring.

"Maybe you can get more girls from Tucson or Vegas?" Candie wanted to draw Jonny's attention away from the little boy.

"Maybe you can get off your lazy ass and go get ready. I expect you and the other bitches to make up for what I'm losing tonight. Consider your quotas doubled. No one comes back here till they've got it either, unless they want a beating."

Candie held her hand out to the frightened girl trembling in the corner. "Come on. Let's cover up that bruise. No john wants to start their date with a blackened eye blinking at them." The girls walked together toward the stairs, and Candie motioned for Steven to join them.

"Leave him here. We've got work to do." Jonny pointed to his bedroom door.

Candie couldn't bear to look at the boy's innocent, frightened face. She gripped the other girl's hand tight and pulled her toward the stairs. "Let's get ready to go before the others wake up." She practically pushed the girl down the stairs.

"Hey, knock it off."

"Shut up and get dressed. I'm first in the bathroom." Candie shut the door behind her and leaned over the toilet. She thought she might be sick, but at the same time wondered why. It wasn't the first time she'd seen Jonny groom a fresh whore. Desperately, she tried to harden her heart and mind against what she knew the little boy would go through. Most nights she had to shut out the sound of his cries for his mommy when she tried to sleep. Her mind closed an iron curtain on the memories of her first days and weeks with Jonny, and even more so on the life she had before he kidnapped her from the park where her brother played baseball.

"No!" She glared at herself in the mirror. "Stop it. Remembering only make things worse." Candie wiped tan foundation into the tears dripping down her face and started on creating the dark, smoky eyes her dates liked to see. She rolled her long brown hair in large hot-rollers before painting her lips a fire-engine red. The tight gold skirt offered a glimpse of where her fishnet covered legs curved into her ass, and she pushed her young breasts up in her bra until they spilled out over her fuzzy pink top. Candie teased and sprayed her curls and then added the final touch—over the knee, high-heeled black boots.

"I'm done. I'll wait for the rest of you bitches upstairs." She was glad for the slight break before heading out to meet her first date. Jonny had her booked for the night in a room at the motel down the road. She preferred that to walking the track. Her earnings were more reliable, and Jonny would be pleased with her at the end of the night. Sometimes, he even let her sleep in his bed with him on those nights. When

Jonny was happy with his take, he remembered to tell her he loved her. He remembered his promises of how one day it would be just the two of them. Tonight wouldn't turn out like that though. He yelled again at someone on the phone. Jonny was already having a terrible night.

This time, when Candie sat down on the couch to wait, she turned up the volume on the TV. She didn't want to listen to Jonny screaming anymore. Nor could she bear listening to Steven cry when Jonny got off the phone and returned his focus to the boy's *education*.

Chapter Four

E l stifled a deep sigh. She knew that most, if not all these girls would end up back on the streets. No matter what kind of help she offered. They didn't trust her. They didn't trust anyone, except maybe their pimp. A prostitute's relationship with her pimp was a twisted, convoluted one similar to that between slave and master, an association El understood was difficult to break free from. Clinically, the diagnosis was Connection Trauma, or Stockholm Syndrome, combined with PTSD.

These girls, children really, did what they had to do to survive, and during the process it was their pimp who fed them, clothed and sheltered them, told them he alone loved them. After he *disciplined* them, beating them into submission, it was he who tenderly cared for them. Warping reality until their tortured minds broke, and they offered their love and loyalty in return for being forced to sell their bodies to strangers to make money for their pimps.

"You have no right to keep us here, you know. We didn't do anything wrong. You have to let us go." The self-proclaimed spokeswoman for the group of castaways sneered at El, breaking into her thoughts.

"You are all minors, so in truth, I cannot release you unless it's into your parent's or guardian's custody."

"That's bull-shit. I'm twenty. Lola's nineteen, and the others are all eighteen. So, you have to let us go."

El glanced at the youngest girl in the bunch and knew she couldn't be more that eleven years old. Her heart wrenched, and she bit down on her lip waiting for the familiar pain to wash through her. "Unless you have ID, I have to assume that you are all minors."

The girl, Lola, spoke up. "This is false imprisonment. I know. I saw it on Law and Order."

"Even though you may have to spend the night in a jail cell, you are not under arrest. I haven't been able to find other placement for you yet, but by tomorrow you'll have a more comfortable place to go."

"Until when? We were supposed to meet someone in Denver, for work. You're ruining that for us." The oldest girl stepped toward El threateningly.

El's spine tingled, and she straightened to her full height, prepared to defend herself if necessary. "Is that so?"

A female police officer approached. "We'll have everything set up for you in about an hour. We had to make a few adjustments."

"Thanks. I appreciate it." El smiled. The girl took a step back, and El resumed their conversation. "What kind of work are you here for?"

"We're waitresses."

"Waitresses being smuggled into Denver in the back of a trailer with no windows?"

"Whatever, you have to let us go."

El's frustration built into a headache, and she pinched the

bridge of her nose. She gazed over her knuckles at the youngest girl standing at the far side of the room. Maybe it was still possible to reach her. One thing El realized through her years as a social worker was you could only help people if they wanted help.

"For tonight, you all will stay here in the jail. I have a bag of clean clothes in my car that you can look through to find something to wear. Tomorrow, a judge will decide what happens next. It's out of my hands."

Leaving the small group in the capable presence of the female officer, El made her way out to her car to retrieve the bag of cast-off clothing. Once outside, she took a minute and leaned against the still warm, brick wall of the station house. She drew in several deep breaths of fresh air, glad for a break from the stench of jailhouse humanity. The girls, she knew, put on a tough-guy act because they were scared. They didn't know who to trust or how much trouble they would be in for telling the cops anything. Some kids didn't survive the beatings they got if their pimps suspected disloyalty.

El rubbed the goosebumps from her arm that still ached after being broken in such a beating, years ago. It had never been set properly, didn't heal correctly, and continued to cause her pain now and again. With one last fortifying breath, El pushed herself off the wall and made her way to her car. She considered the strategy of talking with the smallest girl on her own. Possibly, she was new enough to this wicked world that she still remembered her family. Perhaps she knew someone who could take care of her—who wanted her back. El let out an enormous sigh. More often than not, there wasn't a helpful support system at home either, and unless she could place these girls in decent foster care, they were destined to wind up back on the streets. Life sucked sometimes. That was all.

Her mind wandered to the woman who had helped her. The group that rallied to support her and the therapist who worked with her for years. She remembered the promise she made to herself when she decided to turn her life around and she spoke the words into the night. "If I can help even one kid escape the torturous life of human trafficking, all this hard work will be worth it."

She nodded and stood taller as she grabbed the bags from her car and strode back to the station. Renewed focus strengthened her resolve.

The girls ran fingers over the various clothing, trying to act bored but secretly pleased to have something new to wear. El took the opportunity to pull the youngest girl to the side.

"What is your name?"

"Princess."

El smiled at the girl. "Do you remember your name before? Before they called you Princess?"

A shadow passed through the girl's eyes, and she shrugged. "I'm not her anymore."

"Yes, sweetheart, you are. You just pretend to be Princess when you need to be someone else—and that's okay. Princess protects you. But who are you on the inside?"

The little girl stared at El for a long time before she whispered, "Teressa".

"Hi, Teressa. I'm so happy to know you. You are safe now. I promise." El felt certain she could find placement for this darling child. She was still young enough to attract a family willing to help her through. The older girls were a different story. If they agreed, she could help them with a place to live and the counseling they needed. But, they had to want it.

While the girls selected clothes to wear, El ordered burgers and fries for delivery. She sat in a molded plastic chair lined up against the wall in a row of six identical seats. Chewing her salty fast food, she observed the scene. Famished, the teens ate their food greedily, causing El to wonder when they had last eaten. Teressa sat next to her, leaning against her arm. Gradually, the girl slumped, and El eased the sleeping child down until her head rested on El's leg. She brushed a few strands of hair from the child's soft cheek.

The oldest girl stared at them from across the room. Eventually, she approached. "Why are you doing this? What's in it for you?"

El held the girl's gaze as a familiar dagger pierced her heart.

Chapter Five

Robert stacked the papers on his desk and added them to a file resting in his outbox for his Teacher's Assistant to deal with in the morning. He slid his glasses off his nose and rubbed his tired eyes. It had been a full day, and he definitely needed a drink before he faced going home.

The house wasn't what he dreaded—*it* was everything he'd dreamed of—understated wealth with top of the line accoutrements. They'd even paved the circular drive with marble. His family lived in the enviable Cherry Hills neighborhood of Denver. Their lifestyle was far more than he could afford as an economics professor at Denver University, but he held that knowledge to himself. Robert loved the mansion; it was the occupants that kept him away at work, and at play, late into the night.

Play. He could use a bit of that tonight along with that drink. Robert picked up his phone and called his local provider.

"Hey, Prof. In need of a little TLC?"

"I can be there in forty-five minutes. Did the shipment

arrive?" Robert ran shaky fingers over a blemish on his left cheek.

"No, sorry man. A slight problem came up. It won't affect you though. I got you covered."

"You have one that's ten?"

Jonny sighed, and Robert's chest constricted. He'd been fantasizing about this for a week. His index finger snagged the base of his mole.

"Close. You'll never know the difference. What do you like? Knee socks and Mary Janes?"

A hot gust of anger filled Robert's head. "God damnit, Jonny! You promised me. I don't want a used up twelve-year-old." Surprised by his own outburst, Robert steadied his breath and quieted his tone. "What happened? Is your problem with the shipment going to affect the party?"

"No. No way, Professor. I'll deliver what I promised by then. No worries, man. The driver got pulled over, but we have plenty of time to replace your merchandise."

"The consequences of failing the 'big man' would be dire. You better provide what we expect." Robert knew this was no hollow threat. George didn't tolerate it when people let him down. He never had, not even in their college days.

"No, I promise, man. I got you. You'll get what you ordered."

"Then what about tonight? You know what I want, and you can't deliver."

His slippery voice paused on the line before Jonny continued. "You want young, right?"

Robert didn't answer, but his pulse accelerated, and he closed his eyes.

"How about trying something new?"

"What do you mean?"

"I just acquired a rare gem. A nine-year-old... named Steven."

Robert's racing heart slammed into his rib cage, and he sucked in a breath. Robert had never imagined... He'd seen it in some videos he watched online, but... "I don't know."

"You're right. It's too soon. He's not ready, anyway." Jonny took back his offer like a snap.

Robert reeled with confused emotions, his imagination causing his pulse to throb in response to the titillation.

"I got what I got tonight. Take it or leave it."

"Yes. I'll be there."

"Room 22." The call ended.

Robert leaned back in his chair, considering. After several minutes, he reached again for his phone.

"Bob, how the hell are you? I didn't expect to hear from you this evening. Everything all right on your side of the range?"

George Baron and Robert James had been best friends since they were college roommates forty-some years ago at Cornell. Robert had earned a scholarship to the prestigious school but George had enrolled like his father and his grandfather before him. George came from privilege and from a world of experiences completely unknown to Robert with his down-home, Midwest upbringing. Their friendship opened doors for Robert he'd never known were available.

His friend studied business while Robert focused on economics. After college they moved to Denver, which suited them both. Since then, George made his fortune in oil and gas, and after earning his PhD, Robert secured a position at the illustrious DU School of Economics. However, Robert's real money came from his private stewardship of George's second set of books—records only the two of them knew about.

"Hey, George. Things are okay here. How's the ranch?"

"Best time of the year up here. I spent the day in Telluride with some prospects today. I think they're in."

"Good to hear."

"What's eating you, Bob? I can tell something is off."

No sense putting off the unwelcome news. "The shipment that should have come in tonight was... confiscated."

"By the cops?"

"Yes."

"Damn. I've already taken substantial deposits for invitations to that party, Bob." George's voice lowered, menacing in its quietness.

"Everything will be fine. Our supplier has guaranteed a new shipment in time."

"How did he guarantee it? With his life?"

Robert swallowed. He knew those were not empty words. "Yes, I made sure he understood."

"Why else are you calling? Something you need to tell me?"

"Nothing bad. Jonny offered me a fresh game tonight. It surprised me, but the more I think about it, the more I want to try it out."

"You know I don't care what you do on your own time, so are you thinking about including this new entertainment at the party?"

"Maybe. It might prove even more lucrative than what we have going now." Robert thought of at least two politicians he knew who would snatch at the opportunity—men they could blackmail with the evidence of their dark tastes. "Tonight, Jonny will provide me with an unspoiled nine-year-old."

George coughed. "Nine?"

"Boy."

The phone line hummed in the silence. Robert picked at the edge of his mole, waiting for George to respond.

Finally, his friend's voice sifted through the speaker. "Yes. You're right. This offering could be very profitable indeed—and not only with money. We could write our own policies, pass our own laws. Bob, you have made my night. Get in touch with the supplier. We'll require more than one, and they will need to come with at least a little know-how."

"I'll tell him. On my way over there now."

"Enjoy yourself."

"Always do." Robert chuckled and ended the call.

Chapter Six

The following week, Clay drove an unmarked SUV down a strip of cracked and pitted asphalt in a line of slow-moving cars. They cruised past a selection of prostitutes of all ages, shapes, and genders standing in front of gated and barred storefronts, and calling out to the men driving by. A couple of the street walkers, though dressed like women, Clay suspected were actually men. Drivers slowed down to view the available options.

"Hey, mister, want to party?"

"You lonely? Need a friend?"

The Denver vice cop whom Clay partnered with for the night rolled down his window letting in the stench of rotting urine-soaked garbage and weed. Ranger sat in his kennel in the back watching the scene from behind tinted windows.

"Hey, boys" A woman with huge breasts straining her black-lace push-up bra bent forward to display her wares. Smudged mascara settled into the circles under her glassy eyes. "Want to give a girl a ride?"

"Where you going?" The cop asked with a grin.

"Anywhere you want, baby." She teetered up to the window on spindly spiked heels. "Depends on what kind of time you got. We can pop around the corner real quick-like, or I got a room..."

Clay's body weighed heavy on his bones. This woman—all of them—selling themselves to strangers made his chest hurt. Didn't they know the danger they put themselves in? There were some crazy psychos out on the streets.

"Where's the room?"

"Motel just up the road." The woman showed the direction with her head, then smiled displaying two broken teeth. Had that happened at the hand of her pimp? He forced himself not to survey the area like a lawman would. He'd already taken in the dim lighting from the caged storefronts, the gang tagging graffiti, and the array of people abused by life.

Instead, he leaned toward her. "We were told to ask for one of Jonny's girls. Would that be you?"

Her smile dropped away. "No, sugar. Those skanky hos are two blocks down." She rested her ample offering on the window ledge. "I can make you a better offer, anyway. Why don't you take what you want from here?"

"Tempting." The cop chuckled. "But, we're already hooked up. Maybe next time."

Clay pressed the gas as the hooker stepped away, and they drove further down the dingy road. "I've been on tons of streets like this when I was in the Marine Corps. They're all over the world, and they're all the same. But, I never slowed down and really considered. I mean, looked at the faces. Under the makeup and fakeup, this scene is truly sad."

"I hear you. The worst thing is these girls just keep getting younger and younger. It fucking breaks my heart. I've got a daughter of my own. I can't imagine..."

Clay coasted as they approached the next block of people calling to the cars. He touched the brake. "Look, over there." Clay pointed with his chin to a darkened part of the street. An adolescent girl hanging on a man's arm walked with him into an alleyway. "Let's go."

He pulled over and parked. Both men opened their doors, and Clay let Ranger out. They drew their weapons and followed the couple, positioning themselves on either side of the alley before peering into the shadows. Clay had seen a lot of things, but witnessing the immature girl on her knees before a man easily three times her age made his stomach turn. He choked back bile along with an intense urge to grab the guy by his throat and slam him against the sooty brick wall.

"FBI—Nobody move." Clay called out as he leveled his weapon at the man's face. Ranger stood poised to charge, a low growl rumbling in his chest. "What's going on here? You paying this little girl to do nasty things to you?"

The two lawmen made their way carefully toward the couple.

The girl, who looked to be fourteen or fifteen, turned terrified eyes to Clay and cried. "No." She sniffed. "It's consexul."

"Consensual, you stupid—" The man fumbled with his zipper.

She'd obviously been coached on what to say if she was ever busted, but she didn't remember the right word. Clay's partner gestured to a roll of money sticking out of the girl's low-cut tube top. "Then what's the cash for?"

Clay shook his head in disgust. "Cuff this bastard and read him his rights," he said to the officer. "I'll talk to this young lady separately." He stepped toward her with Ranger on his heel and helped her to her feet.

The girl stared at his dog with terror in her eyes. "Is that a wolf?"

"No." Clay patted the silky head of his black Malinois. "This is Ranger. He won't hurt you. He only growled at the man who brought you into the alley. He knows who the bad guys are—he can tell."

"He can?" Her voice filled with wonder.

"What's your name?" Clay crouched down next to Ranger so he didn't tower over the girl.

"Fancy."

"No, your real name."

She shook her head. "We weren't doing anything wrong."

"That's not true. Even if he didn't pay you, performing a sex act in a public place is illegal, and you're under the age of consent."

Her eyes filled, and her lip trembled. "I'm eighteen."

Right, and I'm twelve. "Listen. I want to help you. This is no life for a girl like you. Tell me, do you know a man named Jonny?"

Abject fear flashed in her eyes, and she clenched her teeth together before gathering herself. "I'm not supposed to talk to you. You're trying to trick me. I don't know anyone named Jonny. I didn't do anything wrong. This is my own money."

Clay sighed and stood to his full height. "Then, you leave me no choice. If you don't want my help, then I have to arrest you and take you to jail. You can tell your bogus story to the judge."

Clay loosely cuffed the girl's thin wrists, wondering if the bracelets would simply fall to the ground. The poor child was scared beyond reason, and he wished she'd let him help her. Ranger sniffed her and licked her bound hands. The girl reached to stroke his muzzle.

The cop called for a back-up squad car so they could keep

the suspects apart in separate vehicles. A female cop arrived and took custody of the girl. Clay and his partner followed them with the john to the station to process his arrest. Speaking with dispatch, Clay asked them to call El Clark in to meet them. He hated arresting this kid and adding to her juvenile record. She was a victim, not a perpetrator. But one thing was certain, she'd be safer in jail all night than on the streets.

Chapter Seven

Clay helped the young girl who called herself Fancy out of the car and opened the kennel for Ranger. His dog hopped out of the SUV and walked next to the tense girl, occasionally bumping her fingers with his nose. He remembered how protective Ranger had been with the youngest kid they brought in from their highway checkpoint a week ago. Smiling to himself about his sensitive attack dog, he almost bumped into El who stood waiting for them inside the double doors of the police station.

"Excuse me. I'm sorry, El." An overwhelming wave of pine-scented cleaner rushed out the door failing to cover the fog of filthy humanity. He scrunched his nose. "Thanks for coming in on such short notice."

"I'm glad you had them call me." El held out her hand to the adolescent standing next to him. "I'm El Clark. What's your name?"

The girl, who looked even younger under the bright lights of the PD, tossed her head with a false air of insolence, and ignored El's hand. "Fancy."

El lowered her arm. "It's nice to meet you, Fancy."

Clay gestured to the hall that housed several cramped interview rooms, and they moved toward them.

El worked to put the girl at ease. "Let's sit down and talk for a minute so we can figure out the best way to help you. Okay?" She guided the girl into one of rooms. "Have a seat. Do you want something to drink?"

"Why are you being so nice to me?" Fancy narrowed her eyes at El.

"Is there a reason I shouldn't be nice to you?" El countered and received a shrug topped with a dramatic eye-roll.

Clay rubbed his jaw to hide his smirk. In many ways, teenage girls were all the same. "How about a soda?" he asked and turned to El. "I'm gonna grab a cup of coffee. Do you want anything?"

El's gaze narrowed at him then too, though not as dramatically. *What the hell? Do all the women around here suspect ulterior motives when I offer to do something nice?*

"Sure, coffee for me too. Black." El smiled then, and the light reflecting in her hazel eyes struck him.

When Clay returned with the drinks, he interrupted the girl insisting she was eighteen and only guilty of partying with a man in an alley.

El's brows gathered into a skeptical line. "What's your address?"

The girl almost answered, but she caught herself. "The street. I live on the street. It's not against the law to be homeless."

"Where is your family, your parents?" El took the steaming cup from Clay. Her mouth curved, and she bobbed her chin in thanks. She continued interviewing his suspect, so Clay remained quiet. With a pop and fizz, he opened a can of Coke and set it on the table in front of Fancy before he slid into his seat.

"What does that have to do with anything? I'm eighteen."

"I want to help you, Fancy." El canted her head toward Clay and Ranger. "We all do. But you're making that hard for us. If you are eighteen, the police will arrest you and try you as an adult. The judge will sentence you to the adult jail, not juvey. And that's not a benevolent place."

Ranger whined and moved next to Fancy, resting his chin on her lap. She stared at him while she scratched behind his soft black ears.

"But if you're honest with us, starting with your actual age, we can help you. There are places you can stay and people who want to give you a hand up. Tonight you have an opportunity to change your life for the better. We want to help you do that." El's words tripped over a slight laugh. "Even Ranger there wants to help you."

"What do you know about my life? My life is just fine." Fancy glared at El.

Clay leaned his chair back against the wall next to the door and sipped the surprisingly fresh coffee. Someone on the night-shift must have had mercy and made a fresh pot. El tapped her pen on the tabletop. She stared the young prostitute down until the girl dropped her gaze. "Are you telling me you enjoy performing sexual acts on men you don't know, in a dark alley? For money you have to give to some other man? That *this* is the life you dreamed of when you were a little girl?"

Fancy's face reddened as though someone had slapped her, and she fluttered her eyelids against the moisture gathering in their corners.

"What *did* you dream of being when you grew up?" El continued.

Fancy closed her eyes, pressing the tears out. The drops ran down her cheeks. Rivulets of mascara and blush left clean tracks across her overly made-up face. She didn't speak for several minutes. In the silence, they could hear the ticking of the clock above the door.

In a tiny voice, Fancy murmured, "I wanted to be a zookeeper."

El reached across the table and squeezed the girl's arm with encouragement. "I think you'd make a great zookeeper. Ranger here is the proof. He's very smart, and he knows you love animals. Look at how he responds to you."

As if he knew what El said, Ranger let out a friendly little yap and wagged his tail. Fancy pressed her face into the big dog's neck and cried. Clay's jaw fell open, but El acted. She stood, rounded the table, and squeezed into the space next to his dog. She put one arm over the girl's shoulders and the other around Ranger and waited until Fancy sat up. Clay, with his mouth still ajar when El looked up at him, was utterly shocked that two strange women sat draped over his fierce and deadly attack K9 partner.

"Close your mouth, agent. Dogs, as I'm sure you know, are way smarter than we are." El laughed and even Fancy smirked a little. Clay clamped his lips together and shook his head in disbelief.

El remained in her crouched position next to Fancy's chair. "Okay, now. Please, tell me your real name."

After a lengthy pause, the girl inhaled a deep breath. "A long, long time ago, I used to be called Kelly."

A brilliant smile lit El's features. "It's very nice to meet you, Kelly."

HOURS LATER, EL AND CLAY HAD KELLY'S WRITTEN statement. Though she admitted she knew Jonny, the man Clay wanted to find, she refused to say any more about him. She was terrified of what he would do to her or the others if she said anything. El arranged for placement until Kelly's hearing and explained the steps they needed to take for her extraction from a life of sexual slavery. The miserable existence her pimp had forced her into.

When Kelly went to change into other clothes, El touched Clay's arm. "Thank you."

"For what? Just doing my job."

"No. You're doing more than that, and I truly appreciate it." She bent down to rub Ranger's head. "You know, your dog here would make an exceptional therapy animal."

Clay barked out a laugh. "He's a highly trained FBI-K9 officer. An apprehension and attack dog."

Humor sparked in El's eyes when she stood to face Clay. "Yeah, he's tough, just like his handler. But both of you stayed and cared for an adolescent girl that the world threw away. Maybe you're *both* a little more than FBI Agents?"

A warmth radiated through Clay's chest at her praise, and he ducked his head, attempting to hide the grin that stretched across his mouth. When he felt he had a bit more control, he glanced up at her and smoothed his tone. "So does this mean you'll let me take you out for dinner this weekend?"

As she considered him, the light in her eyes dimmed, and she swallowed hard. "Maybe we could grab a cup of coffee sometime?"

The cold brush-off punched Clay in the gut. He scrunched his brows, but nodded. "Sure. *Sometime.*" Going nowhere fast, he turned on his heel. "*Knoze.*"

Ranger jumped to Clay's side and together they strode out of the station house. Clay looked down at his dog. "What the hell just happened?"

Chapter Eight

George sat on his wide veranda overlooking the moonlit valley of his 9500-acre ranch in the Rocky Mountains near Telluride, Colorado. He lived there with his wife, and those who served them, took care of his house, and worked the land. He savored the flavor and aroma of his Arturo Fuente cigar while sipping on a velvety, twenty-year Macallan and reveling in the richness of his kingdom. A self-satisfied grin bunched up his fleshy cheeks, and he closed his eyes in certain satisfaction.

A buzz vibrated near the cut-crystal decanter standing on the table next to his chair. George let out his breath and peered at the lit phone screen. His smile broadened, and he answered on the next ring.

"Peter. To what do I owe the pleasure of your call?"

Colorado State Representative, Peter Spiel, responded in a familiar, friendly tone. "Good evening, George. I hope I'm not calling too late."

"Not at all. What can I do for you?"

"Well, I've been looking forward to the, uh—party you're hosting at the end of the summer."

"Yes. You've sent your preferences and requests. Is there something else?"

"Actually, I'm wondering what you would think about my extending the invitation to a couple of friends of mine?"

George sensed an opportunity, but he had to be careful. One false step and he and Robert would be in more trouble than even his fortune could buy them out of. "Well, I don't know. My guests are all vetted and known to be secure..."

"I understand that, and I promise that the security of your events is all of our utmost concern. Obviously."

"Yes..." George was eager to learn who else he might catch on his line, but he had to play it cool. Peter should have to beg. He sucked a puff of the flavored cigar into the back of his throat and breathed it out, waiting.

"These men would bring more legitimacy to your... parties, and I have no doubt that you can accommodate their more exotic tastes."

George laughed, coughing on the smoke. He sipped a soothing, buttery swallow of scotch. "Legitimacy?"

"Well, what I mean is that my friends are both senators. Once they taste what you have to offer, your bottom line could increase exponentially. You, of course, should still vet each participant with great care, but think of the potential connections you could build. The money you will certainly make."

And the power I will wield. George's chest puffed, and he stood chewing the end of his cigar. "I'll take your suggestion into consideration. Send me the names of the prospective guests—I'll look into them. Do us both a favor though, and don't say anything to them until I give you the green light. The last thing we want is for the authorities to shut down our fun." George laughed a roughened smoker's hack and cleared his throat with another swallow of the golden whiskey. "Text me their contact information, and I'll get back to you." He ended the call.

AFTER POURING MORE SCOTCH INTO HIS GLASS, GEORGE dialed Robert. "Bob. Where are you?"

"At home. It's game night. Hold on."

George waited while Robert moved into a room away from his family so they could talk.

"What's up?"

"Our fortunes, my friend. That's what." George's prodigious belly pressed tight against his waistband when he laughed and he slid a thick finger between the fabric and his rolls to ease the pinch.

"Sounds good, but what are you talking about?"

George recounted his phone call with Peter. "It'll be ideal to get a string of senators on the line. Not only will we blackmail them for money, but we can start making governmental policy! Just think of the power we'll have over them, Bob. Makes me hard merely thinking about it."

"Who are they? How do we know they aren't investigating us?"

George sighed. "Bob, you've always been a worrier. Even in college." He thought back to when they first started doping girls at frat parties. "I told you back then nothing would go wrong, and it never did. Those silly bitches never remembered what we did to them." George's laugh echoed through the hills surrounding his massive log cabin home. "But we have a slight challenge."

"I figured."

"Not *a problem*, Bob, a challenge." The muscles at the back of his neck strained. For the first time since college, George wondered if Robert had enough vision—sufficient courage. Until now, George's business suited Robert because it gave him carte blanche to feed his own twisted fantasies. But his nerves could end up getting in the way and getting them busted. He'd have to keep a close eye on his best friend. "In order to benefit fully from our new associations, we need to add digital surveillance cameras to every room. We can capture all the weird shit that goes on here along with the faces of respected government officials, movie stars, whoever. What do you think? It's just a little insurance."

A lengthy pause stretched over the line. "That's a brilliant idea, George, it is. But what about us? When we..." Robert cleared his throat. "What about me?"

"Oh, for God's sake, Bob. If I wanted to blackmail you, I'd have done it a long time ago. We're friends, we've been through a lot together. We've both made fortunes and had tons of fun doing it. I don't care what you do behind closed doors. I never have. There is no need to have a camera in your room—unless, of course, you want one." George chuckled.

"I know, George. I just get nervous."

"Leave the worrying to me, for now. First, we need to hire someone to wire the ranch with video and sound. Who could we hire that we trust? We have to think about how to get it done with no one knowing. How will we keep the technicians quiet?" George heard Robert's kids laughing in the background and was once again thankful that his own kids had grown and moved away. They were such a pain in the ass. "Up the order with our supplier too, but wait until we find out if any of these senators have particular requests."

"Got it."

"Are we all set for the mid-summer event up at the oil-fields in South Dakota?" George chuckled. "That game is small potatoes these days. But it's been part of the bread and butter up till now."

"Yeah. We're lined up for that. Dakota is straightforward, no special demands. Those men don't care what they—"

"Dad! Come on - it's your turn." Robert's teenage daughter's voice echoed from the other room.

Robert must have cupped his hand over his phone because he sounded like he was in a cave when he continued. "I've got to go, George. I'll think about the surveillance."

"Okay, Bob. Have fun playing games with your family. And hey—this is excellent news. I promise. Don't start worrying."

"I won't. I trust you."

"Like a brother."

"Right. More than a brother." Robert clicked off.

George ran his hand across his sweaty forehead. He hoped the freight-train they just hopped aboard wouldn't get away from them. Yet, the political influence and extreme wealth his efforts would bring them made it worth the risk.

Chapter Nine

✣

E l let herself into her small two-bedroom ranch-style house. The gloomy silence pressed down heavily on her loneliness. She flipped on the living room lights, kicked off her shoes, and dropped her keys into a pottery bowl on the table by the door. Once again, she considered getting a pet. Not a dog—they needed too much attention, and El was rarely home. Maybe a cat. She would love to come home to a friendly face, and to be responsible for another creature besides herself. To have someone happy to see her at the end of the day.

Clay's rugged features snuck into her thoughts but she abruptly shook them away. She dumped her tote and purse onto the maple dining table that divided her tiny kitchen from the living space. In the kitchen, she slid a wineglass from its hanger under her cupboard. She filled the balloon-shaped goblet to the brim with cranberry juice and seltzer before she wandered into her bathroom to turn on the tap for a bath. It had been another day from hell and a hot soak was exactly what she needed.

After adding an extra measure of lavender-scented

bubbles to the water, she undressed while the tub filled. El could view the TV in her bedroom from the bathtub, so she turned on the evening news. Not tremendously relaxing, but she liked to know what went on in the world. Her stomach gnawed on itself and El remembered she hadn't had dinner—again. Sometimes, on busy days that were filled with damaged kids, it was hard to remember to eat regularly. Today had been one of those days.

Wrapped in her midnight-blue silk robe, El returned to the kitchen and sliced some Gruyere and laid it on a plate with some crackers and grapes. She carried her makeshift meal back to the bathroom and set it next to her glass on the teak tub tray before lowering herself into the almost scalding water. For several minutes she closed her eyes and allowed her muscles to unwind. She'd caught the tail end of the hour on the news, and the weatherman droned on about the summer heat and fire restrictions. El reached for her glace, took a sip, and let it roll around on her tongue. Pretending the juice was wine didn't really help.

Commercial ditties flitted at the edge of her awareness as she slid further into the soothing suds letting the hot water cover her shoulders. The theme music for the top of the hour broadcast blared, announcing the headlines, but she remained focused on the bliss of the steamy bath.

"In breaking news tonight, the FBI confirms there may be a serial killer on the loose here in the Denver Metro area. Two days ago, police found a deceased adolescent female in a dumpster behind the Dollar Discount Store on East Colfax. Earlier this evening, police discovered another dead girl in a motel on Syracuse Street. Evidence points to similar injuries in both cases."

El bolted upright. "Oh, God," she said aloud to the room. Her heated skin puckered in the coolness of the air conditioning. Both East Colfax and Syracuse were well known locations for prostitution and gang violence. Did she know either of the dead girls? With cold fingers of dread clutching her heart, she reached for the remote and turned up the volume on the TV.

"Both victims appear to have suffered multiple stab wounds and bear bruising on their necks consistent with strangulation. Denver Police do not yet know the identities of the victims, but acknowledge neither of them fit the description of any known missing persons in the area. Police are asking, if you were near the area and saw anything out of the ordinary in either of these locations, to please call the FBI hotline set up for this case. We do not have photos of the murder victims at this point, but the Coroner's Office believes them both to be Caucasian females with long brown hair, fourteen to sixteen years of age. Again, please call the number at the bottom of your screen if you have any informa tion involving this case."

El rose from the tub and reached for a bath towel. As she pulled it off the rack, it brushed against her glass. The goblet shattered against the porcelain. Splinters of glass and blood-red juice splashed across the floor and onto her white bath-mat. *Damn it!* El shuddered at the sight, and bent over the side of the tub to sweep away the mess with the terrycloth. She dried off with another towel as she rushed to her phone.

Desperate to help protect the kids on the street, El considered her contact at the Denver PD. Maybe she could go on some ride-a-longs. She knew the street kids better than most cops—knew where they worked and was familiar with many of their faces. Perhaps she should go down to the Coro-ner's office and see if she could identify either of the murdered girls, though that was the last thing on earth she wanted to do. She swayed as the blood drained from her head, and sat heavily on the edge of her bed.

Shaking off her light-headedness, El picked up her phone

to dial the police station but hesitated over the keypad. The person she truly wanted to call had texted her earlier, so she'd have his number. His text still glowed on a banner across her lock screen.

Here's my number in case you change your mind about going to dinner.

More than anything she wished she could call Clay and borrow his strength to bolster her flailing resolve. She knew he'd be happy to hear her voice—figured he'd probably come to her and hold her in his arms if she asked him to.

She threw her phone across the comforter and buried her face in her pillow. Her eyes burned with hot tears and her throat ached like she'd swallowed a stress ball. No matter how much she desired to be with a man like Clay Jennings, it wasn't possible. He liked what he saw on the outside. He may even think he liked the person he was beginning to know, but he would never hang around once he knew the truth. Women of her kind didn't deserve men like him and that was all there was to it.

El clenched her molars together and pushed herself up to get dressed. She needed to get a grip and get going. This tragedy wasn't about her and it was time to push her personal garbage back into the dark compartment of her mind where it belonged. Children were in danger on the streets of Denver and she had to do what she could to help.

Chapter Ten

❧❀❧

Jonny's cell phone rang, and he answered from inside his bedroom. He shouted a line of expletives at whoever called. His mood had been dark and awful lately and he had been hitting her and the other girls more often than usual. But, tonight whoever called distracted him from his focus on Steven. Relieved, Candie took the little boy's hand and led him downstairs to the mattress covered floor.

"Over there," she pointed to the lumpy pad in the corner she had claimed as her own. "Get under the cover and go to sleep." Her blanket was a tattered quilt she'd found at a nearby thrift-store for a dollar once when Jonny felt generous. "It's late, and you need to stay out of Daddy's way for the rest of the night."

The little boy stared up at her and whispered, "I want my mommy."

Candie's heart splintered into pieces that dropped into her stomach almost making her retch. "You've got to get over that, Steven. For your own good. Come on now, lie down."

"Will you tell me a story?" His small voice twisted in her already churning gut.

"I don't know any happy stories, Steven. The trick to this life is making it through, one day at a time. Surviving. Hopes and dreams—they only hurt. Tonight, just think about sleep, and be quiet. With any luck, Jonny might forget you're down here. He's got a lot on his mind, and he's in a sour mood. It's best to keep out of his sight."

"Will you stay here with me?" He gazed at her from large blue eyes set above little round pink cheeks. His expression held such hope, it scraped her raw inside.

"I've got to go to work tonight, but I'll lay by you when I get back, okay?"

"Okay." Steven reached up and touched her cheek with gentle fingertips. "See you later."

Candie stroked his soft hair, and then against her better judgement, she bent down and brushed a quick kiss against his forehead. "Go to sleep." She stood and walked away before he could wrap anymore tentacles around her sore emotions.

At the top of the stairs, she practically ran into Jonny who paced the living room floor.

"Why are you still here?" His angry eyes flashed at her.

"I–"

"Never mind. I need to talk to you, anyway. Fancy's been arrested."

"When?"

"'Bout an hour ago. She got picked up while working the track." Jonny turned and strode to the end of the room, then pivoted and walked back. "She'll be in juvey for at least three months. Damn it!" His dark eyes searched the ceiling and then drifted down to Candie.

"What?"

"*You're* my new bottom-bitch." A sleazy grin slid across his face.

Bottom or bottom-bitch was the term pimps used for the

top whore in their stable. The title belonged to the girls they expected to keep the other hos in-line and working. In that moment, Candie became responsible for the others when they were out on the street. Snitching to their "daddy" was another part of her new job description. It meant more work, but sometimes the position offered a little more freedom too. It definitely meant she'd get more of Jonny's attention, which was a double-edged sword. Candie was only fourteen, and usually Bottoms were older. At fifteen, even Fancy was young for the job, but Jonny liked his girls young.

Candie pasted a smile on her face. "Thank you," she spoke the words she knew he expected from her.

"You start tonight, right now. Let the others know what happened and that they will answer to you from now on. Also tell everyone you all need to make up Fancy's quota until I get another ho. I'm not losing any money just because she was stupid enough to get arrested." Jonny stepped off again on his path across the worn, stained carpet.

"I should go. I've got a date at ten." Candie turned toward the door. The motel where she worked was two blocks away, and the walk would give her some time to think about how to use her new position to her advantage—and maybe to Steven's as well. She could tell Jonny that she would take over grooming Steven. She couldn't save him from the horrors that he faced, but she could help prepare him and hopefully put off the inevitable as long as possible.

Jonny's hard tone stopped her in her tracks. "Where's that little boy? He needs training for some parties coming up this summer."

Icy dread trickled down Candie's spine. She froze in place with her back to Jonny. She couldn't make herself turn to face him. "He's sleeping right now. Why don't you let him rest? I'll work with him in the morning."

She heard the springs complain when Jonny dropped onto

the couch. "Yeah, okay. I'm beat tonight, anyway. Have him watch those videos first thing. The ones with the boys. That's the shit he needs to learn."

Bitter disgust climbed up her throat. "I will." Candie was glad he couldn't see her face. She was sure she was some horrid shade of green. If there was any way she could help Steven escape without being killed for her effort, she planned to find it. She couldn't stomach the life he would face otherwise. He was only a child.

Chapter Eleven

❧❀❧

George leaned against the railing on the deck and watched the blazing coral sun sink below the indigo horizon of his own personal mountain valley. He listened to the final evening calls of the blue-jays. Everything came together nicely for his and Robert's sex party next month. They had ordered the props and role-play costumes which were on their way. At first, he laughed at some of the strange requests, but the more he thought about them, the more curious he'd become. That's how porn had always been for him. The more he saw, the more he wanted to try. His current fantasy was to dress as an Arabian king and enjoy a harem clad in golden lingerie and colorful scarves. Six girls at once performing whatever acts he commanded. He closed his eyes and let his imagination slither around. *I need to be sure there are plenty of little blue pills and cocaine on hand.*

Startling him out of his reverie Bess, his wife, joined him on the deck. "What are you doing out here all by yourself?"

George adjusted his trousers, glad of the darkening sky. "I was about to pour myself a drink. Care to join me?"

"I have some lemonade." She held up her glass to show

him. "I just got off the phone with Bella. We've finalized the details for my visit. Texas is boiling in August, but I want to spend time with the kids before they have to go back to school."

"How long will you be down there?" George didn't really care as long as she was out of the house for his event.

"The entire month. That is, if you don't mind me being away until September." Bess moved to the dry bar inside the French door leading to George's office and poured him a scotch, neat. "You should join us for a few days. The grand-kids would love to see you. How many years has it been?"

"August is such a busy month." George didn't enjoy father-hood the first time around, and grand-parenting was worse. "You're right, it's been too long and I'll miss you and the kids, but it can't be helped. Take them some gifts from me, will you?"

"Of course," Bess sighed. "Europeans have the best idea, taking all of August off to go on holiday. Think how much fun we'd have traveling with the entire family down to Nassau to stay for a couple of weeks at the Atlantis resort. The kids would love the water park and the beach." She passed George his glass and tapped it with hers. "Cheers."

"Cheers." George tilted his head and regarded his wife. She'd never been a beauty, but she was a striking woman with her coffee-colored hair and strong features. Bess had been on the women's rowing team in college when they met and had maintained her athletic build after all these years. He pictured her having the time of her life with their grandkids at a water-oriented resort.

Originally, George had wooed her for her father's money, but she'd been a suitable wife and mother over the years. When her parents died, his net worth tripled. During their lives together, Bess never suspected him of ulterior motives or of his darkest desires. She was happily unaware of his other life, or perhaps she simply didn't care. They loved each other like one loves a favorite dog. They shared no passion, but they enjoyed a comfortable companionship when they were together. Primarily, George used Bess as an integral element in his cover as a dignified, legitimate businessman, and she unknowingly played her part beautifully.

The phone on his desk—his private office line—rang, causing his muscles to jolt. That phone never rang unless he expected a call from someone to whom he had personally given the number. Even Robert didn't use that line. He chewed on the fleshy inside of his cheek, determining whether to answer. In the end, he decided the call might lead to more money, so he turned toward his office. "You'll excuse me, my dear. I need to get that." George closed the French doors behind him, leaving Bess outside on her own. He lifted the receiver from its cradle. "Hello?"

"Is this George Baron?"

"Who is calling?"

"Never mind names. A mutual acquaintance gave me your number and told me you were the man to contact to procure certain specialized party... favors."

George paused, considering how best to handle this strange call. "Who is the acquaintance that suggested you contact me? Obviously, I need to know that, at the bare minimum."

The voice chuckled, "You haven't asked what type of party favors I'm requesting."

"That's something I'm sure we can work out once I know you're a legitimate caller. First things first." A small "thrill of the game" zinged through George's belly, and he took a large gulp of his whiskey.

"A certain government official, one whom you've invited to your upcoming event, recommended your services."

"Is the gentleman from my own home state?"

"I believe so, yes."

"Are you seeking an invitation to the mentioned event?"

Condescending anger laced the caller's tone. "Certainly not. I'm preparing for my own private soirée that I plan to hold at one of my estates in early September. Is this something you can handle or not?"

George's blood simmered at the man's insinuations. First, that he was some sort of glorified pimp, and second, that the stranger questioned his ability to deal with such arrangements.

"What is the general locale of your property?"

"Florida."

"Of course location is not a problem as long as a jet can land nearby. With the proper vetting, I'm sure we can come to a mutually pleasing arrangement. I'll put my top man on this job. How would you like him to contact you?" After exchanging the various emails for contacting each other with more specific details and off-shore account numbers routed through IP proxy servers all around the globe, the men ended their call.

George gripped the receiver, practically crushing it in his fist. Greedy energy raced through his veins but it was laced with apprehension. If this deal was real, their business was about to skyrocket. If not, they could go to prison for a long time. The thrill was almost too much to bear. He punched Robert's number into the phone.

Chapter Twelve

❦

Clay and Ranger sat in the dark SUV with yet another cop. He'd only had the same partner twice. That was the way with the K9 positions on the joint FBI, State, and Local Law Enforcement Task-force. He supposed, over time, he'd get to know the regular handful of guys. So far Clay enjoyed working with all of them. He'd learned a lot and hoped he'd shared his piece of the knowledge pie too. Cross-pollinating was an excellent thing, when egos didn't crash into each other. So far, so good.

They passed the time by teasing each other with inner law enforcement rivalry, each insulting the other in good fun. In reality, they respected each other's positions and wanted the same things—to protect the innocent and put the bad guys behind bars. Street cops always seemed interested in the K9 faction of the FBI, and this guy was no different. Ranger appeared to like him, and that went a long way with Clay.

Clay pulled into a busy truck-stop on I-70 and settled into the shadows where they could observe the trucks parked in the lot for the night.

"I'm going in to get a burger. Want anything?" The cop reached for the door handle.

"Yeah. Grab me the same with fries and a Coke." Clay opened his wallet and tossed his partner a twenty. "I'll let Ranger out to stretch his legs while you're inside."

He climbed out of the driver's seat and worked through some kinks in his own body before he opened the customized K9 kennel in the back of his vehicle. While Ranger sniffed around the scrub at the edge of the parking lot, Clay leaned against the car and watched the busy nightlife at the truck-stop. Cars lined up in the gas lanes to take advantage of the lower gas prices, and many of the passengers made pit stops to use the restrooms and to buy coffee and snacks for their drive.

Truckers left their semi engines running, most likely to keep the batteries charged for watching movies, and the cab temperature cool for a few hours of sleep before they hit the highways again. Clay coughed away the diesel fumes that fogged the lot. He wondered how it would be to live on the road like truckers did. *Must be a lonely life.*

As his partner exited through the front doors of the diner, Clay noticed two young women walking in. He watched them through the large plate-glass windows of the restaurant. They scanned the place before separating and sauntering between rows of booths and tables. One girl, who had packed herself into a micro-skirt, displayed a bare mid-drift under a fake, pink-fur crop jacket. She leaned on a table with her elbows. The men eating dinner sat taller and peered inside the coat. Clay shook his head.

The cop approached and leaned against the car next to Clay, handing him a to-go bag filled with a greasy burger and fries. Clay opened the bag and breathed in. "God, that smells good. Thanks, man." His gut growled in agreement.

"Sure."

"You notice those two girls going in as you were coming out?"

"Yeah. I'm guessing fifteen, maybe sixteen. It's hard to tell with all the make-up."

"How do they get way out here?" Clay stuffed a handful of salty fries in his mouth.

"Oh, man. This is a lucrative spot. Think about it. Their pimps drop them off. Here they don't even have to pay five bucks an hour for a room. These jack-offs come with their own private compartments."

"Yeah, and complete privacy to do whatever they want. God—these girls are totally vulnerable."

The cop swallowed a huge bite of his sandwich and sucked in a mouthful of soda to rinse it down. "Right? Like the two murdered prostitutes. The ones the sergeant briefed us on tonight." He scarfed another mouthful.

Clay nodded and pulled a drink of Coke through his straw. His gaze never wavered from the girls. They moved from table to table. The shorter girl sat down in a booth next to a hefty man eating alone. Facing him, she slid her arm around his shoulders. A few minutes later, they both got up. The man tossed some cash next to his plate, and they left together through the glass doors. Clay watched them walk down a long row of parked trucks to one at the very back.

"Here we go." He bunched his trash up and tucked it behind the front seat. He grabbed Ranger's lead and called, "*Kemne.*"

Ranger quit his sniffing mission and sat down on Clay's left side. Clay clipped the lead onto the dog's vest, and checked his weapon. "Ready?"

"Let's give them a few minutes to settle in. If we get there too soon, they'll say they were just watching TV."

"I hate this part." Clay swallowed a rush of disgust down his throat. "I don't want to see what these sick bastards pay these kids to do to them. I just want to get the girls, drive them back to the station, and pass them off to El Clark."

"I know, but without any evidence, you can't take them in. It sucks, but that's the job."

Clay's partner finished his fries and licked his fingers. He sucked his straw until loud bubbly noises echoed in the cup. "Okay, we can head over there now." He chuckled.

"How long did it take before you got so callous?"

The cop laughed. "Not long, my friend. Not long. The more you're out here, the more you realize nothing changes, no matter how much you do."

"Pretty cynical," Clay commented while at the same time realizing his own heart was already hardening too. Guys went into law enforcement to defend and serve, but the more he was out here, the more he realized no one wanted defending, and his service was the wrong kind.

The lawmen silently approached the enormous truck. The cop slapped the door and yelled. "Open up. Police." The cab shook with movement from within, and the officer climbed up on the step, shining his flashlight into the dusky interior. "What's going on in here?" Thick sarcasm salted his words. "Come on, open up."

The large door swung open, and the cop jumped down out of the way, keeping the light aimed in the truck driver's eyes. The man practically tossed the girl off his lap before wrestling with his pants. The cab smelled like stale cigarettes and sex.

Ranger growled, and the driver's eyes widened in his puffy face. "What's wrong officers? We're not doing anything wrong."

"No?" Clay stepped forward. Ranger's tense shoulders were poised to spring. "You think having sex with a minor is perfectly fine in the State of Colorado? And worse," he pointed at a stack of bills on the dash, "paying for it? That's two laws broken right there."

"You've got it all wrong, officer."

"Do I?" Clay raised his chin toward the girl. "How old are you?"

Her heavily lined eyes glared at him. "Old enough. This is none of your goddamned business. You guys are just using your badge to get a free peek."

"Free? Do you usually charge for a peek?" The officer goaded.

The girl looked momentarily confused before her expression hardened again. "Nobody's charging anyone for anything."

"Let's see some ID. How old are you?" The cop held out his hand.

"Old enough. But, I left my purse at home. Sorry, boys," the girl sneered.

Fat fingers fumbled through his wallet, and the trucker held out his driver's license. "Listen guys. I'm sorry. I didn't know she was a minor. You've got to let me off with a warning. You know how it is—I've got a wife and kids. If you arrest me, it will ruin my life."

Clay's chest constricted. *What an asshole.* "So getting caught will ruin your life, huh? Not the actual paying for sex while you're out on the road. Cheating on your wife. There's nothing wrong with those things?" Clay glared at the man, sickened by his backward logic. "Get out of the truck."

"You can't take me in. I've got a strict schedule to keep." It was ugly and pathetic to see a huge man whine. "Can't you just give me a ticket or something?"

"Get out of the truck right now, on your own, or I'll have my dog drag you out."

The man's eyes popped, and he wriggled his heavy form out through the door. The prostitute followed him, snatching the cash on her way out.

Clay's partner cuffed and patted them both down before

he called for a second unit to transport the man to the station. Clay escorted the girl to the K9 vehicle. He opened the back door for her. "You know, we just want to help you. This is no kind of life."

"What the hell do you know?" She stopped before getting inside and turned to him, sidling up to his chest. A seductive smile slid into place. "Listen, you're a good-looking guy. Anything I can do to convince you to let me go?" Her natty fake fur brushed against his arm as she pressed and slid her body against him.

Clay stepped back. "No ma'am. Nothing will keep me from trying to find you the help you need to get out of this life."

"You don't know what you're missing." She tossed her head and let him help her into the seat.

Ranger loaded up through the back hatch, and Clay drove straight to the station.

A WOMAN SCREAMING ABOUT HER FALSE ARREST BROUGHT El out of the small police department conference room where she had posted an informational flyer about human trafficking on the board. She'd seen this girl before, on several occasions. Her arrest record was extensive. If only these girls would point the finger at their pimps, the system would consider them victims, rather than perpetrators. Law enforcement changed slowly, but more and more, under-aged prostitutes were not being arrested. Instead, they were brought in and put into the social system where hopefully they could get the help they needed. But some, like this young woman who was eighteen or close enough to believe, would face another arrest on her record making it even harder for her to escape her life of bondage.

A sharp bolt of electricity shot through El's body when she realized that Clay was the officer escorting the girl into the station. She didn't think he was scheduled to work. She was both pleased to see him and dreaded talking to him at the same time.

Clay guided the prostitute to the intake desk, his dog keeping his place on his handler's left side. He glanced in El's direction and when he saw her, a smile brightened his face. El had never met anyone with such startling light-blue eyes and wondered if Clay came from north-German descent or maybe he was Scandinavian. She pictured him as a Viking and smiled at him in return, with more enthusiasm than she should have allowed. The worst thing she could do was encourage him.

After Clay dropped his charge off in the capable hands of the intake officer, he and Ranger made their way over to her. "Hi. I didn't expect to see you here this late."

El checked her watch. "Yeah. I don't normally come in at this hour, but a couple of kids were brought in earlier, and I wanted to get them placed. They left about a half-hour ago." She scratched Ranger behind his ear and he licked her fingers with his rough tongue in return. "I dropped off some human trafficking fliers while I was here." El shifted her weight back, uncomfortable standing so close to Clay. "I've seen the girl you brought in before. She's a hard nut."

"We found her soliciting at a truck stop."

"That's fairly common, though it's getting better now that an organization called Truckers Against Trafficking is helping get information out and watching for victims."

Clay glanced over to where he'd left the girl. "If I didn't know better, I'd believe she liked this life."

An old sorrow draped around El's shoulders like a shawl. "Trust me, she doesn't. It's just that everything gets worse for her if she tries to do anything about it."

"I don't know how you do it."

"What do you mean? Do what?"

"I don't know how you face trying to save kids who don't want help, day after day. I've only been working this gig for two weeks, and already I feel like giving up."

Without thinking, El reached for Clay's arm and grasped hold. "You can't give up. I promise you're making a difference, even if it doesn't seem like it."

' Clay glanced at her hand and her skin grew hot. She released him immediately. His eyes softened, and his mouth twitched up on one side. "Maybe you're a better person than me."

Heat flashed across her face. "No." El shook her head. "No. I'm not. Not at all. But I *do* know that you're helping just by trying. Your presence on the street shows that you care. I wish I could make you understand."

His eyes narrowed slightly as he watched her. "I want to understand." He leaned his muscled shoulder against the doorjamb. "The invitation to dinner is always open, you know. We could talk."

The initial bubbles tickling El's belly were what she figured any regular, untarnished woman would feel when a good and handsome man asked her out, but the sharp pins of reality popped those lofty balls of hope instantly. She wanted to say yes, wanted to get a new dress and go somewhere nice with this man, to laugh and feel safe and beautiful, but she knew all of that was an impossible dream. Her head wagged slowly back and forth, and the light in his eyes dimmed. "I'm sorry, Clay. My life is so crazy right now."

"Sure." He glanced down at Ranger who muzzle-bumped his hand as if in solidarity. "Time to get you home to bed, boy. Ready to go?"

Ranger stood to follow him.

Something like panic pinched the walls of El's chest. "Wait." She grabbed his bicep again.

The muscles in both his arm and his jaw flexed. He tossed a frustrated expression at her, raising his eyebrows in question.

"Have you heard anything about the two prostitutes who were murdered?"

He released a sigh. "Not really. We had a short briefing on the situation before our shift tonight, but that's all. I have a joint task-force meeting at FBI headquarters tomorrow. I'm sure the team will know more by then. They'll at least have worked up a profile of the un-sub."

"The what?"

"Un-sub—unknown subject."

"Oh, right. I'd love to learn more about that..." El could hardly believe the words tumbling their way out of her mouth. "Maybe over coffee?" Her heart thudded.

Clay studied her, and she wished she could evaporate into thin air. She had just told him no, and then she said she wanted to go somewhere with him. El gave him mixed messages, and that wasn't fair. He *should* tell her where to get off, and El bit down on her lip bracing for Clay's rejection. Ranger stepped toward her and leaned his weight into her leg, and she knelt down to cover her awkwardness by petting his shiny black coat.

Clay cocked his head and swallowed, causing his Adam's apple to slide up and down. "How about lunch on Friday?"

Tension flew from her shoulders, and she smiled uncertainly. "Okay. Yes. Lunch. We could meet somewhere."

His rugged smile rewarded her. "Great. Text me the time and place. I'll be there."

Chapter Thirteen

❦

Clay and Ranger were up early and on their way to Denver's FBI headquarters. They had a meeting with the Human Trafficking Joint Task-force and even though they'd had a late night, Clay's attendance was required. When Clay signed up for the task-force, he imagined all the good they could do—the help the unit could be in getting victims off the street and missing children back home. It had come as a punch in the face when most of the young girls he'd tried to help didn't want his interference and told him so in the ugly, hateful language of the street. The language itself didn't shock him. He'd heard that and worse as a Marine. But hearing the coarse words coming out of the mouth of a twelve-year-old girl made him cringe.

He pulled into the parking garage and let Ranger out of the back. "This is the big leagues boy. Let's go impress the team with the K9 contingent."

Ranger wagged his tail and licked Clay's hand when his handler stroked his head. As if he understood, Ranger walked stoically with his head up next to Clay through security and into the conference room on the third floor.

"Jennings," Agent Rick Sanchez, the Special Agent in Charge of the joint task-force, and the husband of one of Clay's best K9 agents, greeted him as he entered the room. "Good to see you—and you too, Ranger."

"Sanchez." Clay nodded to his friend and glanced around, looking for Agent Dean. He spotted her at the far end of the conference table, standing with her K9 partner, a chocolate Labrador named Annie. After smearing half a bagel with sweet, strawberry-cream cheese, he joined her at a spot against the wall. The dogs sniffed the air, but with impeccable discipline did not sniff each other. Clay bobbed his chin at his co-worker.

"Hey, Jennings. How's it goin' working the streets?"

"Hi Dean—or are you going by Sanchez now?"

A bright smile lit her face. "I'm Kendra Sanchez in all things personal, but I'm keeping Dean professionally."

"How long do I have to put up with you being so sappy?" Clay teased, secretly wishing he had someone he felt that way about.

"I don't know... probably forever."

Clay rolled his eyes dramatically. "Great," he chuckled.

Rick Sanchez called the meeting to order. "Thanks for coming, everyone. We'll have reports from each of the Federal, State, and local law enforcement representatives gathered here, but before we get to that, I'd like to share what we know and what our profilers have come up with regarding the recent prostitute murders."

The conference door opened and Burke Cameron, another agent Clay knew, entered. He approached Sanchez and handed him a folder. Every eye in the room focused on the file.

Sanchez motioned for an agent to turn off the lights, and he clicked the keyboard on his laptop. Images of two average, teenaged girls appeared on the Smartboard screen. Sanchez positioned himself before the board. "These girls are the most recent victims of what we have come to believe are serial killings. They were both found in Denver, but the victimology matches two other fairly recent prostitute killings in Kansas City. All four young women were between the ages of fourteen and seventeen, all had long, light-brown hair, and all worked as prostitutes when they were abducted and murdered."

"Is there a commonality to the method of killing?" A state patrol officer asked.

Sanchez nodded at Cameron who manned the laptop. Recent photos flashed on the screen. This time, the photos depicted the dead bodies as the police found them at the crime scenes. "Yes. All four women were strangled and then stabbed multiple times in the abdomen—postmortem. That is the total information we are allowing the press to have at this time."

Sanchez nodded again to Cameron. Close-up photos of the girls' faces, garish with smeared make-up on pale skin, caused Clay's throat to thicken, and he tapped his head back against the wall. He pictured the faces of some of the young prostitutes he'd come in contact with while out on the beat.

"Our un-sub has stabbed the dead bodies each precisely 21 times, indicating extreme emotion. He then poses the girls with their arms crossed over their chests, which suggests remorse. He also cuts a lock of hair from his victims, either as a signature, or as a trophy. Maybe both. This more specific information, along with the number of stab wounds, must remain between those of us in this room."

Dean asked, "Is there enough of a connection between these women to surmise a motive?"

Cameron slid a pen behind his ear. "Obviously he's targeting prostitutes with a certain look, but other than that we have discovered no other links. The girls don't work for the same pimps, and there is no evidence as of yet that they knew each other, or came from the same area. The depth of the stab wounds indicates the killer is emotional—angry or upset—but the fact that the wounds are postmortem presumes he didn't want the victims to suffer. We suspect he may be punishing someone else in his mind. Perhaps another prostitute whom he believes wronged him in some unforgivable way. That's all we have at this point."

"Go back to the last slide." When it flashed on the screen, Sanchez pointed out the girls' injuries. "Each victim has exactly 21 stab wounds to the abdomen. As you see the women were stripped of their clothing except for their shoes. Unfortunately, since they were working as prostitutes at the time of their murders, it is impossible to tell if the murders were sexual in context. The DNA testing of the semen found in the victims shows there is no match between them, though the un-sub could have worn a condom. However, the fact that the stab wounds are limited to the victim's lower abdomens, might mean the motive has something to do with womanhood."

Cameron continued. "The direction of the stab wounds also suggests the killer is right-handed."

A uniformed cop cleared her throat. "Are you sure the killer is a man? Couldn't it be a woman? Maybe a wife who'd found out her husband snuck off and paid for sex?"

"It's a good question," Sanchez answered. "We aren't ruling anything out, but we think it was a man because it takes significant strength to subdue someone and strangle them with bare hands. Women rarely use strangulation to murder. They're more likely to use a gun. Also, though women do use knives, the depth of these stab wounds indicates a strength that would be more common of a male."

Clay pushed up from his position against the wall and Ranger stood with him ready to follow. "We'll leave the profiling to you guys and go with what you're telling us, but what is our mission? Do you want us to hit the streets and warn people?"

"Yes." Sanchez pointed to a stack of print-outs in the center of the table. "Everyone take some of these photos. Ask around if anyone recognizes either of the victims. Also, warn people that there is a murderer targeting young women with long brown hair."

"Won't that cause a panic?" The female cop asked.

"It's possible, but I'd rather these girls be afraid and cautious, than unaware. We may get some good leads from them, too."

"I doubt it." Clay didn't realize he spoke the words out loud until everyone in the room turned to look at him. He cleared his throat. "I only say that because most of the kids I've talked with are suspicious of cops and don't want our help. If it weren't for Ranger, who seems to connect with these kids, I probably wouldn't get anywhere."

"Well, maybe a little fear will be a catalyst then." Sanchez addressed the room. "Let's take a five-minute break and then meet back here for the unit reports."

Clay reached for his phone and found El's number in his contact list. He pressed the message button and texted her. *New info about murdered girls. Can we make that lunch meeting for this afternoon instead?*

Chapter Fourteen

✦

Candie couldn't sleep, though she was exhausted from pulling double duty to cover Fancy's quotas while she was in juvey. Steven had been crying into his pillow all night since she'd come home. His anguish squeezed her heart in a vice she couldn't loosen with any of the usual false justifications. Finally, she pushed herself to her hands and knees and crawled over the mattress strewn floor and sleeping bodies to the dingy pad he lay upon.

"Hey, little man. You've got to get some sleep," she whispered as she rubbed a spot between his slight shoulder blades.

"I want my mommy," he whimpered.

"I know." Candie pulled him up into her lap, his skinny arms and legs still knobby at the joints. "Listen. Your life has changed. You're not going to see the people you knew anymore. I know that's sad, but you have a new family now."

"Jonny hit me. He slapped my head until I... did something." Steven crumpled into tears and buried his face in her chest. "I don't want a new family. I want to go home."

"Sh, sh." Candie stroked his head and held him tight. "Sometimes we don't get what we want, and it goes better if we just accept our new life—if you just do what they expect of you. And besides, you have me. We can be our own family, how about that?"

Steven stopped crying, but he didn't respond.

"There's a lot of crap you will have to face, but it'll be better if you can learn to deal with it. Okay?"

"Like what?"

Candie closed her eyes against the truth. She wished she could protect him somehow, but knew there was no way. If there was a way out of this life, she'd have found it already. "We'll talk about that tomorrow. I have some videos to show you so you can learn. It's better if you know."

"Know what? What kind of movies?"

"Movies that will show you what you're expected to do when you have a date—so you'll know how to act. It's important to learn to pretend you like it."

"A date? Like movies and dinner? With a girl?" Steven's little face screwed up with disgust, like a normal little boy's.

Candie let out a long, pain-filled breath. "No. Not like that. Let's get some sleep, we'll talk more about this tomorrow."

"Can I sleep in your bed?" His damp blue eyes looked at her with such trust her heart shattered.

"Sure, come on." They crawled back to her slightly bigger mattress, and Steven curled his little body into hers. She pulled the musty, thin blanket up over them, and wrapped her arm around him. Memories of cuddling with her own mother filled her mind, and she fought them off. *What would mama think of me now? She'd be so disgusted with who I am—the things I've done. I never want her to know. It's better if she remembers the little girl I once was.* One hot tear escaped and rolled down her cheek, disappearing in Steven's blond curls.

.   .   .

AN ARGUMENT BETWEEN TWO OF THE GIRLS UPSTAIRS IN the kitchen woke Candie from a fitful sleep. Steven sat next to her, watching her.

"Have you had breakfast?" She wiped sleep from the inner corners of her eyes. The old digital clock across the room flashed a red 1:30 pm. Candie usually slept until two or two-thirty after getting in around 4:00 am.

Steven shook his head.

"Let's go get something to eat and tell those idiots to shut-up."

Jonny's angry voice entered the fray above them, pissed off that the girls' argument woke him. A crash sounded, and one of the girls cried out. Closing her eyes for a second, Candie pictured the blow Jonny had given the girl that likely sent her sprawling into the counter. Candie waited until she heard Jonny storm out the front door before she took Steven by the hand and started up the stairs.

Bright sunshine assaulted her pupils as she and Steven emerged from below. Lacy and Trixie stood in the kitchen. Trixie held a paper towel to her bleeding nose as Candie and Steven entered the room. "Are you okay? Do you want some ice?"

"I think he broke my nose!" the girl cried.

"When are you two going to learn not to piss Jonny off? It always ends up the same. Someone gets hurt, and the rest of us have to cover her workload." Candie pulled the girl's hand away from her face. "Let me see." She studied her nose. "I don't think it's broken, thank God. Let's get you some ice. We can cover any bruises with make-up." She opened the freezer. "Lacy, get Steven something to eat."

"He can get his own food. I'm not his mom, am I?"

"No, but you could make yourself useful."

The girl sighed and tossed a cereal bowl onto the table. She plunked a box of cereal next to it, and pulled a jug of milk from the fridge. Steven took everything in without saying a word. His eyes looked bruised in his pale face from crying all night and lack of sleep. He seemed to sink deep inside himself, and he had seen nowhere near the worst of things yet.

Candie watched him pour the cereal into his bowl and knew she had to help him. Somehow, she had to get him away from Jonny, but how? One thing was certain. If she helped Steven escape, it would cost her her own life.

Jonny burst back into the kitchen. His eyes seemed unfocused like he was on something. He was unpredictable when he'd been using, and Candie casually stepped between him and the little boy having breakfast.

"I just got off the phone with Fancy." Jonny slapped the box of cereal off the table, sending sugar-coated flakes flying across the floor. Everyone froze in place and stared at him. "She has to stay in juvey for six months instead of three. Do you know how much that's going to cost me?"

Nothing, but it will cost the rest of us dearly. Candie's skin tightened, but she didn't answer him, knowing that she and the other girls would have to wear themselves out to make up for Jonny's potential loss of cash.

Jonny's gaze panned the faces staring at him and settled finally on Candie. "Have you started managing these hos' schedules yet?"

Candie nodded once.

"Listen up—all of you. We have a big event coming up. Something special—bigger than the Broncos' playoff season —even bigger than the Stock Show."

Apprehension expanded through Candie's chest like a cloud of noxious fumes.

"It comes with a special order. Eight girls and three boys. Young ones." Jonny popped his chin towards Candie. "You're too old. The man said the younger the better."

Candie shuddered while keeping her expression bland.

Jonny grabbed a bottle of vodka from the counter and knocked back a swig. "I've already called my contact in Las Vegas. Between us, we can fill the order, no problem." His hazy gaze floated to Steven. "Get that boy ready. He's got a weekend gig in Ft. Collins when you bitches are in Dakota."

Candie moved toward Jonny and stretched a hand toward him. "Jonny, he's too young. Give him some time. He doesn't understand."

Like an unexpected snake strike, Jonny's fist flew through the air and smashed into Candie's jaw. Pain radiated through her skull as her head snapped back. Stunned, she lost her balance and fell to the floor, hitting her skull on the table on the way down. She reached her hands up to her face, unknowingly leaving her belly open to attack. Jonny's boot swung savagely into her gut, once, twice, three times. Candie's body curled into itself like a squished spider. Screams echoed in the room, but sounded far away. Then silence.

Candie became gradually aware of a cool cloth touching her cheek followed by soft kisses. Jonny whispered, "Candie? Wake up."

Her eyes fluttered open and watered at the vodka fumes on Jonny's breath.

"I hate when you make me do that, baby. We're supposed to be on the same team, right?"

Nausea roiled through her sore stomach, threatening action, as Jonny lifted her off the floor and pulled her onto his lap. "Don't ever argue with me again. A' right?" He kissed her temple and ran his fingers over her hair. Jonny pushed up to his feet, holding Candie in his arms, and carried her into his bedroom. He laid her on the bed and fluffed a pillow for her head. He kissed the sore spot where he'd punched her, and helped her lay back. "It won't be much longer. Just think, with a couple special events like this one, we'll be set. We can finally get out of this racket. Buy that house we used to talk about. Have a good life." He kissed her lips. "You want that, don't you, baby?"

Candie closed her eyes. That was the story he'd told her the day he'd stolen her from the ballpark where her brother had been playing in a baseball game. She had argued with her mom and had stormed away, angry. Jonny approached her at the playground and sympathized about how unfair her parents had been. He'd told her they didn't really care about her or they would have apologized.

"What's your name, beautiful?"

No one had ever called her that before, and she'd smiled at him. "Lilly."

"Will you let me buy you an ice cream, Lilly?" He pointed at the shop across the street.

She had nodded and followed him inside. He bought her a double-dip of chocolate fudge in a waffle cone. They ate it in his car and then he'd taken her for a ride. She'd felt so grown up.

When she realized Jonny didn't plan to return her to the park, she panicked, but he'd calmed her by explaining to her that he'd fallen in love with her. That she was beautiful for her age and that he wanted to marry her when she got a little older. "Besides, your parents only care about your brother. They don't love you like I do."

"But, you just met me."

Jonny took her hand and kissed it. "Haven't you ever heard of love at first sight?"

Lilly's body had warmed at his romantic words. The boys she knew never talked like that.

Over the next weeks, Jonny bought her gifts and new clothes. He made her feel so grown up. They stayed in motels, but he never touched her other than to cuddle and give her an occasional kiss. He started calling her Candie as a pet name.

The night before they arrived in Denver, things changed. He left her in the motel room and went out for pizza. When he got back, he was angry. When she asked him what was wrong, he slapped her so hard it loosened two of her teeth. Confused and rocked emotionally, Candie stared at him, not knowing if she should apologize for something or run and hide.

Jonny gathered her into his arms. "I'm sorry, baby. I'm frustrated because I need you. I can't wait any longer. You drive me crazy, baby. Take off your clothes."

She shook her head. How could he ask her to do such a thing?

The second slap came as fast as the first. "I said, take off your clothes. You love me don't you? You said you did. This is what people do when they love each other. I need you. I've given you so much, and you've given me nothing in return. Now, take off your clothes. You want me to be happy, don't you?"

Candie's mind closed a curtain on what followed. That night became a void in her memory. But she remembered the following day when Jonny drove her to his dumpy house in Denver. He led her inside to meet three other girls who were also his girlfriends.

He had tossed her backpack down a steep flight of stairs to the basement. "All my bitches sleep down there. Find a free mattress." That night they indoctrinated her into her new family. The other girls told her the cold, hard facts of her changed life, and Candie cried herself to sleep. Her first *date* was the following night.

Candie's life hadn't changed much over the past three years. She'd been used more times than she could count, and Jonny's violence had gotten worse, but the routine was the same. Abuse, apologies, empty promises, and the inevitable claim that he wished she didn't have to sell herself either. He'd insist she had to do her part if they would ever have the life they'd dreamed of, right before he drugged her, and sent her out to the street again.

His voice brought her back. "You have a bruise on your jaw, but nothing makeup can't cover. Rest for a bit, but then I need you. We've got to get ready to go on our road trip up to Dakota. Plenty of oil-workers with too much cash on their hands and nowhere to spend it. God, I love this time of year." Jonny kissed her cheek. "Want some tea? You forgive me baby, don't you? You know I didn't mean to get so angry. You can't sass me though. You're sorry too, right?"

Now, lying in his bed, her body screaming in pain, Candie listened to him apologizing while blaming her at the same time. He bounced between that and planning his next money-making scheme. Inwardly, she recoiled from him and her resolve strengthened. She would not stand by and let this horrible life become Steven's.

Chapter Fifteen

✻

C lay left Ranger at the K9 facility kennel and drove
to meet El for their lunch date. He parked in the lot
behind the shops at Northfield and walked to the
Mexican restaurant El suggested. The entryway was dim and
Clay waited for his eyes to adjust as the cool air-conditioning
soothed the heat from his skin, raising goosebumps on his
arms. He breathed in Mexican spices wafting from the
kitchen and his mouth watered.

El already sat at a table on the colorfully decorated patio
and he told the hostess he was meeting her. The girl smiled
and handed him a menu. It occurred to him that many of the
kids on the street were around the same age as this one, and
he wondered at the fates that changed some people's lives on
a whim. If this girl wasn't careful, could she be the next
victim? His mind was constantly barraged with these
concerns lately. They colored all his thoughts about the world
around him. He missed the days when he was more carefree,
and less informed. As soon as that notion gelled, guilt
followed on its heels. Sure, life was simpler for him when he
wasn't aware, but ignorance didn't change the fact that real

people suffered in trafficking every day—whether he was aware of it or not.

With a gentle shake of his head, he forced his lips into a grin as he approached El. "Hey. Thanks for meeting me."

El's gaze appraised him before she returned his smile. "You said you needed to talk." She glanced behind him. "Where's Ranger?"

"I rarely bring him with me to restaurants."

"Oh." El seemed genuinely disappointed and Clay wondered if she had agreed to lunch so she could spend more time with Ranger. *Can a guy be jealous of his dog?*

They ordered their meal and tossed a bit of small talk back and forth while they waited, nibbling on the complimentary chips and fresh, spicy salsa.

"This is a nice place." Clay leaned back in his chair. "I've lived in this area a long time, but I've never been here."

El sipped on a tall glass of iced-tea. "The food here is really good."

"Have you lived in Colorado all your life?"

A shadow darkened the greenish-blue of El's eyes before she lowered her gaze to her plate and hid behind a curtain of auburn hair. "No. I've lived all over."

Clay wasn't sure why that question threw her. He wasn't trying to pry into her personal past. Their meals arrived and after the first few bites, Clay jumped in. "I wanted to speak with you about your work involving human trafficking and the kids we see every night on the streets."

El blew to cool her bite of piping-hot enchiladas. She raised her eyebrows in question and nodded for him to continue.

"You know there has been two murders."

She nodded.

"Well, it looks like we have a serial killer on our hands who is targeting young women between the ages of fourteen and seventeen. The victims have all had long, light-brown hair, and all were working as prostitutes when they were murdered."

"That's horrible! "We need to get the word out on the streets to be on the look-out for this guy. Do you have a description?"

"No, not yet. Is there a way to let the girls, especially brunettes, know they need to be careful?"

"I'll try to get the word out. That kind of news will spread fast. Is there anything else I can do?"

"I don't think so, but thanks." Clay lifted a bite dripping with cheese and paused. "You know, I've hauled in handfuls of young, underaged prostitutes, arrested almost as many johns, and on a good night I might actually get ahold of a pimp to bring in on charges, but it seems like no matter what we accomplish, we aren't making a dent in the problem. The girls don't seem to want our help either. That's the hardest part for me to understand."

"It's not black and white, Clay. Most of them are addicted to drugs. Drugs that their pimps provide for them, that they believe are the only way to make it through each day. Many don't have anywhere else to go, or any way to take care of themselves. For them, the devil they know is safer than the devil they don't. Some of the kids come from families that are worse than what they deal with on the streets. Still others come from families they love and the pimps threaten the lives of their loved ones. Pick a reason, or two."

"God." Clay's intestines turned to stone. "So, how do we make a difference?"

El wiped her mouth, sat back, and spread her napkin on her lap. "Honestly? We probably aren't even scratching the surface. The sex trade makes so much money for these guys, as soon as you get one pimp off the street, two more show up to take his place. The sex trade brings in more money than drugs and illegal firearm trafficking combined.

"That's hard to believe."

"Believe it."

"Then what are we doing? Is there no way to stop it?"

"The only way to stop it is to kill the demand for it. Sexual exploitation, slave labor, illegal adoption—all types of human trafficking—have been going on since the dawn of time."

"I know that, but it's so bad now. The problem seems bigger than ever."

"That could be. It's probably because there is so much cash to be made. It's all about the money."

Clay swiped at the icy condensation on his glass and blotted his fingers on his napkin. "You say we have to stop the demand. How do we do that?"

El huffed a sad breath. "First, you need to understand how an ordinary guy, like yourself, ends up paying for sex."

Clay's brows shot up. *For God's sake, does she seriously think I'm the kind of guy who would hire a prostitute?* El's cheeks flushed and she looked young and vulnerable in that moment. Clay resisted the urge to take her hand.

"I don't mean *you*, specifically." A self-conscious smile graced her mouth. "Just any regular guy. Anyway, it starts off with young kids seeing so much sex on TV, in the movies, and even video games. They get desensitized to it. Some of them move into watching porn and for a while that gives them plenty of titillation. Many become sexually active at a young age. Then when that thrill dulls, they look for videos with a bit more edge. Maybe some bondage or S and M play. There's a plethora of that kind of thing on the web. After a while, watching isn't enough, but many men in this situation don't want to ask their wives or girlfriends to do anything kinky, so they pay a stranger to act it out with them. That's probably the main path of the demand. There are, of course, others. And when people follow that path long enough, their desire to try more and more twisted fantasies increases. I think that's why we're seeing such an increase in child pornography and younger kids for sale and on the streets."

Clay's appetite flattened, and his food was no longer appealing. He gulped down some water. "So, are you saying directors need to stop showing so much sex in movies? That would diminish the demand?"

El sighed. "It would help, but it's far more complicated than that. Don't forget the money side of this business. It represents enormous dollar amounts, and with big money comes powerful people. Greedy people. They're even harder to fight. They're ultimately why when you pull one kid from the street, another one shows up."

"God. The problem is insurmountable." Clay studied El over the rim of his glass.

"It can feel that way." El sipped her tea.

Clay studied El over the rim of his glass. "How do you continue working at a job that's so discouraging? How do you stay positive with such a low success rate?"

El lifted a shoulder and pulled one corner of her mouth back.

HIS WORDS WRENCHED HER HEART. EL REACHED ACROSS the table and squeezed his forearm. "I take it one day at a time, remembering that every single life that we can help change, matters. I don't think of all those I'm not reaching, but focus on the individual I can affect today. Even if I help only one person's life to change, it's worth it." Clay stared at her and she wondered if he thought she was crazy.

"I don't only focus on the dark side of trafficking, either. I volunteer with a recovery group that assists people transitioning from human trafficking to a new life. The girls coming out have no property of their own—no clothes, no personal care items, no comforts, no family, no home. One thing I like to do is collect items to fill backpacks that the group gives to the victims."

Clay relaxed back in his chair. "You work for the kids at your job *and* you volunteer for them too? I didn't even know groups like that existed." A cloud slid away from the sun and light splashed into the pool of his eyes. He lowered his sunglasses from the top of his head to his nose, and El was deprived of the expression hidden behind the mirrored lenses.

She swallowed her sudden sense of separation and continued, "Yes. Groups like these are crucial not only to help people through their transition but to keep the victims safe. In that way, the recovery centers are similar to centers for abused women. The women's identities and locations are kept secret."

"Makes sense. So, even the volunteers don't know?"

"Right. Well, for the most part. I know, but that's because of my job."

"Does the group provide a place for them to stay?"

Uncomfortable with her sense of exposure, El reached in her purse for her own sunglasses to hide behind. "There are a few temporary rooms. Some people who escape are older and require assistance to make it on their own. But the minors who find their way there are the ones I work with to either find their families or foster placement."

Clay leaned forward and reached for his tea. He held the glass between his hands. "Are a lot of kids reunited with their parents?"

El sighed and shook her head. "Precious few want to return to their families or even have families to go back to.

Most of the kids come from unstable, dysfunctional homes. They are the kids predators focus on as easy targets in the first place."

"Sick bastards." Clay shoved his glass away and adjusted his seat. "As if those kids don't have it tough enough already." His jaw muscles bunched.

His frustration was familiar to El. She dealt with those feelings every day. "The recovery groups do all that they can. Every single person who escapes from trafficking needs love and patience. Most need time in detox or addiction rehab. All require long-term therapy."

"Does the group get funding from the state?"

"Some, but mostly they work on donations. Many of the counselors volunteer their time."

"Like you?"

El shrugged, uncomfortable with the admiration in Clay's tone. "The people coming out of human trafficking are similar to prisoners of war. They're disoriented and afraid, and desperately need help. They suffer from connection trauma, and PTSD, and most likely will never completely heal from their torturous imprisonment and abuse."

Clay covered her hand with his. "You have such a good heart. You're an incredible person. I have to admit, I want to see results. I want the kids we help to be glad for the hand up and take advantage of it. But, more often than not, they act as though we're the enemy." He dropped his gaze to his plate briefly before looking back into her eyes. "You're an amazing woman, El. I hope you'll let me get to know you better."

El pulled her hand free. She'd done it again—sent him a message she didn't intend. She should have kept her hands and her thoughts to herself. El bit down hard on the inside of her lip. God, how she wanted what he offered. She fantasized of life with an honorable man. It didn't hurt that Clay was handsome, but that wasn't what she cared about. He was honest, caring, and strong. Integrity rolled off him in waves. He saw the world in black and white, and stood firm for what was right. El found it difficult to believe that men like Clay truly existed, but it didn't matter, because if he knew the truth about her, he would not be asking to know her better. Clay Jennings would turn and walk away, like every other man she had ever known.

Chapter Sixteen

The day had come. Giddy—either with excitement or the effects of cocaine—Jonny showed Candie and the other girls the dark-blue passenger van he rented to drive them all up to the oilfields in South Dakota. This was an annual event that Candie had learned to tolerate. She would have her own room which was a welcome change. At night, Candie could check out to her imaginary world while men pawed and mauled her body. The secret place in her mind allowed her to be free, lying on a beach somewhere like she'd seen in commercials on TV.

Of course, it would be a little different this time because she was Jonny's new bottom-bitch, which meant she'd be responsible to collect the cash and make sure the others made their quotas for the week. Jonny made a ton of money during oilfield week. So much that he vied for more days, but someone kept the scheduled time slots in the Dakotas well organized, and the men wanted variety. Pimps from all over the Midwest brought girls there.

At the end of the week, if Jonny was in a generous mood, he usually stopped at the outlet mall in Loveland on the way back to Denver and let the girls do a little shopping as a reward. She knew he wanted to get everyone some new clothes in preparation for some big event he was even more excited about than the party coming up in late August.

Their make-shift family boarded the van, each girl toting a bag of clothing and cosmetics for the week. Jonny was the last out of the house, holding a backpack in one hand and gripping the back of Steven's neck with the other. Candie chewed her lip and anxiously moved to nibbling the hangnail on her ring finger. Poor Steven. This was his first full weekend on the job.

Steven climbed in the van and sat next to Candie. He leaned forward, propping his elbows on his knees and didn't look at her. He was the only one Candie wasn't responsible for this week. Jonny had made a special arrangement for him to spend some time with 'the professor', a long-standing client of theirs, up in Ft. Collins.

"I'm sorry," Candie whispered. He reached for her hand. They sat side by side on the drive to Ft. Collins without saying a word. Jonny told her that Steven's "date" had borrowed a vacant house from another professor friend so no one would disturb them during their extended time together.

Ft. Collins was a pretty city. Streets shaded by big old trees were lined interesting sounding shops. Most of the college students had gone home for the summer, but some remained. Young men and women played frisbee in the park or walked dogs and talked. They lived such carefree lives. *What's it like not to have to worry or be afraid? To never have random men grope and use your body? To have cute boys flirt with you, and want to do nice things for you?* Candie wondered if any of them even saw her. If so, what did they think about a van full of teenaged girls driven through town by a squirrelly, little man? Whatever they thought, she knew they couldn't imagine the truth. If someone told them, they wouldn't believe it, or it would disgust them. If she could manage the chance to ask, would any of them help her get Steven to safety? She doubted they'd give her the time of day. When Candie was ready to make a move, she'd have to be sure it would work. Her life, and Steven's, depended on it.

Jonny drove up to a tall, stately home constructed in a different era. The house was two stories tall and built with red brick. A large front porch welcomed folks to sit and visit awhile. Double entry doors hinted at impressive rooms on the other side. Jonny turned off the engine and said, "You bitches wait here. Steven, you're on." He turned and glared at him. "Don't you disappoint me either, boy. This is a big client. I want him happy. Do you understand me?"

Steven barely bobbed his head and stared at the floor. Candie's belly squirmed like oily eels as she squeezed his hand, but she had no words. How could she encourage someone to face the torture she knew would be his?

Jonny opened the side door and yanked Steven out. "Toss me his pack."

One girl kicked it toward the opening. The mood in the van turned heavy. No one looked at anyone else. At the last second before Jonny slammed the door, Steven glanced back at Candie. She tried to smile, but her lips wouldn't move. She pressed her hand against her heart, and he gave her a single nod. Jonny led the boy up to the doors and knocked. The entrance swung open, but Candie couldn't see the person inside. Jonny pushed Steven through and closed the door. Several minutes later, Jonny sauntered down the walk with a bulge in his front pocket—his commission for selling a child.

"What are you cry-babying about, Candie? That kid?" A girl behind her scoffed. "You better get over that."

Candie touched her wet cheek. She hadn't realized she was crying. Fast, before Jonny noticed, she wiped her face dry. He hopped into the driver's seat, whistling a toneless tune, and drove them back out to the highway. Candie did her best to keep her thoughts off of Steven. She tried to escape to the secret place in her mind, but Steven's big blue eyes kept interrupting her fantasy. Six and a half hours later, Jonny pulled up to a row of oil field barracks that would be their home and workplace for the following week.

Jonny handed Candie a key ring that held keys to their rooms, and a spreadsheet with the girl's dates already printed on the schedule. He pointed at the paper. "See those empty spots? I expect you hos to fill them. The money you collect better amount to what a full schedule brings in. If not, I'll take it out of your hide. Hear me?"

Candie swallowed hard. She was foolish when she thought she'd have a little more freedom as Jonny's bottom. Now she realized *she* would have to make up for the flagging quota if there was one. She needed to get these girls working right away.

As soon as everyone ambled out of the van, Jonny drove away, leaving them standing in a bunch with their bags at their feet in the dirt. Candie drew in a full breath. "Okay. Get your bags and pick a room."

"I'm hungry," Trixie whined.

"Me too." Lacy crossed her arms. "I'm not doing anything until we get something to eat."

Candie lifted her bag to her shoulder. "We'll get dinner as soon as we're settled. We have two hours before we start work tonight. Come on." She marched toward the barracks without looking back, but she didn't hear anyone following. Candie chose the room in the middle of the row, so she could keep a better eye on the girls. After trying three keys, she found the one that fit her room. Without turning around she shouted. "It's up to you, but no food until we're unpacked." Resigned to her fate, she opened her door, stepped through, and closed it behind her with a bang.

A double bed sat in the middle of her room next to a small table with two chairs, and a tiny bathroom. A counter in the back corner held several unmatched glasses. Below them sat an empty mini-fridge except for a tray of ice. The only window looked out the front. The dirt covering the glass rendered the torn curtains unnecessary.

Candie set her bag on a chair and slipped off her shoes. A knock sounded from the entry. She assumed the girls were ready to walk down to the canteen to find some food, and she yanked open the door. A tall, wiry man, dirty from his day's work stood before her. He took a step inside, body odor wafting in with him, and Candie backed up to give him space. The man grinned, displaying tobacco stuck in his yellow teeth. He closed the door. After tossing several bills on the table, he undid his belt, pulled it from the loops and snapped it. Candie flinched.

He chuckled. "Ready to party?"

Dinner would have to wait.

AFTER A LONG, HARD WEEK, CANDIE'S BODY WAS SORE ALL over. She dried off from a noontime shower, relieved not to have to reapply heavy makeup to her face. She slipped into a loose T-shirt and shorts that wouldn't rub against the handful of bruises and welts she'd sustained over the duration of the past days. Usually, the oil workers were merely interested in straightforward sex, but this week had been different. Her tongue ran over a stinging cut on her lip, and she was glad to be going home. Candie wished Jonny would give them a day off to recuperate, but she doubted it. She shoved her few belongings into her bag, added the zippered bank-bag filled with the week's cash, and left the room with its nightmares behind. She and the other girls gathered out in front of the barracks to wait for the van.

Jonny's band of disconnected children sat on the temporary porch sharing the same space but were in no way together. No one looked in another's eyes—no one spoke. The sun beat down on them, and Candie absently swung her legs to move the hot air pressing against her skin.

Eventually, in the distance, a whirl of dust wound up the road. Jonny's van came into view and Candie stood. The tires crunched the gravel when Jonny parked next to his stable of girls. She noticed three forms sitting side-by-side on the bench seat in the back of the van. She opened the sliding door, hoping to see Steven—wanting to know that he was okay—that he had survived.

Steven sat wedged between two other boys about the same age, whom Candie didn't know. Their glassy eyes floated in slack expressions. Obviously, Jonny had drugged them for the long drive. *Where did these boys come from? Did Jonny steal them from a park somewhere? Kidnapped them the way he did me?*

The new kids stared at her and the other girls. Tiny flecks of terror flashed in their dopey eyes. One of the unknown kids had wet his pants and the sharp scent of urine permeated the air inside the van. Steven's empty gaze rose to her throat, but he didn't look up at her face. His body sat on the bench seat, but he didn't seem to be inside of it. Candie closed her eyes against a piercing jab that radiated pain through her chest.

"Who are these boys, Jonny?" She moved away from the door so the other girls could load up.

Jonny wheezed out a sketchy smoker's laugh. "They're a new addition to our family."

"But where did they come from?" Candie swallowed back a lump of bile.

"That's the best part." Jonny chuckled. "I used the old

remote-control car trick at Park Meadows Mall. That little blond kid back there chased the car right up to the side of the van. The grab took less than ten seconds. The kid didn't even have a chance to fight before Tito popped him with the syringe of smack. It worked so well, Tito and I did it again at the Aurora Mall an hour later."

Candie shuddered. Even the mention of Jonny's friend's name made her nervous. Tito was the leader of a gang that ran the streets in Aurora. He and Jonny grew up together, and now Tito protected Jonny's territory in exchange for free use of Jonny's girls. Tito was mean for being mean's sake. Candie hated the thought of his vicious hands anywhere near those scared little boys.

"Why did you steal them?" She clenched her molars together in sorrow and frustration. Afraid to show Jonny that she cared about them, she changed her tack. "The house is already full. Where will they sleep?"

"Bitch, why do you think your opinion matters to me? I don't care where they sleep." Jonny returned to the driver's seat. "I'm a business man, baby. I'm expanding, remember? I need them for the kiddy porn site I'm building, besides I also need them to fill a party order."

"Jonny—"

"Shut your fat suck, and give me my money. You better have enough too, you lazy hos. This wasn't a fucking vacation, you know."

"I've got it." Candie opened her bag and handed the pouch to Jonny.

"Come to Papa," he said, and snatched the bag away from her. He pulled out the cash and counted it. "No tips?" He glared at Candie.

"It's all in there." *Nobody better have kept any cash back.* If Jonny found a ho keeping back any bills both she *and* Candie would pay the price.

"Come on, girl, get in the van, before I drive away and leave you here."

Candie let a pent-up breath out and climbed into the van. She squeezed herself into a spot next to Steven, nudging his seat mate over.

"Are you okay?" she whispered to him.

Steven dropped his chin to his chest. He didn't answer, didn't even acknowledge her. She understood that he probably thought she betrayed him. He might even blame her for letting this happen to him. She wished he knew that if she could have stopped it from happening, she would have.

Jonny pulled away from the barracks and found his way back to the road. "I know a guy who's part of a nab and grab gang that works Park Meadows regular like." He eyed Candie in the rearview mirror. "They have all sorts of tricks. One of their boys is young looking and he flirts with the teeny-bopper, rich-bitches 'til he gets one to go outside with him. Then wham! She's tossed in their van." Jonny's hands gripped and re-gripped the steering wheel as he got caught up in his story. "They've also grabbed chicks right from the parking lot when they go to get in their car. Simple too. All they do is zip-tie her wiper blades together and when the mark gets back out to undo them—pow—they grab her. Best part of that scheme is they get the girl *and* the car. Fucking brilliant! And it takes way less work and time than grooming a kid on social media."

Candie leaned close to Steven's ear and spoke so only he could hear. "We will escape. Somehow. I promise. We just have to survive until then."

A single tear trickled down Steven's cheek as his blank eyes stared straight ahead.

Chapter Seventeen

❧❧❧

El helped fill donated backpacks with items the Hope Recovery Group had collected for teens during their recovery and transition. She worked alongside a group of wonderful volunteers, who had incredible compassion for the victims of human trafficking. They offered their time and efforts faithfully for people whom they would never meet, but who desperately needed their help. The volunteers understood how crucial it was to protect the identity of the victims to keep them safe from their abusers.

El toted a large plastic bag filled with toothbrushes and tubes of toothpaste. She moved through stacks of donated items, placing a set in each pile. A woman in front of her passed out sketch pads and colored pencils. Today, they had fifty-five backpacks to fill. Later, El would drive to the different police stations around the city and drop off one or two full packs to have on location in case their departments brought in kids in need of help.

After El set some toothpaste on the last pile, she went to the front of the room and addressed the band of helpers. "Excuse, me." When she had everyone's attention, she continued. "I want to thank each of you for coming in today and every day that you work to assist the victims of human trafficking. You should know how necessary your efforts are, and that you are changing lives. In my job, I see the faces of these kids. They are lost and alone. They're scared. Receiving this gift, a bag of items they can call their very own, is a first step in rebuilding their faith in humanity, and in believing they might have a different kind of life. You all are amazing, and I thank you."

The workers clapped and returned to their tasks with renewed energy.

El's cell phone buzzed in her back-pocket. Clay's number lit up her screen. Torn between excitement that he'd called and the knowledge that she should discourage him, she drew a deep breath and shoved her fingers into her hair. With the next vibration she answered. "Hello?"

"Hey, El. It's Clay. I wondered if you'd meet me for a beer this afternoon? It's a beautiful day, and it's just about beer-thirty. Ranger and I like to go to a place that has a big patio and is dog friendly. Want to join us?"

El hesitated, torn between the desire to enjoy a relaxing afternoon with a new friend—behaving like regular people, and knowing that was impossible because she was anything but regular.

"Come on. Ranger is staring at me with hope in his eyes and that silly dog grin of his. He really wants you to come." He waited, and she tried to come up with an excuse. "It's just a drink, El."

She sighed. "Okay. That sounds nice. I can't leave for another half-hour though."

"Where are you?"

"I'm at a church in Centennial, working with a group here that gathers items for people escaping human trafficking."

His voice deepened. "You're really something. I don't

think I've ever met anyone so willing to give of themselves. You're a way kinder than I am, that's for sure."

"I'm not."

"Yes, El. You truly are an unselfish person. A wonderful human being. You inspire me to get off my ass and do more."

"You wouldn't say that if you knew me."

"I think I would, but let's find out. Come have a beer, and we can talk. I'm betting I'll still feel the same way." When El didn't respond, he continued. "I'll text you the location and meet you there in an hour. See you soon." He ended the call and within seconds a tone alerted her to his text.

What will he think when he finds out about me? El sighed. *I suppose he deserves to know, and then he'll stop trying to get me to go out. That will be better for both of us.*

EL DROVE PAST THE CORNER BAR. CLAY WAS ON THE PATIO, leaning back in his chair with a pint of beer in his hand, enjoying the sunshine. Ranger lay at his feet underneath the table. With his black coat he probably preferred the shade. They made an alluring pair. Grasshoppers leapt around in her stomach at the thought of spending time with them. Parallel parking was not her strong suit, so El parked several blocks away where she could pull forward up to the curb. Walking the three blocks back to the pub would do her good. The leafy trees in the old Denver neighborhood were tall and full, shading the street and keeping the summer heat at a pleasant level.

When El approached the corner, Clay grinned and stood up. "I think you have to go inside to get out here to the patio." Ranger's tail thumped the cement.

El made her way through the restaurant out to Clay's table. "This looks like a fun place."

Still standing, Clay waited for her. "Yeah. Cheap beers and

they always put a bowl of water out for dogs." He pulled a chair out for her.

"Thanks." El smiled at him and sat down, bending forward to greet Ranger. He licked her hand and seemed to smile as he lolled his tongue out the side of his mouth.

"I've got some buffalo wings on the way. What kind of beer do you like?"

"Actually, iced tea sounds good to me right now."

He waved to call the server over. "I'm glad you came."

"Me too. I wanted to talk to you about something."

Clay raised a blond eyebrow.

"Have you ever heard of animal-assisted therapy?"

"Yeah, but I don't know much about it." He snickered. "I guess you could say our K9s do a type of crime-prevention therapy."

El shook her head, and a slight smile played at her lips. "No, I mean helping people heal through the use of animals."

"I know they take dogs and cats to nursing homes sometimes."

"Yeah, like that—in a way. Those animals help the older folks to express and feel love. It helps relieve their loneliness and boredom."

"Okay... what does this have to do with me?"

The server brought the wings, and El ordered her drink. She dipped a fiery wing into ranch dressing and bit into it. "Oh, that's good!" She finished chewing, the creamy sauce soothing her burning tongue. "Anyway, I've noticed several times when you've brought kids into the police station, how sweet Ranger is with them. He seems to understand their need for a friend and for protection."

Clay quirked his brows and gave her an incredulous expression. "Ranger is *not* sweet. He is a highly trained, vicious attack dog."

El laughed. "True." She rubbed Ranger's head. "I didn't

mean to insult you, boy." Her mango tea arrived, and she drew a long, icy sip through the straw. "I'm serious though. I know he's an amazing FBI K9 agent, but I think he also has an innate intuition. I've seen him naturally comfort some of those kids."

Nodding, Clay studied her from behind his mirrored Oakleys. "I've noticed it too. He likes kids."

"I once went to a workshop given by a social-worker in Castle Rock. She worked with teens in the foster-care system using equine therapy. Her work fascinated me, and recently I've been wondering if animal therapy could help kids who break free from trafficking."

"How? What would that look like?"

El took another long drink before answering, pausing to garner her courage. "To start with, dogs could offer unconditional love and acceptance to people who don't believe they are worthy of any love at all. Like kids afraid of the judgement they will face from people that don't understand their situation. Dogs don't ask questions, or scowl, or offer pity. They simply love. I think it could truly be beneficial."

"I have to agree." Clay sat forward, resting his forearms on the wrought-iron table. "What about linking up with an animal shelter, or something?"

"Maybe. I'd like to have a team of dogs that kids could build a relationship with, though. It might be worse if a survivor made friends with a dog one week only to come back and learn he had been adopted out of the program. These kids have already dealt with too much loss."

A genuine smile spread across Clay's face.

"What?" Self-consciousness sent blood to El's cheeks. Had she been too enthusiastic? Too dramatic?

"You never cease to amaze me."

She lowered her gaze to her hands and shook her head, wishing he would stop.

"Seriously. You give all of your time and effort to assist people who are less fortunate. I know lots of people who talk about helping, or who write a convenient check to support a cause, but I've never met anyone whose work and free-time are both given to help others."

"It's not a big deal."

"I doubt the kids you've helped would agree with you." Clay cocked his head. "Why do you do it? Spend all your time helping others?"

The air surrounding them grew dense with meaning. El stared at the chiseled features of the man seated across from her while she stirred her drink with the plastic straw. The beginnings of sentences ran in and out of her mind. Finally, she settled on a simple and vague explanation.

"Someone helped me once. I'm paying it forward."

"El, when I first met you, I thought you were beautiful and that it might be fun to go out with you. Since then, I've gotten to know you a little more. You're someone I'd really like to spend time with." Clay removed his sunglasses and leaned forward, his eyes pleading. "Please let me take you out for a nice dinner."

HE'D NEVER HAD TO TRY SO HARD TO GET A DATE. EL obviously didn't dislike him, or she wouldn't have met him and Ranger for Happy Hour. His dog sat up and leaned against his leg. *Maybe it's Ranger she wants to see? Am I being out manned by my dog?* "Come on, El. I'll take you wherever you want to go."

El shook her head, and a long sheath of silky russet hair slid over her bowed face. "You don't understand."

"You're right. I don't. Did I do something to offend you? Are you seeing someone? What? You think I'm a creeper?"

She looked up at him then, with laughter in her eyes. "No. It's none of those things."

Relief loosened the muscles in Clay's shoulders. *So, she's not seeing anyone. Nice.* "Then what is it? What don't I understand?"

El stared at him. He imagined the gears clicking in her brain, and he waited. She had something to say, and he sure as hell wasn't going to rush her.

El pulled a long drink of tea into her mouth and swallowed before she spoke. "I don't want to get into the details, so don't ask me to."

Clay nodded, wondering where she was going, but remained quiet.

"When I was young, I was a victim of human trafficking."

As though someone punched him right in the gut, Clay let out a gust of air. He knit his brows together and reached for El's hand.

She drew her arm back and clasped her hands in her lap. Ranger stood and approached her, resting his chin on her knee. A slight smile brushed across her mouth, and she petted his head. "Thanks Ranger. You're a good boy. You get it, don't you?" Her gaze rose hesitantly to meet Clay's. "This is exactly what I'm talking about. He senses my emotions, and with no judgment or need for an explanation, he comes over and gives me love. This is what the kids we meet every night need more than anything else."

She had deftly changed the subject, and he knew he had to let her. She warned him ahead that she didn't want to talk about it. A protective rage coursed through him, and his muscle groups flexed with adrenaline. He wished he could ask who he needed to hurt to make them pay for putting her through—through whatever nightmare she had survived. Clay had learned over the past several weeks that no two trafficking stories looked the same. He wanted to hear about what happened to her, but at the same time, the last thing she needed was to relive it all only to satisfy his desire to know.

"So... now that you know, you can see why we can't go out. I get it. So, let's just leave it at that. Nothing else needs to be said." Her words took on speed. "I hope we can keep working together, and I want you to think about gathering a few dogs to spend time with a recovery group I work with. Please, just think about it."

She stood and looped the strap of her purse over her shoulder. Bending down, she kissed Ranger's nose. He reached his paw up to her, trying to say something. Maybe he hoped to stop her from leaving. Clay remained speechless. She didn't want him to say anything, that much was clear. And even if she did, what words could he offer?

Clay stood as she wrestled with her chair. "El—"

Her eyes took on a frightened, trapped look, and as she tried to rush away, she tripped on the leg of her seat, toppling it to the ground. She ducked her head and lunged toward the patio door.

Clay reached out to steady her, but she jerked her arm away and ran inside. Ranger sat down, staring at the door through which she disappeared, and whined.

Chapter Eighteen

❧❦❧

C lay selected a cinnamon-apple muffin from a tray, filled a paper cup with coffee, and found a seat at the far end of the conference table in the FBI situation room. He bit into the sweet bread, and Ranger laid down next to him, lapping up his fallen crumbs.

Agent Sanchez brought the meeting to order. "Let's begin with reports from each participating police department. Do you think this task-force is making a difference? If so, what? If not, why not, and how can we do better? Go."

Each department presented their experiences. A sergeant from the Denver PD spoke first. "The task-force brings more awareness to both officers and the community. In our department, it's also a big help to have extra boots on the street. The K9 faction is more beneficial than I expected it to be. Folks on our beat won't mess with a police dog, whereas before they gave us shit all the time."

Thornton's Human Traffic Detective also ended his report with a kudo to the K9 assets. "Even though these dogs can be crazy scary, the kids we want to help seem to relate to them. It's an in-road as far as we're concerned."

Clay considered what the officers reported along with El's desire for a K9 enhanced therapy group. The connection seemed to happen naturally between the kids and the dogs, and he liked the idea, but as the head of the FBI K9 Unit, he had to think through everything, including liability. These K9 officers weren't trained to cuddle.

"Thank you for your input. We'll consider all of it. For now, I'd like to move on." Sanchez bobbed his head at an agent manning the lights, and the room dimmed. "There seems to be a rash of abductions in the metro area. Two boys, ages nine and ten have gone missing in the Denver area over the last week. There are no pleas for ransom, no word from their kidnappers, and so far, no signs of their bodies found anywhere. At this point, we're assuming that they're still alive even though it's been longer than 24 hours. It's possible, and even likely, that their abductors have forced them into trafficking." School photos of the two young boys flashed on the smartboard. Clay's gut tightened to a hard fist. Cases always seemed more real when pictures of victims glowed larger than life on the screen.

"It's common for traffickers to transport abducted children to different cities, but I want everyone to keep their eyes out for them in the Denver metro area, anyway. Talk to your contacts." Sanchez nodded to Clay. "Agent Jennings will pass out articles of the boy's clothing to the K9 teams for the dogs to track. It's a long shot, but we'll take any information we can get."

One of the street cops spoke. "Nine- and ten-year-old *boys*, sir?" Her eyes darkened in her now pale face.

"It's a sick world out there, officer. Let's hunt the twisted bastards down and bring those children home." Sanchez rested his hands on his hips. "We've sent the link for these photos to each of you. Take your iPads and ask everyone on your beat if they've seen these boys or heard about them. Ask the people you come across on the streets during your shifts, even talk to the johns. Do what you need to do. We want these kids back with their families as soon as possible." He sighed. "Now, Agent Cameron has more information on the recent serial murder case."

Cameron tapped on his laptop keyboard, and the images on the board changed. The fresh face of a pretty teenager smiled out at them. "Police found another girl, approximately sixteen-years-old, with long brown hair, in an alley outside of a seedy motel in Aurora. Same victimology as our previous victims. Same MO and signature. This girl was also nude except for her high heels. Official cause of death is asphyxiation by strangulation, and there were 21 postmortem stab wounds to the abdomen." He flashed to a second slide depicting the bloody crime scene.

Sanchez took over the presentation. "This is our newest victim, Jennifer McNab. Since each of the victims has a similar appearance, he is likely finding surrogates for punishing a particular woman again and again. The lab results have not found matching semen in the victims, but because the un-sub stripped the women of their clothing, we're assuming that this is a sexual crime. The un-sub likely rapes his victim while wearing a condom, strangles her, and after she is dead, he stabs her in the abdomen, the specific place of childbearing, 21 times. He then takes his trophy—a lock of hair." Sanchez scanned the faces all staring at the photos on the screen giving them time to absorb the information. "The murder victims have all been prostitutes. We believe women —prostitutes specifically—with this similar look are his target and seeing them sends him into a murderous rage. The woman he is ultimately punishing in his mind is either a prostitute, or he sees her as one."

Clay tilted his head to the side, studying the images.

"Maybe she was someone he loved who was unfaithful to him?"

Cameron nodded and took up the narrative. "It could be that the un-sub murdered the original woman in a jealous rage. Perhaps she was carrying another man's baby, or she terminated a pregnancy with his child. If so, we have six murders instead of five."

Sanchez pointed at the final slide. "Our un-sub is most likely a white male between twenty-five and forty." Photos of all the similar-looking victims side-by-side filled the screen.

A uniformed Denver officer raised his pen in the air. "How'd you come up with that profile?"

"Statistics, primarily," Sanchez answered. "This type of emotionally motivated crime is most often committed by white males. We believe the murder is emotionally driven by the fact that the cause of death is strangulation, and because the stab wounds were inflicted post-mortem. Strangulation is a highly personal method of killing someone and then, once dead, the stabbing is unnecessary. This leads us to conclude the killer is not satisfied with the death itself, and continues to spend his rage on the body. We determined both the age and gender because of the strength and stamina it takes to stab a body to the depth of these wounds—twenty-one times."

The officer nodded, and wrote several notes on his pad.

Sanchez made eye contact with the others in the room. "Needless to say, we need to find this guy. Get the word out on the street. Everyone must be on the lookout for anyone who fits this description, but especially girls in the sex trade who have long brown hair." He picked up his papers and tapped their edges on the table to straighten them. "We're giving a press release in one hour, so the warning will go out across the news channels too, but we want you out there talking to the regulars on the street. Find out if anyone has seen or heard anything."

Clay swallowed hard. Little boys stolen, murdered girls— he'd seen some sick shit in the war during his deployments to Afghanistan, but the crap going on right here on the streets of home was difficult to digest. He reached down and gave Ranger a pat, more to reassure himself that there was still something good and solid in his world than for any other reason.

Sanchez approached him. "Hey, Jennings." He stuck out his hand. "How's it going out there on the streets? Do you think the dogs are helping?"

Clay pushed himself away from his position leaning against the wall, and shook Sanchez's hand. "It's nice to hear that the uniform cops think they're beneficial. Honestly, they're probably more help during roadside stops than on the beat, as far as locating smuggled people. But, and I can only speak for Ranger, he does seem to sense the vulnerability of these kids and makes some kind of connection with them. His presence helps the girls I've brought in to feel more relaxed and willing to go through the process."

Sanchez nodded. "That's a terrific thing, but it will be a hard sell for continued financing for the mission if the greatest benefit is comfort. Let's focus on the traffic stops."

Clay released a pent-up breath. "Yes, sir."

"You disagree?"

"No. In fact, I completely agree with your logic, but one of the social workers I deal with almost every day is interested in using dogs as a means of therapy for the kids she's trying to get off the streets."

Sanchez shook his head and gave Clay half a smile. "That sounds like volunteer work to me. Not a job for a highly trained and *expensive* FBI-K9 unit."

"I hear you. In fact, I wouldn't even believe it if I didn't see it with my own eyes. Ranger has been specifically trained to apprehend and take-down criminals. But, he's a different dog with these kids."

"Your compassion is commendable, Jennings, but frankly, I don't think the FBI wants him to be a different dog." Sanchez clapped Clay's shoulder. "Be sure to get the boys' clothing articles out to the K9 teams right away. I want to find those boys yesterday."

"I'm on it."

"Thanks, Jennings. Keep me posted."

"Yes, sir." Clay picked up the bags of clothing to take to the participating K9 teams. Sanchez was right. He needed to maintain his focus. El and her recovery group could use any dogs for the type of work she was interested in. He'd talk to Kendra. It might interest her to do some volunteer work with her dogs, Baxter and Annie. *But, Ranger just might be the perfect dog to help El deal with her own personal trauma during their private time.*

Chapter Nineteen

C lay drove to the FBI-K9 facility. He needed to run Ranger through his drills to keep him sharp. His dog had been spending too many hours in the back of the SUV and loving on lost kids. Clay called El on his way there.

"Hello?" She sounded tentative.

"Hey, it's Clay. I just got out of a task-force meeting and wanted to talk to you about a few things." He figured if he made the call sound official, she'd agree to speak with him. He wasn't sure where he stood after she ran off the other day.

"Oh?"

"Yeah. Mostly grim news. They found another girl murdered at a motel in Aurora."

"Oh, God." El's voice dropped

"On top of that, two local boys have gone missing. The collective thought is, since they've found no bodies, that someone may have lured them away from their families and forced them into trafficking." Clay pulled into his parking spot at the facility, but kept his engine running for the air-conditioning. "Also, my boss said he wants the K9s out on traffic stops, and to take part on search and rescue missions—that it's not financially feasible to have them working with victims if they're not using their training."

"But, the dogs are so good for the kids. Did you explain that to him?"

Clay closed his eyes, regretting the strain that filled her tone. If the mission schedule was up to him, he'd have Ranger work with El's kids every day. He'd do anything to bring a smile to her face and lighten the weight she carried across her shoulders like a yoke. "I did, but he has to justify the expense to his superiors. I'm sorry, I wish I could do more. It seems like the more we accomplish, the worse things get."

"I know it seems that way, Clay. But you have to remember that for each kid we reach, the work we do means everything to them. We are changing lives. You have to focus on one life at a time."

"And one should be enough. I know—you're right." Clay turned off his car and opened the door to let some fresh air inside. "I have an idea, though. I'd like to talk with you about it, but I'm heading into the K9 facility right now to work out with Ranger and catch up on a few admin tasks."

"I thought you were off today."

"Well, I had to attend the meeting, and training has to happen, even on non-work days. You're off today too though, aren't you?"

She hesitated. "Yes."

"I should finish around four-thirty. Want to meet for dinner to talk about my idea? It involves the dog therapy you were talking about."

Silence answered him, but he waited. He wouldn't make it easy for her to decline him.

A long minute later, El said, "Okay, Clay. I'll meet you."

Yes! He pumped his fist.

EL DROVE TO THE NEW COUNTRY-WESTERN restaurant/bar on the northwest side of town where she agreed to have dinner with Clay. He was persistent, that was for sure. She had no choice other than to tell him her story. Then he'd realize why he wouldn't want anything to do with her. She wasn't the kind of woman a man wanted a future with. The sooner she got that through his head, the better.

When she arrived, Clay was waiting for her at the front of the restaurant. The smile he greeted her with made the edges of her resolve crumble. He held the door open for her, and the hostess seated them right away at a table near the bar.

"Want a beer or something?" He pulled her chair out for her.

"Just tea. Thanks." A cold drink would help her relax. The conversation she had prepared for wouldn't be fun. El put off the inevitable by watching a three-person band playing from a platform set up in the corner of a small dance-floor on the far side of the bar.

When their drinks came, they ordered their meals. The restaurant served basic country fare, and El asked for fried chicken and mashed potatoes. She sipped her iced tea while she and Clay made small talk.

Their waiter brought hefty plates of food, and Clay cut a bite from his steak. "So, I don't think Ranger can play a big part in working with the kids you have in recovery, but one agent who works with me has a Bloodhound who was injured, and is now retired. She also has a sweet Labrador whose job is Search and Rescue. I thought Kendra's dogs might have time to do the kind of therapy work you're looking for."

"That would be amazing, and maybe Ranger could volunteer on a few of his days off? He's a natural." El was buoyant. This man—this tough former Marine—understood. He saw the potential of dogs helping the trafficking victims through the first tough days of their recovery. "Thank you, Clay."

"For what? I haven't done anything yet."

"Yes, you have. You're willing to figure out a way to help kids beyond the requirements of your job. You're a good man, you know that?"

The grin that spread across his mouth made her breath catch in her throat. If she were another woman, with a different life, she would reach over and touch his square jaw, maybe even pull him toward her so she could kiss his warm smile. El blinked and looked away. She shouldn't dream of the impossible. Those kinds of fantasies inevitably caused her heart to shatter, and putting the pieces back together was a painful task.

Clay described his friend Kendra, and her dogs over dinner. He talked about K9 training and breezed over his time in the Marine Corps and the war. El understood. *We all have things we don't want to remember. Things we don't want to re-hash by talking them out.*

After their meal, Clay ordered dessert. "We're practically obligated to have apple pie and ice cream after that meal." He laughed as he stood and held a hand out to El. "Want to dance while we wait for dessert?"

El's face flamed. She glanced around the bar and to her horror, saw a group of people stomping out a line dance on the other side of the room. "I don't know how to dance like that."

"It's easy. Plus, not knowing how is part of the fun, and you'll pick it up quick."

"No, really."

"Yes, really. Come on. It'll be fun. One dance, and I bet our dessert will be here before it's over." He took her hand and gave her a gentle tug. "Give it a try."

El peered at the dancers again and saw that several of the

people on the edge of the group stumbled through the steps, but were still having fun. She laughed. "Okay. One dance."

Clay kept her hand in his as he led the way to the floor. He spun her into the line, and they tried to catch up for about five measures before the song ended. A slow song followed, and without asking, Clay pulled El into his arms. He held her loosely at her waist, so as not to spook her. "You promised me one dance, and I'm collecting on your promise."

El rolled her eyes, but despite herself, a laughed bubbled out of her chest. She rested her hands on his shoulders. As the band played, their bodies edged together. His arms tightened, and she leaned against his chest, closing her eyes. For this one moment in time, El let herself enjoy the solidness and strength of his body—the feel of him drawing her close. She breathed in his subtle fresh-cotton scent.

When the music wound down, Clay touched her chin and lifted her face. His glacial blue eyes stared into hers, mesmerizing her. He lowered his mouth to hers and kissed her sweetly, but the kiss intensified.

An alarm shrieked in El's head, and she jerked away from him, startled. His brows scrunched together, but she barely registered his confused expression before she turned, and bolted toward their table. Warm apple pie, with melting vanilla ice-cream stacked on top, awaited them, but she barely noticed as she dashed for the door.

Clay caught up to her by the time she ran half-way through the parking lot. "Wait, El. What's wrong?" He grasped her arm, but she pulled away. He released her. "I'm sorry. I shouldn't have kissed you." The emotion in his voice, and the remorse etched across his face caused her to pause.

"It's not you. You didn't do anything wrong." Tears blurred her vision. "It's me. I'm screwed up. You should leave me here, and get away as fast as you can."

"What are you talking about?" He reached out to her, but

then dropped his hand to his side. "I'm not going anywhere. Will you talk to me? Tell me what's going on?"

El burst into tears, and Clay gathered her in his arms. She let him, needing his strength as she fell apart.

"It's okay. Go ahead, let it out." He held her tight, rubbing her back, until her tears calmed and she pulled away.

"Sorry about that." El wished the pavement would suck her down into it so she could disappear. Clay probably thought she was a complete nut-case now. She couldn't meet his gaze.

"You have nothing to apologize for, but I'd like to know what the matter is. Maybe I can help?"

A sorrowful half-laugh, half-honk squawked through her throat. "There's nothing you can do. Nothing anyone can do."

"Okay. I get that." He took one of her hands. "When I was in Afghanistan, I saw some horrific shit. No one can make me un-see it. No one can take away my memories. But sometimes, talking with my buddies about it helps ease the weight. So, maybe I can't do anything, but I *can* listen."

El believed in what he said. She'd based her professional life on that very concept. *But can I really tell him? What would it be like to unburden myself for a few minutes? The risk is always in the cost.* She chewed on her bottom lip. *I really like this guy. If I tell him, will he judge me? Be disgusted by me? Reject me?* If he was, if he did, then at least he'd stop asking her out. That's what she wanted anyway—wasn't it? El risked a peek at his face.

"Come on. Let's sit in my car." He opened the door.

She nodded once and let him help her into the passenger seat of his Tahoe.

"I'll be right back. I have to go pay the bill and I'll get your purse. You left it at the table."

El nodded and he closed the door. Certain dread pressed down on her as she waited for him to return.

Minutes later, his door swung opened and he slid in.

"Okay." He pivoted to face her. "Now we have some privacy. Do you want me to drive somewhere or...?"

"There's a lake a couple of blocks away."

"I know the one. Good idea." They rode in silence until he parked where they had a view of the water. A family of ducks paddled in a line across the lake's surface. Clay remained silent, allowing her to find her words, and her timing.

"Remember what I said at the pub the other day? Before I... left?"

"Yeah." He took her hand in his and rested it on his knee.

Her chest constricted, making it hard to breathe past the ache in her throat. "I'm going to tell you my story, so you know exactly who I am—who you're dealing with."

The warmth from his fingers encouraged her. "Okay." He canted his head to listen.

"First of all, I'm sorry I ran off the other day. I just couldn't..."

"It's fine. I understand."

El leveled her gaze on him and tried, but failed, to smile. "You can't possibly understand, but thanks for being open. You see, when I was a little girl, my mother was a junkie." El sucked in a huge, fortifying breath. "Often times, I had to take care of her. She'd forget to eat unless I made her something." El chewed on a loose piece of skin on her lip. "My mom had men over all the time. Mostly, they sold her drugs or gave them to her in exchange for sex." She glanced at Clay to see if she had shocked him yet. Satisfied that he was still with her, she lowered her eyes and stared at their joined hands. "Eventually, she was so used up, her suppliers only wanted cash, which she didn't have, or..." her voice weakened and she could barely force out the words, "or me."

El felt the muscles in his hand tighten, and she couldn't bring herself to look at his face. She pressed on, "So, my mother began trading me to her dealers in exchange for her fix. It wasn't a big leap for her then, to sell me off completely to a dealer, who then sold me again to a different man who forced me to have sex with lots of men—every night." A hot tear scalded her cheek, but she didn't bother to wipe it.

Clay covered their joined hands with his other. "How old were you?" His voice was low and steady.

El shook her head. She coughed, gagging on her shame. "Thirteen."

"My God, El. I'm so sorry."

"That's not all." Her throat tightened on her words—they barley squeezed through. "He doped me up with heroin. Soon I was using regularly. It was the only way I could face the nights. The only way I could survive the abuse. By the time someone rescued me, I was a full-blown addict." El stared a hole through the dashboard. "So, now you know." She drew in a shaky breath. "Can you see why you shouldn't want to go out with me? Why you shouldn't want anything to do with me? And don't worry, I completely understand. I wouldn't want to be around me either."

Clay sat quiet for a long time, but he kept her hand in his. Finally, he reached up and pushed the strands of hair that were hiding her face behind her ear. He tilted her chin toward him. Her eyes burned. She didn't want to see the rejection she knew she'd find in his eyes. She steeled herself against the pain, and lifted her gaze to meet his.

Clay's expression was soft, and he searched her eyes with his. "Thank you for sharing that with me. I can only imagine how hard that was."

El jerked her head in what she meant to be a nod, but it felt stiff. She lowered her gaze to her lap.

"El, look at me. Please. I want to say something, and I want to look into your eyes and know you're hearing me."

She fluttered her lashes against fresh tears, but managed to look up at him.

"None of what happened to you was your fault. You were only a child. The horrible things that other people did to you has no bearing on your value. None."

Hot tears flowed at his words, and her shallow breaths barely moved her aching lungs.

"Look at how you choose to live your life now that you've escaped. You worked through rehab to get sober. The career you picked is all about helping others. Even in your spare-time, you help people take their lives back. El, the person you are right now is someone of extreme value. I admire you, and wish I was more like you."

El shook her head. "No, Clay. You don't want to be anything like me."

"I wouldn't want to go through the horrors you survived, that's true. But, I do want to be more like the person you've become. El—you are kind, caring, and selfless. Sure, you're a beautiful woman, but it's not just your looks that make you desirable. You're the most loving and giving person I've ever known. And now that I know what you had to live through? You've become that much more amazing in my eyes. Truly, El."

"How can you say that?"

"How do you view the victims of trafficking that you help every day? Do you judge them? Or, do you understand their plight?" Clay leaned toward her, intensifying his words. "And isn't that what you appreciate about Ranger? That he looks beyond someone's appearance and life situation, and sees their intrinsic value? Their pain?"

"How could I judge them? I've experienced what they've been through." El's heart nudged her to believe him, but she'd grown so used to not trusting men that her mind resisted.

"You're right about Ranger, but he's a dog. You're a man. You know that's different."

"True, but still, I could never judge you—except to say that I'm in awe of your strength and resilience. You're a wonderful woman, El. I'd be honored if you'd let me be a part of your life." Clay's expression was earnest as his eyes bore into hers.

Can he mean it? Could I ever hope to believe that he does?

Chapter Twenty

El I had plenty of time to think about Clay, and whether or not she could trust him, on her lengthy drive across the state. She committed to spend the next five days touring with a human trafficking prevention organization who visited several small towns along the mountainous section of I-70, and Grand Junction. They also planned stops at some ranching and farming communities between there and Durango.

A wealthy benefactor had gifted the prevention group with a fifth-wheel trailer and matching F350 painted with their anti trafficking logo and message. They outfitted the rig so people could walk through and gather all types of information regarding what human trafficking is. The trailer contained mixed media presentations on how to keep kids and women safe, as well as, how to recognize someone enslaved in trafficking. Pamphlets described how to assist suspected victims and listed the links to many helpful organizations. The team gave talks at libraries, schools, and other public venues. People were often shocked to discover the prevalence of human trafficking in the United States, even in small rural areas, like these. El spent part of her vacation every year joining these volunteers to get the word out.

Most towns welcomed them, organized central locations for their presentations, and advertised the presentations to their communities, but on the third day out, El hit a roadblock. She gripped her phone tighter. "But your town council agreed to have us. We're on your schedule."

"I'm sorry, ma'am, but someone must have changed the schedule." The receptionist sounded genuinely bewildered.

"So, can we set up somewhere else in town, then? Maybe by the library, or a park? There's still time to get the word out. We'd be happy to pass fliers out to stores and post them on community boards."

"Hold, please."

El covered her phone and whispered to Lynn, the woman in charge of the trip. "They're saying we're not on the schedule, so we won't be allowed to open the trailer or give our presentation."

"That's weird. I spoke to one of their council women myself."

El shrugged. "I'm trying to find another venue."

The receptionist clicked back on the line. "Ms. Clark? Thank you for waiting. I looked into the situation, and I have a directive from the city council president. He asked me to tell you, that now is not a good time for the town to host your presentation, and that you should just drive on through."

"What?" A ball of furious energy swirled behind El's sternum. "We've driven a lot of miles to visit your town. Our event organizer spoke with one of your councilwomen and set this date. Now, we understand if someone made a mistake in scheduling, but why can't we set up at an alternate location? We've come a long way, and we're only here for one day."

"I'm really sorry." The woman's voice softened, and it sounded as though she was speaking in a tunnel. "I tried, but the answer was a hard no. It's probably best for you to just skip our town and go to the next one." She paused. "But, as far as I'm concerned, I think what you're doing is so important. I have a teenaged daughter. If you let me know where you end up, I'd like to drive her to you, so we can hear what you have to say."

"Thank you. I'll call you, but can you tell me who is standing in the way of our presentation here?"

Another, longer pause. "Oh. Well. Let's just say it's the powers that be."

"The president of the city council?"

"No, not exactly. More like someone who knows someone on the council, I'd guess. I really can't say anymore. It's all speculation, anyway. I wish you good luck, and I do hope you'll let me know where you end up."

"I will. Thank you." El ended the call.

Lynn sat next to her. "What's going on?"

"I'm not sure, but it sounds like somebody in the community has some serious sway over the city council, and that person doesn't want us informing people about human trafficking. It's suspicious, isn't it?"

"Definitely. But, we have little choice. I guess we'll just drive on to the next town on the list."

"I suppose." El didn't plan on leaving it at that, however. "Let's grab some lunch here, either way. No one can prevent us from parking on Main Street while we eat. The trailer's paint job advertises nicely what we're all about, and before we leave town, maybe we could pass out some fliers at local businesses?"

Lynn clapped her hands together. "Sure. It's worth a try."

The driver pulled their rig up along the curb at the edge of the main drag. El opened the truck door and waited for the diesel fumes to dissipate in the fresh country air before she jumped down. Armed with handfuls of pamphlets and fliers, the team walked down the street to the local BBQ joint for lunch. Honky-tonk music greeted them as they went through the door.

"Welcome to Wiggle Pig's Barbeque." A tall, but stooped elderly man in a red plaid shirt approached them with menus.

El smiled. "Thanks. We're visiting from Denver. Are you open for lunch?"

"Yes, ma'am." He led them to a table.

When he returned to take their order, El showed him their fliers. "Would you mind if we put one of these in your front window?"

The man scratched his grizzly chin as he read the page. "Not only can you hang one in the window, I'll put a stack by the register, if you like. It's awful what some people do to kids."

"Yes, but thankfully there are kind people like you in the world too. Thank you so much." El gave him a bunch of pamphlets and then shook his hand.

After enjoying tangy pulled pork sandwiches, El, Lynn, and the others, encouraged by the BBQ owner's openness, split up to canvas the other Main Street businesses. When El stepped out of the barbershop, she noticed a sheriff's deputy standing next to their truck, writing on his ticket pad.

"Good afternoon, Deputy." El approached him. "Is everything all right? We're not parked illegally, are we?"

"Yes, ma'am you are. I'm writing you a ticket for taking up more than one parking space." He didn't look up at her.

"Do you have trailer parking in town? There are no signs saying that using over one space is illegal." El swept her arm, gesturing up and down the road. "Not to mention, there are many vacant parking spots all along the street."

"Just doing my job, ma'am."

"Or perhaps more than your job?"

He raised his head and stared at her from behind

mirrored sunglasses. "It would be best if you all move along. I'll make this ticket a warning, if you leave now. If not, the fine is a hefty one."

"Okay, we'll go, but your town has an odd way of welcoming strangers. We only stopped here for lunch."

"We both know you're doing more than that." He removed his glasses. "Look, I think what you folks are trying to do is important. Personally, I'd like to see your presentation, but my orders come from the city government. So, I suggest you load up and drive on out of here." The deputy tore the notice away from his pad and handed the thin, yellow slip to El. "Have a nice day, and good luck."

El ground her teeth and swallowed back her frustration. Something was going on in this town, but now wasn't the time to address it. "I'll get my colleagues. Thank you for the warning."

Chapter Twenty-One

Clay left Ranger at the K9 facility and drove to the FBI headquarters for the weekly task-force meeting. His mind was on El and their last conversation. Everything was still up in the air with her, but at least he had the chance to tell her that he was interested in her. He was scheduled to work through the weekend and with El away on her trip, he'd miss seeing her at the police station. He parked in the parking garage and Kendra Dean pulled her red Jeep into a spot next to him.

"Hey, stranger." She greeted Clay as she let Annie out of her vehicle. "I haven't seen you for a while. How's it going with the human trafficking work?"

"It's tougher than I expected it to be." Clay reached down and gave Annie's soft head a pat. "Hi, girl."

"Yeah? Why's that?" They fell into step and walked toward the blue-glass building together.

"I thought it would be more about taking down bad-guys. Seems like I spend most of my time hauling young girls off the street and trying to convince them to accept our help, or arresting them to keep them safe for a few weeks.

The crap I've seen out there breaks my heart, Ken. I had no idea."

"How's Ranger doing? Do you think having K9s on the job is beneficial?"

Clay laughed. "Funny you should ask that. He's only had to take one guy down. Mostly, he cozies up to the kids I bring in. He has a way of breaking through their tough-guy facade, helping them relax, and drop their defenses a little bit. Any of the kids that El and I've been able to reach I think is due to his presence."

"El?" Dean smirked and raised an eyebrow at him.

"It's not like that. Eloise Clark is a social worker whose focus is rescuing kids from trafficking, and either finding their families or placing them in foster homes prepared and trained to help them recover."

Dean laughed. "When is it ever 'not like that' with you, Clay?"

"Okay, fair enough." He laughed with her. She was right, he liked women. He and Kendra had been friends a long time and she loved to tease him about how many women he dated. She called him a womanizer which he wasn't—but there were so many women, and so little time. What could he say? "But seriously Ken, it's different with El. She's... different."

Dean stopped and cocked her head to the side. "Will the wonders never cease?"

"Whatever. Come on. I don't want to be late." Clay kept walking, ignoring her teasing. "What are you doing here, by the way?"

"We had some extra time, so I thought we'd stop in and say 'hi' to Rick."

"Still acting like newlyweds, huh?" Clay opened the building door holding it for Dean and Annie.

Dean grinned. "It's only been a month, so we *are* still newlyweds."

Rolling his eyes with drama, he laughed and followed her inside. "Well, it's lucky for me I ran into you. I wanted to talk to you about putting Baxter back to work."

Dean's brows crunched together. She pushed the elevator button and stared up at the light. "He can't work with only three legs, Clay. You know that."

"He can't do the work he used to do, but I think he might be perfect for a different type of job."

She glanced at him then. The sorrow she felt for the bloodhound who lost his leg while defending her life, was still evident in her eyes. "What kind of job?"

"Remember how I told you that Ranger was able to reach some of the kids I've been working with?"

She nodded. The elevator doors opened, and they entered the compartment.

"Well, El wanted him to do some therapy work with a recovery group she volunteers for. I talked to Sanchez about it, and though he liked the idea in theory, he said we couldn't justify the expense of using high-dollar, highly-trained FBI K9s for therapy work. I have to agree with him on that point, but it got me thinking. Baxter might be great for these kids and it would give him something to do besides lie around in retirement. He's probably bored out of his mind."

Dean let out a soft laugh. "He is, poor guy. Every morning, he whines when I load Annie up in my Jeep."

"Well, think about it. El's on a trip right now, but when she gets back, perhaps we could take him to her group and see how he does?" The elevator opened on the third floor and Clay turned toward the conference room. "I'll call you about it later."

Dean waved and headed toward her husband's office. "Sounds good."

. . .

Sanchez came five minutes late to the meeting, and Clay smirked to himself, knowing the dark-haired reason for his tardiness.

"Good morning, everyone. Let's get started." Sanchez took his position at the front of the room. "Two days ago, we received a call from a woman who lives in Banner, a small town near the eastern border of Colorado. She wanted to inform the FBI about some suspicious activity going on in a house down the road from her home. She lives about ten miles from town."

Agent Cameron sat back against the edge of the table. "What type of suspicious activity?"

"Cars coming and going at all hours of the night, seven days a week." Sanchez set his laptop on the table and opened it.

Clay narrowed his eyes. "Why did she call the FBI?"

"Good question." Sanchez addressed the room with his answer. "Apparently, the woman has called the local Sheriff multiple times. The sheriff sent a deputy out to the house one time, but he reported that nothing unusual was going on. He says the cars were family members coming and going and that they had every right to do so. But, Mrs. Coch is certain something illegal is going on. She reports that the vehicles are different every night."

"So, she doesn't believe the sheriff?" Cameron asked.

"Exactly. After speaking with Mrs. Coch, I agree it's possible there's something going on. What she describes is most likely drug related and could also be a brothel of sorts. Last night, two agents surveilled the home. They observed the exact behavior that Mrs. Coch reported. We got the appropriate warrants, and tonight I've ordered an FBI raid. If we find what I think we will, then we'll have to determine if the Sheriff's Department is in on it, or not." Sanchez scanned the people in the meeting until his gaze landed on Clay. "Jennings, I'd like some K9 units involved in the raid."

"I'm on it."

"Good." Sanchez turned to Cameron. "We'll need a SWAT team with us, just in case."

"Yes, sir." Cameron punched numbers on his phone and left the room.

"That's it for today. There's nothing new on the murder investigations to report at this time. We've got a solid profile, but no suspects. Unfortunately, we'll have to wait until someone on the street reports a man fitting the un-sub's description or until he makes another move. We'll gather here again tomorrow, after the raid. Let's get out there. Be safe."

AT 1:00 AM, CLAY LAY PRONE ON A RIDGE OBSERVING THE activity going on in the farmhouse below. He peered through his night vision binoculars. Ranger lay by his side. The team had been in place for over an hour. In that time, Clay counted seven cars arriving, six vehicles with lone drivers, and one with a driver and a passenger—all men. The visitors entered the front door, without knocking. Loud music poured out of the house whenever the men went through the entrance, and fell silent again when the door closed behind them.

Clay, Ranger and three other K9 teams dispersed around the perimeter in support of the SWAT team. His radio receiver crackled in his ear and Sanchez's harsh whisper followed. "Sending in two agents for a closer view."

On high alert, Clay followed the agents with his magnified view. They approached the home unnoticed. After peering in windows on all four sides of the building, they dashed behind the barn, and reported from there. "Windows are mostly covered. Sounds like a party. There's music, dancing, and what appear to be five to seven underaged women present. I am unable to get a clear count of the occupants. A minimum of two, military-grade M27 automatic rifles are present in the room, one propped by the front door, and one held by a man standing on the stairs to the left of the entrance."

"Fall back." Sanchez commanded. "We'll wait it out for another hour."

During the following time span, four men left, only to be replaced by five more—all arriving in separate vehicles. "Mrs. Coch didn't exaggerate about the cars coming and going." Clay murmured to the agent nearest him. His gaze shifted to another vehicle rolling down the drive. "That's a County Sheriff's car. This ought to be interesting."

The cruiser came to a stop in the yard, and a heavy man pulled himself out. He ambled across the grass and up the porch steps. Without hesitating, he opened the door, and entered the fray.

"Well, I'll be damned. Good old Mrs. Coch was right." Clay panned back to the sheriff's car to be certain no one else came with him.

"Move in." Sanchez commanded. "Stay clear of the front. Approach from the back and sides."

Twenty or more FBI agents and four K9 teams crept in toward the farmhouse, black figures moving like specters in the night, Clay and Ranger among them. They circled the perimeter, covering all doors and windows. SWAT members approached the front door with a battering ram, ready to breach the entrance.

"FBI! We're coming in!" Two bashes with the ram, and the door splintered apart with a loud crack. The breach team entered with a well-choreographed attack, each member covering the next.

Four men flew out the back door and ran into a black-clad FBI unit waiting for them. Two men attempted to escape through a side window where Clay and Ranger waited. Ranger's fierce growling barks froze them halfway out the opening.

Clay leveled his SIG P320 and his flashlight at the men. "FBI. Don't move." The men raised their hands.

Someone turned off the music, and Sanchez's voice sounded across the radio above the din, "Bring the dogs in."

Nodding to the SWAT agent standing next to him, Clay left their captives and made his way with Ranger to the back door. He entered the kitchen and found counters covered with thirty or more bottles of booze. Keeping his firearm at the ready, Clay moved across the room toward the front of the house. Ranger stopped and sniffed at a door on their right side of the room.

"Ranger is signaling something behind a door in the kitchen. I'm going to clear the space before coming to you."

"Roger that, Jennings." Sanchez confirmed.

Clay reached for the door handle and silently turned the knob. With his pulse hammering, he flung the door open and swept the space with his mag-light and handgun. No one was there, but the landing opened to a steep flight of steps leading down to a dark basement.

"*Knoze.*" His command had Ranger walking tight to his left side. "FBI - show yourself. Now!" He called into the darkness below.

Silence answered Clay as he took one step at a time, his heart firing so loud he had to focus hard to hear above its rapid thumping. He slowed his breathing and took another step. Something whimpered—it sounded like a dog, or an injured animal. A thin coating of sweat cooled his body as his adrenaline ratcheted up a notch. Clay stepped off the last stair, and crouching, swung low around the wall at the bottom of the steps. He panned his light through the dank room.

What met his eyes horrified him. He lowered his weapon and searched for a light switch.

Large dog kennel sized cages filled the basement. Five of them caged barely clothed young women. Four pairs of eyes stared out at him, dark in their frightened faces. A fifth girl huddled at the back of her cell, crying into her hands.

"Don't be afraid. I'm with the FBI. You're safe now. No one can hurt you." Clay pressed the button on his radio. "All clear in the basement off the kitchen, but I need assistance. There are five victims imprisoned down here."

"On our way," a disembodied voice answered.

Ranger approached the closest cage. He laid down in front of the girl inside and sniffed at the grate.

"Good boy, Ranger." He met the girl's frightened stare. "Don't worry. He's safe. He's the one who found you all. We'll get you out of here as soon as we can."

Loud boot steps clambered down the stairs, and three agents filed through into the room.

"Oh, my God." The first agent lowered his weapon and turned to the man following him. "Call for an ambulance."

The agents pried open the lock on the nearest cage and opened the door, but the girl inside didn't come out.

"It's okay, you're safe now. Come on out." Clay held out a hand to help her, but she cowered back. Ranger stepped inside the cell with the girl and licked her knee. She instinctively held out her hand, and he lapped at her fingers. Clay knelt down. "We're here to help you."

Ranger backed out, and the girl followed him, crawling through the small entrance. The other captives followed suit, except the girl who kept her face buried in her hands and her back toward her rescuers. Clay approached her and Ranger pawed at her cage. He sniffed the back of the girl's neck and head. The young girl peeked out at the dog from under a fringe of stringy hair. He poked his nose into the space and gave her a small lick. She flung herself toward him and clutched his furry shoulders. Once again, the instant rapport his supposedly fierce and frightening attack dog made with these vulnerable hurting kids, struck Clay dumb.

The two, dog and child, sat snuggled together until the paramedics showed up on the scene. They wrapped the other girls in blankets and helped them upstairs to waiting ambulances. It took time and patience to extract the frightened child from her cage. Ranger remained by her side through it all. By the time Clay made it up to the front room of the house, all the girls had been freed and subsequently were tended to by medical personnel. Agents arrested the men who had been partying, and rounded them up outside to await transportation to jails in several surrounding towns. Banner's sheriff stood cuffed among them.

Clay and Ranger joined the other K9 teams in searching the house and surrounding property for drugs, firearms, and more people. They found two crates of automatic rifles and 100 kilos of cocaine stashed in the barn.

Sanchez appeared at Clay's side. "Hard to believe this crap can happen in such a tiny farming town out here in the middle of nowhere."

"I have a hard time believing how prevalent this shit is everywhere, and it pisses me off that the local law was in on this."

Chapter Twenty-Two

❧❧❧

George sat in his Range Rover and watched his plump wife climb the steps of the Falcon 500, his private jet. It hadn't been difficult to convince her to fly down to Texas without him. He waited for the plane to spool up the engines and take off, before he started his car. Telluride's airport was closer to his ranch, but George preferred to keep his jet in a hangar at this airstrip. The smaller airport was shared by several communities on the western slope of the Rockies, but was less crowded than Telluride, and there was far less notoriety.

As he made the long trip back to his secluded ranch, George ran through the details of his upcoming event. The technicians completed the adjustments on the hidden video equipment in each of the guest cabins and bedrooms yesterday. He'd outfitted a large hidden storage closet with monitors and recording equipment so he could watch the live feed and record it for both financial and political blackmailing purposes. He was particularly excited about hosting Colorado's State Representative, Peter Spiel. Spiel's influence would certainly come in useful for manipulating policy decisions in the future. George chuckled to himself. *I might enjoy watching all these assholes hang themselves politically more than any of the other treats on the menu this week.*

When George drove up the long winding drive toward his massive ranch home, he appraised the workers scattered around his property. His chin rose and his chest filled with pride as he regarded his fiefdom. A new crop of undocumented workers snatched up near the border groomed the property around the buildings. Most of them didn't speak English, and none of them knew where they were, or that the only pay they'd receive would be in the form of food and a cramped place to sleep. George waved at them merrily.

The laborers wouldn't even *try* to escape. Where would they go? They'd be afraid of deportation if they went to the police. George laughed again, pleased with the image of himself as a covert, modern-day slave owner.

He wound his way past a group of guest cabins. A handful of dark-haired women in maid uniforms carried fresh linen inside the buildings. Others followed with cleaning supplies. Another group worked inside the main house, cleaning and cooking, preparing for the up-coming event.

He'd noticed a particular woman two days ago—a new member of his herd. He'd call her to his bedroom tonight. Briefly, he wondered how much of a fight she'd put up. He liked it when they fought.

His cell phone rang through the speaker of his Range Rover, and he glanced at his dashboard monitor. Robert's name flashed on the screen. George pressed a button on the steering wheel. "Bob. How the hell are you? Things are shaping up around here."

"Good. Real good."

"What's up?"

"Remember the experiment I told you I wanted to try?" The professor chuckled. "Well, George, I think you ought to take a turn yourself. I've put in an order for several boys to come along with the girls. Some of our guests might enjoy the opportunity."

George laughed a rough smoker's laugh. "I sure as hell hope so. The cameras are all in place. Good God, Bob, we will rule the state after this party. Hell, we need to reel in some senators." They laughed together, giddy with their plans. "Listen, I'm sure I don't need to remind you, but don't forget to have the merchandise well-groomed and well-heeled when they get here. Our clientele will be unimpressed with street filth. That means the works: hair, nails, waxing, and all new clothes. It will be a pleasant treat for the chattel."

"I'm already on it. I spoke to Jonny this morning about that very thing."

"Of course. I knew I could count on you."

"Did you get Nancy off to Texas all right?"

"Sure did, she left about an hour ago. Where are you telling Mindy and the kids you will be?"

Robert chuffed. "I told them I had a conference in Minnesota. Somewhere without a beach so they wouldn't want to join me."

"Good thinking." George pulled into his garage next to five other luxury cars. "Sounds like everything is all set on your end. I've got workers slaving away on the property getting everything ready up here. I guess I'll see you in a couple of days?"

"Can't wait."

Candie and Steven sat together on the couch watching a daytime soap. Steven hadn't spoken a word to anyone since his time at the house in Ft. Collins, but physically he stayed as close to Candie as he could. Her heart ached for him. She wished she could make it better—make all of this end. Since that wasn't in the foreseeable future, Candie did the only thing she could to ease his pain. She offered him a steady supply of the pills Jonny gave her.

When she first came to Jonny, Candie hated taking drugs, but quickly realized that most days its numbing effect provided the only way she could tolerate what he expected of her. Now she couldn't get through the day without them. Surely, the pills were the best way to help Steven survive too. She reached over and took his frail hand. He didn't resist, but he didn't respond either. Steven simply stared blankly at the TV screen.

"Aw, look at you two." Jonny came through the front door. He was in an unusually good mood. "I ought to make a video of you two getting it on. That shit really sells."

Candie's gut coiled tight as a spring, and Steven pulled his hand away. She glared at Jonny. "Whatever. He's not even old enough to..."

"You'd be surprised. Besides, there's other stuff he can do." Jonny's sick laugh turned her stomach. "I'll think about that later. For now, I've got a surprise for everyone."

Candie wasn't interested. Jonny's surprises were only good for him. She turned her attention back to the TV.

"Okay, I guess you don't want to go to the spa."

She slowly returned her gaze to her pimp. "What do you mean?"

"I've been told to get all you hos ready for that fancy event coming up. The man wants you all primped and perfect, waxed clean and polished for his guests—hair, nails, the works. On top of that, you get a bunch of new clothes. So there, smart ass. Still not interested?"

Candie sat up. "Really? When?"

"This week. You need to make all the appointments. Then I'll take you to the mall. Get it done." He turned toward his room. "And Candie, find the cheapest places to get that shit done, too."

She figured Jonny would pocket the expense funds she didn't spend, but she didn't care. They never got this kind of a treat. Of course, they'd end up paying for it during the long weekend foray with a bunch of twisted pervs, but it would be worth it if they got to have an entire day of pampering. Not to mention, the party was at a beautiful ranch in the mountains, not in some seedy motel on Colfax. Staying at a ranch was another unexpected pleasure.

Jonny hollered from inside his room. "How are you coming with the boys? They better be ready for... whatever they're told to do, or you'll pay the price. Get me?"

Candie glanced sideways at Steven. None of this would be a treat for him—or the other new boys. They were all so young. She planned to cut back and save most of the pills she could get her hands on for them. Maybe even ask Jonny for more to keep the boys relaxed. What felt like crushing bands cinched tight around her chest and she closed her eyes, straining her mind to find a way to help them. A better way than just numbing them with drugs. It was too late for her, but not for them. Not for Steven.

GEORGE WANDERED THROUGH THE LABYRINTH OF HIS LOG cabin mansion trying to view the estate through the eyes of a newcomer. He was certain his property would impress new and returning guests alike. The tantalizing aroma of fresh-baked bread drew him to the kitchen. George breathed in the yeasty air as he sauntered into the room. His gaze landed on the woman he'd recently been fantasizing about. "You," he barked. All the women in the galley startled and stared at him. God, he loved the power he had over them. He leered at the woman he desired. "Make me some lunch and bring it, and a beer, to the deck off my bedroom."

Her deep brown eyes held uncertain fear as she gawked at him, uncomprehending. Another woman whispered to her in Spanish, and she lowered her eyes and said, "Sí, señor."

He passed by her, enjoying a handful of her ass on his way. George pictured himself as a plantation owner in the pre-civil war south, or then like a king. He laughed out loud as he left the kitchen. *It was good to be King.*

Meandering, he stopped next in the game room which looked out through giant picture windows to the vista on the western side of his ranch. The usual games were available. A custom carved pool table, shuffle-board, a foosball game, air-hockey, and a dartboard, among several other table games. Three poker tables sat together on the far side by the wall, but none of those benign games held his interest. The display of costumes and props at the back of the room is what drew him. His fingers trailed over a selection of whips, cuffs, and other sex toys. This party was setting up nicely. Very nicely, indeed.

A vibration in his pocket interrupted his musing. He pulled out his phone and answered the "Private Caller" phone call.

"This is George."

"I'm calling to check up on our arrangement for next month in Florida." The anonymous voice slid through the phone speaker.

"Yes. Everything is in place, but before we move forward, I'm still awaiting your down payment."

"I have five-hundred-thousand ready to wire to the account number you gave me at three o'clock this afternoon."

"Excellent. As soon as I confirm the deposit, I will forward you photos of the merchandise."

"I look forward to viewing them."

"You won't be disappointed."

"I'd better not be," the voice hissed.

George balled his hand into a fist. He was uncomfortable doing business with someone he didn't know, even if they did come highly recommended. But in this case, the number of dollar signs made it worth the risk. He'd find out the identity of this clown, and when he did, the asshole would never threaten him again.

Chapter Twenty-Three

❧❦❧

El drove into the parking lot of the FBI K9 Facility and parked in the shade of a big leafy tree at the far corner. She noticed Clay leaning against the railing that divided the parking area from a walkway leading to the front doors. Ranger sat next to him looking up at a brown-haired beauty whose chocolate Lab sat obediently at her feet. She dismissed the strange green twinge that tweaked her gut. After all, the woman was probably his co-worker, the agent whose dogs she hoped could assist with trafficking victims trying to start their lives over.

The two agents seemed comfortable with each other, and El felt another pang of envy at their rapport. She wished she felt that relaxed with Clay, or any man, really. Even though she'd worked hard to get past her nightmares, they still affected her present. El drew in a big breath and let it out in a whoosh before she opened her car door. She walked toward the laughing friends.

Clay raised a hand at her in greeting, and El smiled in return, biting her lower lip as she approached.

"Good morning." His startling clear blue eyes sparkled in

the morning sunlight. "El, this is Agent Dean. Kendra," he swept his hand toward her, "this is Eloise Clark, the social worker I've been telling you about."

"El, please." El stuck out her hand to shake Kendra's firm grip.

"Nice to meet you El." She looked down at the adorable chocolate Labrador grinning at her. "This is Annie."

El crouched down to greet the dog. Ranger wiggled with excitement and looked up at his partner.

"Go ahead, lover boy." Ranger leapt to El's side and licked her face.

Clay laughed. "Ranger is head over heels in love with El. I don't know what to do with him."

Kendra crouched down, so she was on the same level as El. "Dogs have a keen sense of character. Both Ranger and Annie love you, so that means a lot. I can't wait to hear your ideas for using some of our dogs to help people, especially kids, find their feet after coming out of such horrible circumstances." Kendra gave her a warm and genuine smile.

"Okay, ladies. I've done my job introducing you, but now I've got a meeting over at head-quarters. We're debriefing the raid out in Banner."

El stood and reached for his arm. "Clay, do you have a quick minute? I wanted to talk to you about something weird that happened to us when we were on our road trip." El turned and included Kendra. "Last week, I went on a human trafficking informational tour over on the western slope. The organization I went with has a whole mobile set up that guides kids, families, teachers, whoever, through their trailer where they can view videos and tons of other resources informing the public about human trafficking. The group teaches how to both recognize trafficking and prevent it. They're an outstanding bunch of volunteers, and I travel with them once a year." El glimpsed Clay checking his watch. "Sorry if I'm keeping you. I can talk to you about it later."

"No, it's okay. I still have a little time. What happened?"

El described the resistance her group received from the small town's council. "At least the deputy they sent to write us a parking ticket and send us on our way, seemed apologetic—even supportive. I think the push-back came from someone over his head, someone on the city council, perhaps even the mayor. The whole incident was strange. We've never faced that kind of opposition before. I don't know if it means anything, but I thought I'd mention it."

As Clay listened, his brows drew together and he rubbed his chin. "That is odd. Thanks for telling me. Do you have a copy of the warning the deputy gave you?"

El nodded and rummaged in her purse to find it. She handed him the wrinkled paper.

"Good. I'll bring this up in the meeting this morning. See what Sanchez has to say. I'm not sure what we can do with what amounts to a set of vague incidences, but we'll see."

Kendra's face brightened. "Agent Sanchez—Rick—is my husband." She patted Ranger's head. "We'll see you two later. Come on, El, let's get a cup of coffee, and figure out how we can help each other."

El's shoulders relaxed. It felt good to have people who believed in her work. She smiled at Clay when he reached for her hand and gave it a squeeze.

"I'll call you later." His gaze held hers.

The warmth from his hand spread up her arm and settled with a glow in her chest. "Okay." El hoped her smile didn't come across as too soppy, but she figured it did when she noticed Kendra ducking her head to hide a grin.

SANCHEZ STARTED THE MEETING BY DEBRIEFING THE farmhouse raid in Banner. "Good job out there, everyone. We arrested thirteen men, including the local Sheriff, on charges ranging from possession of drugs and illegal firearms, to sexual abuse of minors, kidnapping, false imprisonment, and prostitution. The sheriff begged for leniency, however none was afforded him."

"He'll have a nice time in prison," one of the uniforms commented.

"He'll get as good as he gave," another added.

"Two of the men offered to give up information on the source of the drugs and firearms in return for a plea deal." Sanchez shook his head. "That's up to the DA, but I imagine he'll go for it. This mess has 'cartel' written all over it."

Clay crossed his arms over his chest. "What happened with the girls?"

"After the initial triage, they were dispersed to several Denver hospitals. Once they are released from there, Health and Human Services takes over."

"What a goat rope." Cameron flipped through a file filled with reports

Clay cleared his throat, drawing the attention of the task-force members. "I may have some information on another small town scene we should probably check out." He explained that the situation that happened to El and her group over on the western slope. "They originally had permission to set up their trailer and give a presentation to the town. But, when El called to check on the details, the receptionist told them not to come, that they were no longer welcome. It doesn't sound like the Sheriff's Department is in on any of it, but rather that they are taking their orders from someone else. Probably a councilman who doesn't want the group teaching the citizens how to recognize signs of human trafficking or how to prevent it. It sounded strange to me, so I thought I'd bring it up."

Sanchez's dark eyes assessed him as Clay spoke. "I'm glad you did. Small towns struggle with human trafficking just as much as the bigger cities do." He turned to Cameron. "Call the San Miguel County Sheriff's Department and look into it —try to talk to that specific deputy if you can."

"I'm on it." Cameron took El's warning ticket and left the conference room.

After gathering up his files, Sanchez brought the meeting back to attention. "Thanks everyone. We had a successful raid. One that saved lives and shut down a pocket of corrupt lawmen. Keep up the excellent work. It's one day at a time, people."

The team moved as one restless blob oozing out the door while Agent Cameron attempted to swim upstream. "Sir, I spoke to the deputy. He was open, and receptive to my call. He said that the sheriff put out some feelers—trying to look into the whole thing—but that even he ran into a brick wall from Town Hall."

Sanchez's jaw flexed as he scanned the faces of the few agents still in the room. His gaze landed on Clay. "I don't know if we can do anything with so few facts."

Cameron handed Sanchez a page of information. "The deputy inferred that they would welcome our help. It might be good if you contact the sheriff."

Sanchez reached for the sheet of paper and nodded while reading it. "Okay. Let's get a small team up there to investigate. We'll take the next flight out. Cameron, Jennings, be ready to leave by two."

"Yes, sir," the men replied in unison.

Chapter Twenty-Four

❧❦❧

On their flight to Telluride, the agents discussed their investigation strategy. They planned to interview the deputy who offered to help. He could give them a better idea on how to proceed with the sheriff. Clay hoped they found something they could really sink their teeth into. He trusted El's instinct on this, and a strange defensiveness for her against the unknown powers that blocked her work in the small town flared in his veins.

After touchdown, the jet taxied to the small terminal. Clay peered out one of the circular windows at the airport tarmac filled with a large number and assortment of private jets. "Is some event going on up here this week? There are a ton of planes parked here."

Cameron joined him in looking out the windows. "There's a blue-grass festival in Telluride in the summer. I think that's usually in July."

"Hm." Sanchez stood when the jet rolled to a stop and disembarked as soon as the door opened. A black Suburban waited for them at the bottom of the stairs. "Let's go."

Clay grabbed his go-bag and he and Ranger followed Sanchez to the large SUV. Cameron rode shotgun, and since the vehicle was not equipped with a kennel, Ranger sat next to Clay in the backseat.

Rick drove into the town south of Telluride, making a pass through to check out the local shops on Main Street. At the end of the short strip, he turned around and drove back, pulling into a parking lot next to the town's bar. "We'll start here. Best source of local information available." He backed into a spot on the far edge of the lot that afforded them the best view of the bar entrance and the rest of the parking lot. "I'll go in alone and see what I can find out." Sanchez checked the magazine on his SIG Sauer before sliding it back into his shoulder holster.

"You're going to stand out in there wearing that fancy suit." Clay leaned forward to peer out the front windshield.

"All the better. It'll give me a reason to be asking questions. If I'm not out in fifteen minutes, come in."

"Will do."

Before he closed the door, Sanchez glanced back. "And leave Ranger in the car."

Clay and Cameron watched Sanchez disappear through the front door. "I don't know what his problem is," Clay teased, "Ranger likes a cold beer as much as the next guy."

Cameron chuffed, and they sat back to wait for the fifteen-minute mark.

Ten minutes into their look-out, a dark-blue van with the back windows painted over, pulled into the parking lot. It drove down the aisle directly in front of the SUV, and Clay bolted forward. "Did you see that guy?"

"Which guy, the one in the van?" Cameron craned his neck. "No, why?"

"I could swear that's a guy we've been looking for in Denver. A dirt-bag pimp named Jonny."

"Why would he be all the way over here on the western side of the state? It's a good five or six-hour drive."

Clay's spider senses tingled. "Good question. Is he parking?"

"Looks like he's just cutting through."

Clay climbed into the driver's seat. "Let's follow him."

Cameron grabbed his arm. "We can't just leave Sanchez here alone."

"He can handle himself. We'll be right back."

"We're supposed to go inside to back him up in five minutes."

Clay turned the key. "Then we'd better hurry." He pulled the Suburban forward and turned to follow the van. Coincidentally, the blue vehicle surged forward. Clay pressed the accelerator, keeping tight on the van's tail. Their speed increased, and the van blew through a stop sign, squealing around the corner on to Main Street. Then it shot ahead.

"Light us up." Clay ordered, and Cameron flipped the switches that turned on the lights and sirens hidden in the grill, the sound piercing the tranquil mountain air. The powerful engine roared and they closed in on the van in seconds. Clay pulled up to the side of the other vehicle and edged closer, forcing the driver to the shoulder of the two-lane road. A narrow bridge was fast approaching, so Clay dropped back to allow the van to speed through first. In a flash, they sailed over the bridge and raced up to his side again. Clay sped faster so they could see the driver through the window. Cameron gestured for the van driver to pull over. The driver flipped him off.

"If that's the way he wants it." Clay murmured and bumped the side of the van with the sturdier Suburban.

"Shit, Jennings. Try not to kill us, okay?"

"I got this." He collided with the van one more time before the van swerved and skidded on the loose gravel on the shoulder of the road. The driver slammed on the brakes, fish-tailing to a stop. Clay pulled the Suburban to an angled position in front of the van. He and Cameron got out with their weapons leveled at the driver.

"FBI!" Cameron yelled. "Get out of your van and keep your hands where we can see them."

Clay ran with Ranger around the back of the SUV and they approached the van driver's door from the back. "Come out of your vehicle. Now!"

The van door swung open, and two hands flew out. They were empty. "Okay, come on out." Cameron commanded.

A wiry dark-skinned man slid off the seat and stepped onto the gravel with his hands in the air. "What's the problem, officers?"

"Slowly turn to face the side of your van and place your hands on the vehicle above your head. Are your armed? Do you have any weapons?" Clay approached with Ranger tight to his side.

"No, man. I got no weapons. I didn't do nothing. Why'd you pull me over?"

Cameron kept his gun aimed at the driver while Clay patted him down for weapons. Finding none, he brought the man's hands together behind his back and cuffed him. "Why were you driving 95 miles an hour out of town?"

"Was I?"

Ranger growled, and the man whipped his head around to stare at the sleek black dog.

"What were you running from?"

"You. Why were you chasing me? I thought you were gonna jump me."

Clay shook his head in disgust. "Right. What's your name?"

The driver shrugged. "I don't got to say nothin' to you."

"Do you have a license and registration? You do have to have that. It's the law."

"Yeah, yeah. It's in the glove box."

Cameron stepped toward the door. "Are you giving me permission to look in your car for your registration?"

"Sure, whatever. I got nothing to hide."

Clay nodded to Cameron who took the opportunity to scan the interior of the van while he looked for the necessary document. He found it and brought it out to Clay.

"Are you Jonny Gold?"

"That's me."

"And you're renting this vehicle?"

"Yep. Nothing wrong with that."

"What are you doing over on this side of the mountains?"

Jonny remained quiet for a few seconds before answering. "I'm being a tourist."

"Is that so. What have you seen so far?"

"I don't got to answer you. What you got on me, anyhow? Speeding? So write me a ticket."

Cameron shook his head at Clay. A frustrated gust of air escaped his lungs. "Call the sheriff, Cameron. They'll be the ones to issue the ticket. And there will be an expensive fine for the speed you were traveling."

Jonny laughed a wheezing chuckle.

As soon as two deputies arrived, Clay and Cameron handed their charge over to them. "We had him going 95 miles an hour. I'll be happy to come to his court appearance if, by chance he doesn't pay the fine." Clay grumbled.

The agents climbed back into the Suburban. "I can't wait to hear you try to explain to Sanchez why you scraped up the Suburban by running a guy off the road for a speeding ticket." Cameron laughed as Clay turned the vehicle back toward town. "He'll already be pissed that we left him alone at the bar."

"Shut-up. Did you see anything suspicious in the van?"

"Not really. All I saw was a gold sparkly sweater with a fake white-fur collar on the back-seat."

A bubble of frustration surged up Clay's throat. "Damn it! What would a guy like Jonny Gold be doing with a gold sweater, do you suppose?" Sarcasm dripped off his words.

"Well, that's pretty obvious, but there wasn't anyone else in the van. It's not like we could arrest him for having a sweater."

Clay slammed his fist against the steering wheel. "Shit! Whatever the reason Jonny Gold is up here, it's no coincidence."

Cameron's phone buzzed, and he answered the call on speaker. "Where the hell are you guys?" Sanchez's voice echoed over the line. "Get back here. I've got a phone number."

Clay stopped the huge SUV in front of Sanchez who looked utterly out of place in the parking lot of a bar in a small farming town wearing his dark-blue suit and red power-tie. "Get in before someone tries to buy a car from you."

Sanchez yanked the injured door open with a loud clunk, and Cameron climbed into the back with Ranger, vacating the front seat for his boss. "What the hell happened to the Suburban? I left you two alone for like ten minutes."

"It was more like twenty." Clay pulled out of the parking lot. "Where do you want to go?"

"Find a place to park. I need to make this call." Sanchez held up a scrap of paper with ten digits scrawled across it. "I told the bartender I was in town for the night and looking for company. The guy pointed me to a table in the corner with three men sitting together. So, I bought them a round, and told them the same thing. After giving me a ton of shit, one of them asked the waitress to borrow her pen and paper, and he wrote this number down. He told me not to share the number, or it could mean his job." Sanchez tapped the paper on his knees. "They may have just been yanking my chain, but it can't hurt to call."

He pressed the number into his keypad. Clay pulled into the town's park and found a shady spot under a tree at the end of the lot.

Rick glared at him out of the corner of his eye while he listened to a phone ring on the other end of his call. "Don't think I've forgotten about the Suburban."

Cameron chuckled from the back.

Clay grumbled a word that sounded like "*Shtekay*" and Ranger let out a loud, gruff bark in Cameron's ear.

Cameron sprang sideways swinging his arm up to defend himself. "Shit!"

"Don't be a smart-ass. Ranger doesn't like it." Clay laughed and Sanchez shook his head with an appreciative smirk on his mouth.

His expression turned professional the instant a voice answered his call. "Yeah, I was just over at the Jug and Slug and a man I had a drink with gave me this number. Said I could call it if I wanted some company." He held his index finger to his mouth and pulled the phone from his ear and pressed the speaker.

"Is that so?" An aged smoker's voice responded. "Exactly what type of *company* are you looking for, son?"

Rick paused. "Uh, well, the feminine type I guess."

"You guess? You ever done this before?"

Rick took his time again, and his voice took on an uncertain and nervous tone. "Well, not like this. I mean, I've..." He cleared his throat.

"Fifty bucks, up-front. You take what you get since you don't seem clear about what you want."

"Fifty for how long?"

"One hour - if you can keep it up that long." The ragged voice laughed at his own humor. "Meet us in the alley behind the shops. Same side of the street as Jug's. There's a vacant lot behind the shoe store."

"When?"

"Ten minutes." The call ended.

Rick turned in his seat. "Okay. You guys get out of here and make your way to the meeting spot. Cameron, you get as close as you can while remaining invisible. Jennings, you walk Ranger like you're just a guy out for a stroll. Be at the corner by the shoe-store, ready to cover that half block. I'll drive up in this smashed up mess and see what we find."

"On it." Clay hopped out of the driver's seat and opened the back door to let Ranger out. "I'm not thrilled about taking his vest off, but we'll draw the wrong kind of attention if I don't." He unclipped Ranger's harness, snapped the lead onto his collar, and un-buckled his vest, tossing it into the SUV. "See you there."

Clay made his way with Ranger up the three blocks to Main Street and turned toward the bar. Clay kept their pace at a saunter. He stopped to peer into several of the store-fronts, gauging his time silently. A young mother and her child headed his way. The little girl tugging on her mom's arm.

"Mommy, look! A doggy!" Mahogany curls bounced around the girl's cherub cheeks.

The mother, who had matching hair, only tamer, offered an apologetic smile to Clay. "Haley, you can't run up to strange dogs. He might not like kids."

Clay stopped and waited for the child to approach. "*Sedni.*"

Ranger immediately sat down. Without looking up at Clay, the little girl placed her hands-on Ranger's face and kissed his nose. Clay marveled at them both—the girl for her complete lack of fear and Ranger for his total acceptance of her exuberance. "Good boy, Ranger."

"I'm so sorry." The mom caught up, breathless and wrestling her shopping bags. "Haley—"

Clay grinned, "It's okay. Apparently, he likes kids."

"Thanks for being so nice." The lady said to Clay before turning to her daughter to explain that some dogs bite.

Clay's internal mission-clock ticked louder and louder. "Okay, Ranger, say goodbye. We've got to get going."

The child refused to release his ears, and Ranger looked up at Clay from the top of his eye-sockets.

"I'm sorry, ma'am, but we're going to be late. I'm meeting someone." He appealed to the mother.

She pulled on the girl's arm. "Come on, Haley. Say goodbye now. The nice doggy has to go bye-bye."

"But I want him!" Haley cried.

The woman met Clay's gaze with a helpless expression. His pulse kicked up—he had to be on his mark at the right time. He could just command Ranger to come, but he didn't want to startle the kid.

Ranger licked the girl's face with a slobbery tongue. She laughed and wiped at her cheeks. As soon as her hands left him, Ranger stepped off. Clay followed, acting as if the dog pulled him.

"Bye doggy!" Haley called after them.

Clay raised his hand in farewell, but kept moving. "You're smarter than I give you credit for, Ranger, my boy. Good dog."

They made it to the corner just after an old truck eased down the street toward the alley. Clay stopped as if looking at the shoes in the shop window. The truck made a sliding turn, skidding on the gravel, into the alley. It came to a stop in front of the Suburban, pinning it in. Clay turned down the walk, staying just out of sight, but peering around the brick wall at the back of the building. He could not see Cameron, but trusted he was there somewhere.

Three men piled out of the truck, one carried a baseball bat. This was no hook-up. *Shit.* The men encircled Sanchez and taunted him. Clay couldn't make out their words, but he kept his eye on his boss. Sanchez's posture would inform them when to back him up. For now, he wore a worried expression, and his arms hung loose at his sides.

The volume of the men's jeers increased, and the guy holding the bat took a swing, smashing one of the Suburban's headlights. Broken plastic and glass showered the ground.

Rick held his hands up, and appeared to be reaching for his wallet, though Clay knew he'd come out holding his SIG in his grip. The headlight smasher drew his bat back again, and Clay shouted, "*Drz!*"

Ranger shot forward like a black arrow in the darkening sky. He lunged and caught the batter's arm in mid-swing, knocking him off his feet. Ranger held fast and jerked his head back and forth while growling and pulling on the attacker. The assailant screamed as his flesh tore apart in the grip of canine fangs, and the bat clattered across the pavement. A sense of brutal justice surged through Clay's gut before he clamped down on the raw emotion, and called his dog off.

"Ranger, *pust.*" His dog released the captive, but stood over him snarling as Clay spun him over to his belly, pressed his knee into his back, and cuffed him.

Confusion reigned among the would-be robbers. Cameron leapt out of the shadows with his weapon drawn. His arm lashed around the neck of the thug nearest him in a choke hold, pressing the muzzle of his gun against the man's temple. The captive froze like a statue with his hands in the air.

Simultaneously, Sanchez shifted his weight to his back leg,

and like the Karate Kid, sent his other foot into the leader's chest. The man flew backward into his truck, breaking the window with his skull. The move impressed Clay who hadn't seen Sanchez in action before. *Note to self: Don't piss that guy off.*

The agents patted their attackers down checking for other weapons and lined them up against their truck. Sanchez slid his phone from his coat pocket and dialed 911.

"Who the hell are you guys?" the guy with the torn-up arm asked.

Clay glared at him. "The wrong guys to fuck with."

The sheriff and his deputy arrived in minutes, followed by the town's lone firetruck. After the Volunteer EMT firemen administered the initial first aid, the sheriff took custody of the attackers.

"I thought you and your team would check in with us as soon as you got into town." The deputy rested his hands on his utility belt and scowled at Sanchez. "Imagine our surprise, finding you here in an alley fight."

"Just checking out the lay of the land." Sanchez straightened his tie. "But we appreciate your quick response time, Deputy."

The lawman bobbed his head. "You can follow us to the clinic if you want. We'll go there before we head to the jail."

"We've got a few things to check out first. We can email you our official reports."

The deputy glanced at the sheriff who rubbed his chin. "That'll be fine Agent Sanchez, but keep us in the loop, if you will."

"I will. We'd like your input and assistance with whatever we find."

"Deputy, you drive these boy's truck on over to the jail. I'll follow you." The lawmen nodded at each other before they drove away.

Sanchez glowered at their busted headlight. "That setup

was a complete waste of time, and we better come up with a good story to justify the beating this vehicle is taking." He knelt in front of Ranger. "Good job, buddy. Thanks for saving my head." Ranger licked his hand.

"Where to now, Sanch?" Cameron shoved his hands into his pants pockets.

Sanchez shook his head and bit down on his lower lip. After a few minutes of thought, he said, "Let's go check out the municipal airport. We can probably scrape up some information there."

Clay loaded Ranger into the back and climbed in next to him leaving Cameron to wrestle with the dented front door. Sanchez drove out to the tiny airport.

With his clearance, the vehicle would have been allowed to drive onto the tarmac, but since no one manned the gate, they continued on to the hangars without confrontation. Sanchez parked in the shadow of a hangar. "There's got to be seven or eight jets here, and for what? It's not like this po-dunk town is the new hot spot for the jet-setting elite."

Clay drummed his fingers on his thigh. "Two things are vastly out of place. First, a fleet of private jets show up, and then Jonny Gold drives through town."

"Who's Jonny Gold?" Sanchez turned sideways in his seat to look at Clay.

Clay explained that Jonny Gold was a pimp who ran a string of girls out of Denver. They knew about him, but had never caught him at anything that would stick, nor would any of his girls agree to testify against him. "When we saw him, we chased him hoping to catch him with underaged girls, or some other evidence we could arrest him for."

"Is that how the Suburban got wrecked?"

Clay shrugged.

"I'm with Jennings on this." Cameron shook his head. "I don't believe in coincidences."

Sanchez's dark eyes moved from Cameron to Clay. "Do you think Gold brought girls up here for some... event or something?"

"I can't be sure, but he was driving a van, and Cameron saw a girl's gold sweater in the back seat. It's all conjecture at this point."

As they discussed the possible connections, Clay pointed to a jet coming in to land. They watched it touch down and taxi to a spot near the hangar where they hid. A black Range Rover pulled onto the tarmac and approached the jet as the doorway steps lowered to the ground. Two men hurried down the steps and got into the Rover.

"Let's follow those guys. If they're a part of something, they could lead us right to it." Clay leaned forward, wedging his broad shoulders between the two front seats.

"I agree." Sanchez waited until the Range Rover drove back toward the airport gate before he started the engine. Without turning on the headlights, he pulled out to follow the car. Clay studied the flight crew as they passed by, but they were busy shutting down the plane and securing it for the night.

Sanchez kept a suitable distance behind the Range Rover, which became difficult as they followed it up into the winding switch-back roads of the surrounding mountains. They drove for forty minutes before their quarry turned off onto a long private road guarded by an impressive security gate. A uniformed, and armed, man stepped out of a stone guard-shack and spoke to the driver. After studying his papers, the guard opened the gate, and the Range Rover disappeared up the long, dark road.

Clay ran his gaze up and down the estate's fence line. It appeared like a fancy split-rail fence, but he took in the high-volt electric extensions. "This is no ranch on the open range.

It's more like a fortress. We're not getting past that fence without a tactical team."

Sanchez drove to the next bend before turning around. "We need to find out who lives here and what the hell is going on up at that house."

Chapter Twenty-Five

Candie explored the room they gave her for the duration. She'd never been in such a plush space. The decorations made it appear rustic, yet it was anything but. The bedroom itself was bigger than the whole main-floor of Jonny's house. Full sized logs bolted together framed the gigantic bed. A moss-rock fireplace fought with the breathtaking mountain view out the picture windows for best focal point. On her way to explore the massive bathroom, Candie peeked out a pair of French doors leading to a private deck with its own hot-tub.

The bathroom was large enough to be another bedroom. Exotic looking oils, salts, and creams, surrounded a jetted tub that could hold four or five. Candie ran her fingertips over a stack of thick towels as she stared at the multiple sprayer heads inside the glass shower. Hooks on the wall held thick, matching terry robes.

Her clothes, such as they were, had already been hung in another full-sized room she supposed was the closet. Candie made her way across the rich carpet to that section of her suite. A long counter spanned one side of the space and a delicate chair sat underneath it, in front of a large mirror surrounded by soft lights. A set of brand-new make-up and brushes lay on the counter along with a selection of fancy hairstyling equipment.

"Candie?" Steven's small voice called from the main bedroom, and she stepped out of the closet.

"Hi. Are you all settled in your room?" She wanted to pretend like they were on a wonderful vacation, but she couldn't quite get her expression to go along with the ruse.

"What's going to happen to us here?" He glanced around her room, seeming far less impressed than she had been.

Candie sat heavily on a chair in front of the fireplace, its leather as smooth as butter. "It's a job, like any other. I guess we should try to enjoy the luxury while we're here though, don't you think?" She scanned the bedroom once more. "Have you ever seen anything like this before?"

"I want to go home." Steven's chin trembled, and Candie reached out to hold his hand. She drew him onto the chair next to her.

"I know," she whispered. "Someday we'll find a way, but for now I'm glad we have each other."

He nodded and scrubbed a tear from his eye before it fell.

"Why don't you show me your room. Is it close to this one?"

He shrugged and led her down a long hallway. At the center of the ranch home was a magnificent room with a fireplace so large, Candie could stand in it. Windows at the front and back offered incredible panoramas of the majestic Rocky Mountains. A grand staircase built with golden hued, polished logs swept up both sides of the great room and led to what Candie supposed was the master suite. Thinking of her own richly outfitted rooms, she imagined the master bedroom was probably fit for a king.

In the massive central room, chairs and sofas were gathered in groupings around low tables. Two long wings spread out from the central area. Candie's room was one of eight in her hall. She presumed there were eight bedrooms down the other hall as well. At the backside of the house, floor-to-ceiling glass doors opened onto a flagstone patio. Multi-layered pools surrounded by large plants, trees, and flowers created private nooks. This was the most beautiful place Candie had ever seen, but she despised it. This kind of money only meant one thing for her, Steven, and the others. They were merely party favors for the guests coming to this event, to be used however they saw fit.

Steven's room was located on the far side of the opposite wing. Her leaden heart dropped into her belly. "I have plenty of pills. I want you to take one every time..."

Steven nodded.

She grabbed his arm and opened his hand, pouring a handful of white pills into his palm. "Hide these somewhere in your room." Candie hated giving drugs to a little kid, but it was the only way he'd get through this week.

A bell rang calling all of their group to the center hall for instructions.

Two men stood in the middle of the main room. One was short and fat. He wore creased jeans and black cowboy boots with a yellow button-down shirt under a dark blue blazer. His black eyes flashed at them from his bald headed round face. His nose, and the fleshy skin that hung off his cheekbones were red with tiny veins. Next to him stooped a taller man, with rounded shoulders. Candie thought of him as beige. He had on tan pants and a brown blazer with leather patches on the elbows. His graying brown hair matched his dull dust-colored eyes. Even the large mole on his cheek was brown. It was obvious to Candie which man was in charge, but when his tall partner scanned the room, his eyes landed on Steven who stiffened under their steady gaze. The man seemed unassuming, but he held a frightening dominance over the little boy.

Cue-ball clapped his hands together and spoke. "You all know what you're here for. My guests are used to fine things and getting everything they desire. You are to provide them with whatever they ask, immediately. We have set you each up in a room where you will... entertain my guests unless they prefer to take you somewhere else. You will do what they want, how they want, when they want it. Period. Is that understood? Punishment for any infraction will be swift and painful."

He rubbed his beefy palms together. "Now, go prepare yourselves for the welcoming cocktail hour. I expect you to look your best. Everything you need is in your rooms. Be back here in one hour."

Candie squeezed Steven's hand. "See you back here." She smiled, but there was no joy in it, and Steven didn't return her expression.

DRESSED IN A SILKY GOLDEN SHEATH, WITH HER HAIR hanging long in loose curls, Candie walked on dangerously high heels down the hallway toward the party room. Men's voices, punctuated by occasional loud laughter floated toward her. She entered the room and felt the stares of men considering how they might use her body. A shudder skidded down her spine.

A server swooped by and handed her a glass of champagne. The older Hispanic woman met her eyes with a sad look and whispered, "*Lo siento*."

Not understanding her words, Candie offered the woman a slight smile concerned about what the woman thought of her—of this party. Wondering if she too was expected to sacrifice her body, or if she was a slave of another kind. *Does no one think what is happening is wrong? Is there no one who can save us?*

Candie quelled those thoughts immediately. That kind of thinking led to depression and hopelessness. She thought of Lucky, one of Jonny's girls who had become so sad she finally slit her wrists. Candie couldn't afford to let that happen to her. She opened her tiny purse and pulled out a pill. She swallowed it fast with a big gulp of the dry champagne as a man she thought she recognized from somewhere approached her. He was older and impeccably dressed. She hoped he behaved as civilized as he appeared.

"You look like a girl who likes to party." The man signaled the server to bring more drinks.

Candie smiled at him seductively, knowing how to play her part. "I do. What kind of partying do you like?"

He took two glasses from the tray and handed one to her. "Let's go to the game room and see if something piques our interest." Her date for the evening grasped her free hand and pulled her with him to a set of double doors situated under the staircase.

They entered a round game room. Beyond an ornate pool-table, was a corner filled with displays of what appeared to Candie to be costumes and props. As she looked closer, she realized she was right but the outfits and objects were designed for distinct types of sex play. His grip tightened on her hand while he pulled her along behind him fingering his options.

He stopped in front of a booth containing all sorts of leather, chains, collars, and whips. "This looks interesting. I promised myself to try new things on this trip." He leered at her and murmured. "Think you can wield that riding crop?"

A cold flush of relief washed over Candie when she realized he wanted her to hit him, not the other way around. She ginned up her sexy voice. "Have you been a bad boy? Do you need me to teach you a lesson?"

He laughed and pulled her body into his, grinding himself against her. "You have no idea." He gathered up the items that interested him. "Take me to your room."

Candie led him down the hall. They each changed into the outfits he'd selected, her young body not quite filling out the stiff, lace-up bustier. She'd never done anything like this before, but she'd heard about it—seen it all in the videos Jonny made them watch.

The man asked her to slap him. Candie held back taunting him until he begged her. She led him toward the bed by a leash attached to a collar around his neck. She repeated the words she'd heard the woman in the dominatrix porno film say. She ordered him to bend over the bed. Finally, she snapped his ass with the crop.

Her date growled in pain and spun around, snatching the crop from her hands. "That fucking hurt." He yelled as he drew his hand back and slapped her full force across her face. Pain detonated through her head, and an aura of lights flashed across her eyes. She lost her balance and fell to the floor. Her blurred vision cleared just as the man grasped a handful of her hair and yanked her to her feet.

Candie cried out, her roots on fire. He threw her on to the bed, bending her back over the edge. He shoved his fingers between the skin on her neck and the studded collar he'd made her wear, twisting and tightening it against her throat. With his other hand, he stripped off her leather panties. All she knew was agony and fear. The pill, alcohol, and lack of oxygen worked together against her consciousness. Candie heard someone screaming, but her mind floated away. A flash memory whisked across her dimming mind. She'd seen the man who was attacking her once on TV. Hadn't someone interviewed him on the news?

Stars popped and flashed through her brain, and then everything fell into a silent black hole.

Chapter Twenty-Six

C lay absently stroked Ranger behind his ear as he, Sanchez, and Cameron sat in the Suburban staring at the security gate from their hidden position a quarter mile down the road. A phone buzzed, and Sanchez reached for it. He pressed the speaker. "Agent Ricardo Sanchez, speaking."

From Sanchez's formal answer, Clay figured the local district judge finally returned his call.

Weariness resonated through the female voice on the phone. "Agent Sanchez, this is Judge Meryl Lyndhurst. I'm returning your call asking for a search warrant for the property in San Miguel County. That property belongs to a Mr. George Baron. He pays this county a great deal in tax revenue, so unless you have more evidence than speculation, I cannot give you a warrant. I'm very sorry."

"But, ma'am. We're practically certain about what's going on in there. And if there *are* children there, they are surely being hurt—being sexually abused." Sanchez pleaded.

"Have you seen any of these children?"

He hesitated. "No, ma'am."

"Do you have any actual evidence of anything unlawful happening on that property?"

"Just the facts that recently the town turned away a human trafficking prevention group scheduled for a presentation, and two of my men saw a known pimp from Denver here today in an empty van, one that we suspect he drove a bunch of kids up to that ranch in."

Clay shook his head. They had nothing. Nothing but gut instinct, which though his years in Afghanistan taught him to trust, wasn't enough to get them a search warrant. His shoulders drooped. Right now, this very minute, he was sure children were being abused and there was nothing he—they—could do about it.

"I'm terribly sorry, Agent. I believe you are most likely right about what you think is going on. However, I cannot issue a warrant without proper evidence."

Defeat echoed through Sanchez's voice. "Yes, ma'am. Thank you."

"Agent—if anything changes, if you get any real evidence at all. You call me directly on this number, and I'll issue you that warrant right away."

"Will do, thank you, ma'am."

"Good luck." The call ended.

"Shit." Sanchez dropped his phone on the console.

Cameron bounced his head back against the headrest and let out a gust of air.

Clay leaned forward and addressed his comrades. "We have to do something."

Sanchez peered at him from the side of his eyes. "Any ideas?"

"Yeah. Ranger and I will do a perimeter search."

"We don't even know how far that is."

Cameron sat up and pulled out his phone. Punching numbers in he said, "Let's get that information." He spoke to someone back at headquarters and within minutes, he received several maps of the area on his phone. A satellite view depicted the extent of the ranch boundaries.

"Wow, that's big." Clay calculated the perimeter distance and then, coordinating that information with the topographical map, he silently figured out the best breach point and path leading to the ranch home. "Cameron could start on the left, and I could head to the right and meet him in the middle."

Sanchez chuffed, "And I'm supposed to sit her on my ass?"

"Someone's got to monitor the gate."

"True. And that someone is you, Cameron. If anyone gets into trouble for trespassing, it will be me. Jennings can use Ranger as a distraction and get away."

Cameron nodded, dejected. As the low man on the totem pole, he knew better than to argue. "Roger that. I'll keep you posted if I see anything."

Sanchez reached for his Kevlar vest. "If you see anything we can use to get a warrant, call the judge first. Then us."

"Got it."

Clay secured Ranger's vest and then his own. He and Sanchez exited the vehicle and ran a check on their gear and firearms.

"Ready?" Sanchez's eyes pierced through the night.

"Let's go." Clay and Ranger jogged across the street and along the electrified perimeter fence that bordered the road.

He'd run about a mile when his radio sputtered. Cameron's voice crackled out. "Sanchez, Jennings. Denver HQ just called. There's been another murder."

"Goddamn it." Sanchez growled. "Cameron, call the airline. Get us on the next flight for home. Jennings, turn back. We need to get back to Denver right away. Murder trumps suspected abuse. We'll have the local sheriff surveil the gate for the time being."

Clay ground his teeth together. "Yes, sir." He knelt down and buried his face in Ranger's shoulder. "What the hell, buddy. This evil is all around us—on every side. We've gotta do something to stop it." He sat back and held his dog's face in his hands. "I don't know the best way to help all the people enslaved by these sick assholes, but we're going to make a difference. You and I. Got it?"

Ranger barked.

"That's right. Good boy." Clay sprinted off, running back the way they had come. A mental image of El facing this kind of abuse weighed his stomach down like he'd swallowed ten pounds of buckshot. *What kind of hell had El experienced before she escaped from this twisted darkness?* Kids were abused and treated like garbage, and now the poor girls in Denver had to worry about being murdered by a john if they went to work, or by their pimp if they didn't. Clay dug in and pumped his legs faster.

SHARP LIGHT STABBED CANDIE'S EYES WHEN SHE BLINKED to open them. Her eyelashes stuck together with a mixture of sleep and old mascara. The throbbing in her throat made it painful to swallow. *Where am I?* She stirred and regretted the movement instantly. A small groan pushed through her raw vocal chords.

"Buenos dias, niña." A musical feminine voice sounded before a soft comforting hand rested on Candie's shoulder. The kindness brought tears to her eyes and helped her to open them. "Estarás bien."

Candie didn't understand the words she spoke, but the woman's presence was caring and motherly. The voice belonged to the same woman who served her champagne at the party the night before. Her tenderness made Candie want to burst into tears and curl up in the woman's arms.

"Who—" Candie's throat hurt too much to speak and in a flash she remembered why. She touched the front of her neck with tentative fingertips, while she stared at the woman tending her.

"You're to be okay." The dark-haired woman sat on the side of the bed and held a cup of warm tea to Candie's lips.

She sipped and breathed in the sweet steam. The warm honeyed liquid soothed like balm in her swollen throat. "Thanks," Candie rasped.

"Descanso... rest." The woman set several lozenges on the bedside table next to a beautiful tea-pot and returned to her chore of cleaning the room.

"Who are you?" Candie's gaze followed the woman as she worked.

The lean woman faced the bed with a weary smile. She pressed a hand into her chest. "Maria."

A deep booming voice echoed in the hallway, and Maria's eyes grew wide. She ducked into the bathroom. The heavy-set man whom Candie figured owned the ranch marched by her doorway and then stopped. He took a step backward and stared in at her.

"Well, looks like you survived after all. In the end, girl, you made me a lot of money last night." He laughed as his gaze scanned her room. "Have you seen Maria?"

Candie shrugged and took another sip of tea. She focused on the brown liquid, not wanting the man to read anything in her eyes.

"If she comes in here, tell her I want her. Now." He turned and strode into the hall.

A minute later, Maria peeked out from behind the bathroom door.

"It's okay, he's gone."

Maria slipped out of the bathroom, her eyes furtively darting to the hallway. "Gracias. Thank you." She approached the bedside and gripped Candie's hand.

Another woman entered the room with a stack of fresh towels. "Maria! Mr. Barron is looking for you."

Maria nodded and spoke to the newcomer in Spanish.

The woman sighed, turned to Candie and whispered, "Maria want me to tell you to run if you ever get the chance." She glanced over her shoulder at the entrance. "We had your life once. Now that we are older they force us to work as maids. We can't see our families, we get no pay..." The woman choked on a sob. "Just get out if you can." She rushed into the bathroom to deposit the towels and scurried out the door.

Maria finished her work and stood by the side of the bed. "Si—run." She touched Candie's cheek and left the room.

WHAT MUST HAVE BEEN HOURS LATER, CANDIE WOKE TO movement on her bed. Steven had crawled up next to her. He picked up her hand. "Are you going to be okay?"

Candie nodded and tried to smile.

"Your neck is all bruised." His sad eyes moved from her wounds to meet her gaze. "They said you should stay in bed tonight. You don't have to work."

Candie wept silently, and Steven hugged her. His thin shoulders straining to be something she could lean on. "Steven, we will escape somehow. I've been lying here trying to come up with a plan. I haven't figured out how yet, but we will get away."

His eyes, old before their time, gazed at her in resignation. "It's not your fault." The bell sounded, calling the chattel to the main room. "I've got to go."

"I'm so sorry, Steven."

He cupped her cheek in his little hand. "Will you call me Tom when we're alone?"

Her heart swelled, and she gave him a watery smile. "My name is Lilly."

"Lilly" He whispered, then he turned to go.

"Wait, Tom." She opened the drawer of the night table. "Here, take this." Candie gave him the pill she would have taken to cope with the night. She didn't think he'd overdose on two. She hoped not. But one thing was certain, he'd never get through this party without drugs.

The man from last night appeared at her door. "Doesn't look like you'll be up to joining me again tonight." His ferret's eyes moved from her to Tom. A wicked grin peeled up the sides of his mouth. "No worries, I'm in the mood to try something new." He reached out his hand and stroked Tom's cheek. "Come with me, little boy. What's your name?"

"No!" Candie shouted, slicing her raw throat with what seemed like shards of glass.

The man gaped at her.

"I can be ready for you in fifteen minutes." She rasped. "Please. I think we had a connection. Don't you?" Candie reached her hand out toward the man. "Please. Give me another chance." Desperate to save Tom from a horrible fate, she begged her abuser to let her take his place. Candie shoved back her covers and stood. Every muscle in her body burned as though on fire. She took a step and her personal areas shrieked in pain. "What's your pleasure tonight?"

The offensive man assessed her. "Not you. I've already experienced what you have to offer." His heated gaze moved to Tom. "This boy will be fresh territory for me tonight. Come." He grabbed Tom by the upper arm and pulled him out of the room.

The last thing Candie saw was terrified blue eyes as the

boy she'd come to think of as her little brother was yanked out of her room.

She fell back onto the bed and buried her face in her pillow, sobbing helplessly for Tom's fate. *God, if you exist, protect Tom. Keep him alive.* Was that a fair prayer? Maybe he'd be better off dead. Maybe they all would.

CANDIE HEARD THE MUSIC RISE, AND THE EVENING'S PARTY move into full swing. Maria appeared at her door carrying a tray. "Comida." She placed the tray holding a bowl of soup and iced tea onto Candie's lap. "Eat."

She smiled at the kind woman who treated her like a daughter. Life wasn't fair. It wasn't right that this beautiful, kind woman had been forced to be a slave to the man who owned this place. Her every muscle tensed at the thought.

Candie reached for the woman's hand. "Thank you... *gracias.*"

Maria blushed and ducked her head.

"I wish I could help you. One day..."

Long, warm fingers brushed hair behind Candie's ear. "Si." They shared an utterly comprehending gaze before Maria smiled and left the room, closing the door behind her.

Candie punched the button on the TV remote, hoping to drown out the sound of the abuse that was happening in the rooms surrounding hers. She took a long sip of the soothing soup while CNN flashed on the screen.

The soup bowl nearly slipped through her fingers. There on the television, larger than life, beamed the man who almost killed her. He smiled, shook hands with someone, and laughed. The words running across the bottom of the screen reminded her of where she'd seen him before.

Chapter Twenty-Seven

El bounced on her toes while she waited in the parking lot of the community center for Kendra and her dogs to arrive. She was nervous about how well the dogs would mix with the drug and trafficking recovery group they were meeting with today, but excited too. El believed in this method, her challenge was convincing other therapists without any solid data to back her up. The dogs' effectiveness was obvious when on display though. She glanced once again at her watch.

She and Kendra had agreed that beginning with a group of women who were a year or more along in their recovery and transition was best. If Kendra's dogs were successful, then they could try to integrate canine therapy with women arriving fresh out of the sex trade. El believed their most effective work would eventually be with that segment. The dogs made relational headway much faster than people could. And, for some reason, people seemed to open up more easily when their fingers were coursing through a coat of canine fur.

Kendra's red Jeep turned into the lot and pulled up next

to El. She hopped out of her car, followed by Annie and a Bloodhound El hadn't yet met.

"Hi Kendra, thanks for coming." El bent down to stroke Annie's muzzle. "Hi girl. It's good to see you again." Annie responded with a wagging tail and a few friendly licks.

"Happy to be here. I'm excited about the therapy idea, especially for this guy." Kendra knelt next to her three-legged Bloodhound. "This, by the way, is Baxter."

El ran her fingers over his head and down one long silky ear. "Thanks for coming, boy." The women stood and walked side by side to the door of the building. "The ladies are already here. They start things off with a little social time, so it will be easy for them to meet your dogs before the session starts off, if they want to."

"You said they run this group like a twelve-step program?"

"Yes, similar to Alcoholics Anonymous, in a way. Most of the participants deal with addictions as well as re-integration issues. It's basically a support group with accountability."

"Great. I'll handle the dogs and follow your lead with how you want this to go."

"Sounds like a plan." El held the door open for Kendra and her two dogs. "Baxter gets around so well with only three legs."

"He adapted pretty fast."

"If you don't mind, I'd like you to share his story with the group."

"No problem."

El and Kendra followed the aroma of fresh coffee down a long hallway to the meeting room. About twenty women milled about, sipping either steaming drinks or lemonade and nibbling on cookies. A heavy woman in a shapeless floral dress made her way over to them.

"Hi Nancy, I'd like to introduce you to Special Agent Kendra Dean from the Denver FBI-K9 Unit, and these are her dogs, Annie and Baxter." El ignored the skeptical look pasted across the woman's face. "Nancy is another social worker from Denver County Social Services and the facilitator of this group."

Nancy shook Kendra's hand. "It's nice to meet you, Agent Dean. Thank you for coming, but I have to admit up-front, that I'm skeptical about Eloise's ideas about dog therapy."

"What concerns you?" Kendra accepted a cup of coffee from one of the group members with a smile and a nod.

"I just don't see the point, really. I mean, of course it's nice to pet animals, and I see how that can make a lonely elderly person feel better, but I don't understand how having dogs at a group meeting will do anything but be distracting."

Tension tightened El's jaw. She'd had to fight hard against Nancy's resistance to get permission to try this unusual approach. She touched the woman's arm. "Thank you for letting us come today, even though you're uncertain. I really appreciate you being open to trying new things."

Nancy's brows knit together, and she stammered. El's gratitude was an ill fit to Nancy's attempted obstruction, and it threw the woman off her game.

Kendra interjected, "I agree. It's refreshing to work with innovative therapists eager to experiment with nontraditional methodologies."

"Uh... of course. Come sit down." Nancy waddled away to gather the others. "Everyone, freshen your drinks and find a seat. We'll start in five minutes."

Kendra winked at El, and it pleased her that her new friend acted as her co-conspirator. The attendees filled their cups and found seats in a circle of chairs. Kendra's dogs sat obediently at her feet. After Nancy introduced them, El addressed the group.

"Thanks for allowing us to join you today. We hope to work with survivors, such as yourselves, who are coming out of human trafficking. We believe the dogs can help anyone taking their first steps to a new life to feel accepted and loved. The dog's cheerful faces and unconditional acceptance help all of us to relax and hopefully make it a little easier to share our troubles."

A slight woman across the circle from them sat hunched over her tightly entwined legs and pointed at Baxter. "What happened to him? Was he abused or something?"

Kendra's eyes softened, and a sad smile curved her lips. "No. Baxter was my first K9 partner. I've trained with him since he was six months old. He's the best tracker I've ever worked with, though Annie gives him a run for his money." She ran her hand over the top of his domed head. "Last year, a man attacked me while Bax and I were hiking. Baxter here got shot while trying to protect me. He saved my life, but lost his leg in the process. I owe him everything."

El let the story sink in and took the time to meet each woman's gaze. "His injury forced Baxter into an early retirement from the FBI. Now, he sits at home while Kendra and Annie go to work. I'm hoping that getting to know women like yourselves will give Baxter a useful purpose that he enjoys." She nodded to Kendra, who stood and walked Baxter around the circle, stopping to say hello to each woman.

El continued. "I think you'll find that even though he is damaged, and he doesn't look the same as other dogs, he is still smart and loving and capable. Baxter's value is immeasurable and hasn't been diminished by his injury. He's the same dog he once was, but his experiences make him wiser and more sensitive." She waited until Baxter came full circle. "Does he remind you of anyone you know?" El paused. "Could the struggles you've gone through give you wisdom rather than a label? Baxter's wound is on the outside, but a lot of your wounds are on the inside, yet they can still be crippling. If Baxter doesn't allow his loss to hold him back, maybe you don't have to either. Let's go around the circle and share. If nothing could hold you back, what would you do with the rest of your life?"

Kendra unclipped the leads from both dogs and allowed them to roam around, giving and receiving love and friendship. El glanced in Nancy's direction and caught her dabbing her eyes with a tissue. The social worker's cheeks turned pink, and she waved the tissue as if to brush away her self-consciousness.

Nancy crossed the room and stood next to El. "Okay, you've changed my mind," she whispered.

El's chest expanded with a pure sense of gratitude for Kendra, the dogs, and the work she hoped they would do together. They listened to the women's hopes and dreams. Baxter's example and his calm, encouraging demeanor had helped open their scope of possibilities.

Nancy leaned into El's shoulder, "We need to talk."

Chapter Twenty-Eight

Members of the joint task-force had been poring over profiles and case histories all day. They'd spent the last hour creating as much of a time-line as they could with their limited information. Running on only a couple of hours of sleep, Clay chugged yet another cup of strong coffee, hoping to stay sharp and clear the gritty feeling from his eyes.

Sanchez addressed the group. "FBI Analysts have been searching nationwide for murder victims that match ours. So far, they have found no other prostitutes murdered in this fashion. They did, however, locate a woman who was killed four years ago in Salina, Kansas. After discussing the case with Salina Detectives they discovered the murdered Salina woman had the same victimology—young, with long brown hair, found nude except for high-heels, strangled and had twenty-one postmortem stab wounds to the abdomen." He turned to the photos on the board. "The differences are two-fold. The woman in Kansas was not a prostitute, and she was in the early stages of pregnancy. Salina police suspect her husband of her murder, but they haven't been able to locate him."

Cameron crossed his arms. "Why would a husband stab his pregnant wife in the abdomen?"

Clay ran his hand over his face, his gut cinching. "Either he didn't know about the baby, or he didn't want it. Might have learned that the baby wasn't his." He stared at Sanchez. "Do you think the killer could be re-punishing substitute women for his wife's infidelity?"

"Yes, that's a distinct possibility." Sanchez perched his hands on his hips as he studied the documents spread out on the table. "If so, he's likely choosing prostitutes because that is how he thinks of his wife." He clicked a button on his laptop and a photo of a beautiful, long-haired brunet in her mid-twenties flashed on the screen. "This was Mindy Horton, the woman murdered in Salina. Similar in appearance to all the recent victims." With the next click her crime-scene photos appeared. "Same MO, same signature."

Clay sat forward, bracing himself with his forearms on his knees. "So, we have a serial killer on our hands?"

"It appears that way. The FBI analysts are still searching for other victims, however, the profilers believe our un-sub is indeed a serial murderer."

A third click on the keyboard projected a photo of a stout man in his early thirties with thin, stringy brown hair. "This is our primary suspect, Mindy's husband, Wayne Horton. Local detectives uncovered evidence of the couple visiting a fertility clinic, and they found invoices from a male fertility specialist in the Horton's home office."

"So, the husband's infertile, and his wife shows up pregnant. There's your stressor." Clay stood up and reached for a stack of printouts on the table. "Let's get these copies of Horton's photo out on the streets. Those of us working tonight, our top priority is to get the word out. This additional information could save lives. Let's find this bastard and bring him in."

Sanchez nodded. "Be vigilant and get this guy."

Members of the task-force stood and gathered their papers. Everyone took a handful of the printed photos of the suspect and filed from the room. Clay and Ranger left to start their shift immediately, though technically they weren't on duty for another two hours. Clay choked on his frustration and helplessness. If it wasn't horrible enough trying to survive being trafficked by sex-crazed assholes, these kids now had to fear being murdered every time their pimps forced them out into the night.

EXHAUSTION SATURATED CLAY'S SHOULDER MUSCLES, AND he shrugged them back to stay awake. He cruised the loop around four motels known for their pay-by-the-hour night-time activities. Women in short, skin-tight skirts and tops designed to display their breasts spilling out of lacy under garments led pathetic, desperate men into dingy rooms only to escort them back out half an hour later. The entire scene depressed him to watch, but Clay kept his eyes peeled for any men that matched Horton's description.

Eventually, the grumbling in his belly forced him to find something to eat. Clay grabbed a quick, greasy burger and fries at a fast-food joint, and parked in a dark corner of the lot near one of the busier flea-bag motels. He watched women of all shapes, colors, and ages taking men into rooms. The rotation was blatant, and it shamed him that prior to working with the Human Trafficking Task Force, he hadn't really noticed. It wasn't as though he hadn't driven on these streets at night before. He'd just been blind to what went on in the darkness.

After his last bite, Clay wiped the salt and grease from his fingers, and pulled back out onto his loop. As he drove down a strip known for hookers approaching cars, he noticed a girl with long brown hair in a short dress and over-the-knee, thigh-high boots. She leaned into the window of a sedan which had pulled to the curb. He slowed down to get a look at the driver as he passed by, but the man was bent over, facing the other way, talking to his prospective "date".

Clay turned at the next corner and parked where he could still see the car in his rearview mirror. The young brunette opened the door and slid into the guy's car. Clay waited for them to drive away, before he made a U-turn, and pulled onto the street two cars behind them. The sedan headed toward a block of industrial buildings. Clay switched off his headlights and, keeping as much distance as he could between them, he followed.

Parking a block away, Clay got Ranger out of his SUV. They crept toward the darkened car. With his gun and flashlight poised together and ready, the K9 partners stuck to the shadows as they approached. They were fifteen feet away when the dome light turned on inside the sedan.

The passenger door flung open, and Clay heard the man from inside yell, "Get out. Your price doesn't include a ride back."

The girl backed out of the car door, wiping her mouth with the back of her wrist. "I would have charged a hell of a lot more if I'd known what little I'd have to work with."

The engine roared, and the asshole yelled, "Whore!"

"At least I don't have to pay for it," she screamed back as she slammed the door. The car peeled out, and the prostitute started walking back toward the track.

Clay holstered his gun and stepped into the light.

"Oh, shit! You scared me." The woman held her hand to her chest. She laughed off her fear but sidestepped away from him.

"Sorry, just out walking my dog."

She eyed him skeptically. "Out here?"

"I don't live far."

The woman cocked her head and stared at him. Her gaze dropped to Ranger who wagged his tail. "He's a pretty dog. What kind is he?"

"This is Ranger. He's a Belgian Malinois."

She wrinkled her face. "A Belgian what?" She smiled, and in the light of her expression, looked much younger.

"Malinois."

"Never heard of that. Can I pet him?"

"Sure."

The woman squatted down, balancing on her teetering heels, and smoothed her hands over Ranger's face, scratching under his chin. "Good doggie. You're a pretty boy, aren't you?"

She unfolded her legs and stood, meeting Clay's gaze. "You looking for some company, Mister?"

"No. Actually, I'm FBI." He opened his badge to show her.

"No shit. Well, I was just walking home. Nothin' to see here." She stepped around them and moved to leave.

"Hey, wait a sec. I'm not here to harass you, but I do want to give you some information."

"Yeah, yeah. I know where the church and the mission are. Thank you very much."

Clay chuckled. "Good, but I really do want to warn you about a guy who has been killing prostitutes in this area. Girls, with long brown hair—like yourself."

She stopped in her tracks and turned slowly back to Clay. "I heard about that."

He handed her a printout of the suspect's photo. "This man is a person of interest in the case. Have you seen him around?"

She studied it. "Maybe... but I don't think so."

"Can you show his picture around to the other girls you know?" He opened his wallet. "Here's my card. Call me if anyone has seen this guy. Or, if you see him around, call 911. Don't mess with this guy. He could be extremely dangerous."

She nodded, and when her eyes met his, Clay studied the young woman standing in front of him. Under all the heavy make-up, this girl was probably younger than fifteen.

"Hey, I don't know your situation, and I'm not judging, but if you need help—if you want to start over—I know someone who can assist you. She's been where you are. She gets it."

A brittleness fell across the girl's features, and a hardness entered her eyes. "Sure, whatever, dude. It's not like I can just walk away. If your friend really has been where I am—she'd know that."

"I never said it was easy. If you decide you want to try, call me. There is help available to you."

She considered him for a minute before she held up the card and the photo. "I'll tell the girls." She turned to go.

"Let me give you a ride."

"Nah, I'm good." She spun and walked backwards a few steps, the click-clack of her stilettos echoing against the cement buildings. "Hit me up if you ever want to party. I could show you a real good time."

Clay shook his head. "Stay safe. Be careful out there." He watched her turn and walk away, wondering if this was the last time he'd see her alive.

Chapter Twenty-Nine

A fter all these weeks, El finally agreed to let Clay pick her up for a date at her house. This was their first official date, so he brought her a bouquet of bright yellow sunflowers. They made him think of happiness and hope. The hope reminded him of El. He'd known a ton of guys in Afghanistan that had really bad shit happen to them, but he'd never known anyone whose experience had been as rough as El's. Yet, she had clawed her way to a better life. She figured out how to get an education and had spent her life caring for others. She both amazed and inspired him.

He rang the doorbell of El's single-story cottage home. The tone sounded from deep inside the house and he heard her pad toward the door. She opened it, greeting him with a soft smile that grew when she noticed the flowers.

"For you."

She reached for the bouquet. "They're beautiful." The hazel eyes that beamed up at him, filled with tears and reminded him of the Caribbean Sea. "I love them. No one has ever given me flowers before."

"I'm glad to be the first." His chest broadened with gratitude—it pleased him to hold that distinction. He leaned down to brush her cheek with a quick kiss and was rewarded with a delicate whiff of lilacs. "Ready to go?"

El hugged the bouquet to her chest and peered around Clay's legs. "No Ranger?"

"I didn't want to deal with the competition." Clay chuckled. "He's staying home tonight."

"Let me put these in a vase. Then I'll be ready."

Clay watched her walk toward the kitchen and was filled with contentment. Usually with women, Clay was all about the physical. He went out, had some laughs, and fell into bed. But it was different with El, he simply wanted to make her happy. He'd love it if their relationship could be more than that, but for once sex wasn't his ultimate goal. Instead, he found himself thinking of things that would make her smile. What he felt for this woman seemed richer and more satisfying than anything he'd experienced before. There was so much more to discover about her.

AT THE RESTAURANT, CLAY ASKED IF THEY COULD SIT ON the patio. The balmy evening carried a slight breeze, and dining was quieter outside. He wanted to focus only on El. Their table stood under a burgundy patio umbrella brimming with twinkle lights.

As soon as they got their drinks, they ordered dinner. El twirled the straw in her glass. "How did your task-force meeting go?"

Clay swallowed a mouthful of his hoppy craft brew. "The meeting was fine, but the news isn't good."

El's eyes snapped up to meet his.

He grimaced. "As if human trafficking and murder aren't enough, it seems we now have a serial killer on our hands. The FBI profilers and analysts agree that there's enough evidence to connect the recent murders and conclude a serial murderer is targeting prostitutes."

"Here, in Denver?" Panic laced her tone.

Clay stared into her eyes and gave a single nod. "Yeah. He's targeting girls with long brown hair, who—we believe—resemble his wife."

"He's married?"

"No. Well, he was, but the police have reason to believe he murdered her. That happened in Salina, Kansas four years ago."

"I don't understand. If he killed her, why is he looking for girls that remind him of her?"

Clay chuffed. "The thoughts and motivations of a serial killer make little sense to a healthy mind. But, if he's our guy, he might be continuing to punish, and in this case, kill his wife repeatedly."

"Oh, my God. That's horrible. Why?"

"We don't have all the details at this point, but his wife was pregnant when she was killed. The tipping point for our suspect, we believe, is that he may be sterile."

"So the baby wasn't his?"

"Right. Consequently, he likely thinks of his wife as a whore." Clay's face flushed hot. "I'm sorry. I—"

"No, it's okay. I see where you're going." El swallowed. "So the same killer committed the recent murders?"

"Yes. We're certain of that. We need to get the word out to people on the street. Girls that match his target description have to be aware. What's the best way to keep them safe?"

El closed her eyes and filled her lungs before letting out her breath in a whoosh. "The problem is, the girls have to work or they will be beaten, and possibly killed by their pimp. They're in between a rock and a hard place. We can inform them, but the only way to keep the girls safe is to find the killer." Slipping deep into thought, she tapped her spoon on the table. "We could recommend that long-haired brunettes cut or color their hair. Would that make a difference?"

Clay shrugged. "It might. Can you and your contacts help to get the word out on the street? At this point, the suspect seems to be specifically choosing young women who resemble his wife—but that could change if he escalates. How receptive would the girls be to having undercover cops out there on the track with them?"

"Not at all. Remember, it isn't just a sex trade. There are tons of drugs being used, bought, and sold on those streets. No one will want cops observing their business."

"But is it possible?"

"Maybe, but street smarts are sharp. People are aware of who's coming and going, and who belongs to whom. An unfamiliar face without a connection to a local pimp would make everyone suspicious."

"We just need to catch him." Clay pressed his fingertips into his temples. "It's shocking how far-reaching and dangerous human trafficking is. Anywhere from a single man selling his girlfriend out, to pimps running a string of girls on the street, all the way up to top-level business leaders and politicians. Ridiculously wealthy perverts hosting secret sex parties with underaged kids." His throat swelled like he might choke, and eyes ached as he searched El's. "I don't know where to start, or if we're even doing any good at all. Are we helping anyone?"

El's face softened, and a gentle smile graced her expression. She covered his hand with hers. "The problem is bigger than we can imagine. I understand how helpless you feel. But, please, please remember, even if you help one person reclaim their life, what you're doing matters. What I'm doing makes a difference. What your co-workers are doing could change someone's entire existence. Kendra, for example, changes lives by sharing her dogs to help with the recovery and healing of sex traffic victims. When we add it all together, what we are all doing is meaningful and important. It's crucial." She joined her other hand to his and squeezed. "We'll never end human trafficking. It's been going on since the dawn of time, but we must do everything possible to help those we can."

Holding onto her fingers, Clay lifted his hand and kissed hers. "Thanks. I needed to hear that. Again." He dropped his forehead and rested it on their joined hands. "I rarely get overwhelmed, but this..."

"I know. We're fortunate to have you in the fight."

Their meals came and interrupted the intensity of the moment. Their conversation moved on to what it was like to train and work with dogs, to Clay's time in the military, and on to his childhood. Clay awkwardly avoided asking anything about El's childhood. He wasn't sure how to have a two-way conversation that didn't bring up painful memories.

At the end of the evening, he walked El to her door. He moved to kiss her, but she turned her head. His lips brushed her cheek. He kissed her temple and whispered in her ear. "I'm happy to go at your pace, El. You're in the driver's seat." He drew back and searched her eyes.

She didn't hold his gaze and lowered hers to the ground. "I'm not sure I can do this, at all. You're so good, and true, and pure, and I'm—"

"Ha!" Clay barked out a scoff. "That's not true. I have my skeletons too, you know. Yours aren't your fault. Mine are." He cupped her cheek in his hand. "No one is perfect. I'm not looking for perfect. I'm looking for caring, giving, and thoughtful. You're all of those things. You're beautiful because of those things. I'll wait as long as you need."

A single tear tracked down her cheek, and she blinked. Her mouth moved to smile, but her lips never made it past a flat line. Kissing her own fingertips, she touched them to his lips, and turned to go inside. As she closed the door, she murmured, "Thank you for the sunflowers, and dinner. Thanks for... Thanks, Clay."

His heart weighed heavy when the door latched. Not because he had to wait for her, but because she didn't think she was good enough for him. *I'm the one who's unworthy here. Not El. Never her.*

Chapter Thirty

Jonny glanced at Candie from the driver's seat. "It pissed me off when I saw how bruised you were after the party, but I made a shit-ton of money. You'll be okay in the end, so it was worth it." Jonny tapped his fingers on the steering wheel to the rhythm of the hip-hop blaring through the speakers.

He allowed her to sit in the front seat of the van next to him for the six-hour drive back to Denver. This was her reward. Normally, Jonny made everyone stay in the back. Steven sat alone, leaning his head on the side-wall, staring at nothing. The events of the weekend broke his soul into sharp pieces, and crushed parts of his heart that would never mend.

"When we get home, I need you to get all these bitches ready for the fancy-schmancy beach party." He rattled his fingers around inside a crushed pack of cigarettes, pulled one out, and pressed it between his lips. He spoke around the filter. "Not you, though. This guy—he wants 'em young. You're too old."

It was hard to believe that at fourteen, she was too old.

Candie had wanted to travel to the private beach-house mansion with the others, after all work was work—here or there. But at least there, she could see the ocean and maybe walk along the shore. Instead, she had to stay home, but she'd still have to work. No doubt about that. It wasn't like she would get a break. No, she'd be home, walking the sandy beaches of Colfax.

"We need the full buff and polish again, plus bikinis. You handle that. Got it?"

Candie nodded and stared at her window. They sailed east down I-70 through the mountains toward Denver. The mansions of Vail stood guard over the valley. *What's it like to live that kind of life? Where you could have anything you want—even a slave—and no one stops you?* She shivered and closed her eyes, pretending to sleep.

When they got home, Jonny ordered everyone to meet him in the living room. He told them about the exclusive party he'd rented them out to work. "It will be like the party you were just at, but fancier." Jonny spoke as though he expected everyone to be excited about being used and abused.

Steven slumped on the couch and drew his knees up to his face. Hiding his face, he cried into them.

"Goddamn it, Steven! I'm sick of your sniveling." Jonny yanked the boy's arm. "Man the hell up!"

"I don't want to go," Steven cried. "Please, don't make me."

"Not only are you going, you've got to grow up, 'cuz Candie ain't going with you this time."

Steven stared in horror at Candie, and a giant vice squeezed her chest. She sent him a limp smile."

"I'm not going." Steven yelled, tears spilling through his voice. "You can't make me!"

Jonny took the boy by the shoulders, lifted him up and

threw him to the ground. "Oh, you're going, and I *can* make you." He kicked the boy's ribs. "You belong to me." Kick. "You'll do what I say." Kick.

"Jonny, stop! Please!" Candie ran to her pimp's side and gripped his arm. Her ribs contracted each time Jonny booted the boy. Jonny flung her away, and she crashed into an end table causing the lamp to fall and break. A piece of broken ceramic cut into her knee when Candie crawled back and threw her arms around Jonny's leg. "He's just a little boy. You'll kill him," she cried.

Jonny shook his leg loose and kicked at Candie before reaching down to pull Steven up by his hair. "Get in my room. You clearly have some more learning to do."

"No, no..." Steven's whimpering broke Candie's heart.

"Please, Jonny. Leave him alone. It's been a long weekend. We're all so tired." She stood up and approached Jonny, touching his face. "Let me take care of you tonight."

He stared at her for a moment and seemed to calm down a little. "You're not doing him any favors babying him like you do. He has to get over it someday. You're just making it worse." He swung his glare around the room to include everyone. "Get to bed. I'm sick of seeing you all right now." His black gaze returned to Candie. "I'm taking a shower. Be in my bed when I get out." He stomped to his room and slammed the door behind him.

Candie rushed to Steven. "Are you okay? Can you breathe? Let me see your ribs." She pulled up his shirt, where purple bruises were already swelling on his fair skin. "Trixie, get a cold washcloth for his mouth."

Steven gripped her arm. "I'm not going to Florida without you. I don't care if Jonny kills me. I'm not going," Steven's voice was low and steady.

Candie brushed his blond bangs out of his eyes. "Yes, you

are. You'll have to work either way, so why not enjoy the sun and the ocean? You've got to be brave."

"You said we'd escape," he whispered.

"I'm trying to find a way, Steven. I am. But if you get killed first, then what?" She pulled the boy onto her lap. "Please, be brave. We'll find a way. Someday."

Steven curled up into her and lifted his thumb to his mouth. As he closed his eyes, he sucked. He hadn't done that before. Absorbing his pain into her already tormented soul, she pulled him closer, her tears dripping into his hair.

CANDIE RODE ALONG WHEN JONNY TOOK THE REST OF THE kids to the Rocky Mountain Metropolitan Airport. She sat in the van while they climbed the stairs and boarded the private jet. With the rest of her makeshift family on their way to the exclusive estate in Florida, Candie had Jonny all to herself. She thought back to the days when she believed he thought she was special. The days when she wanted his attention.

Back home, a dark hollowness threatened to swallow her as she deliberately applied her heavy makeup for the night. After lining her amber eyes with thick black liner, she applied bright red lipstick. Candie stared at her image in the mirror and sighed. She unclipped the hot-rollers and let her hair hang in long, loose curls.

Her short, red dress that fit like a second skin, was one that seemed to bring in the money. Jonny expected her to cover more than her usual quota since she supposedly had less competition with the others gone. She suspected he made a mint by supplying the sex-play for the private event. But, no matter how much money he had, it was never enough for Jonny. He even talked about getting into kiddy-porn videos. There was a ton of money for the picking there.

Candie slid her feet into strappy, stiletto sandals and left to take her spot on the track. She sent a prayer up that she wouldn't have to deal with any rough or violent johns tonight. As she teetered down the street to her territory, a car filled with boys who could have been in high school or college drove past, slowing down. They whistled and called out to her. Candie pasted a smile on her face and waved.

"I've got way more than you could handle, sweetheart." One boy yelled as he grabbed his crotch through his jeans.

"Put your money where your mouth is, boys," she called back. They laughed and drove on.

Another car pulled up to the curb. The passenger window slid down.

Candie stopped and bent down to peer inside. A business man by the look of him. "Hey honey, looking to party?"

The man swallowed and appeared nervous. Probably his first time paying for it. "Uh, how does this work, exactly?"

Candie stepped closer and leaned on the edge of the window, giving him a full view of her pushed-up breasts. "Depends on what you're looking for. You tell me that, and we can talk about how to make your wishes come true." She had to be careful about how she worded things in case the guy was an undercover cop.

"I... well... I'm in town for one night and wanted some... company."

Is this guy actually blushing? She glanced at his hand. Sure enough—the tell-tale tan-line. Candie always felt sorry for the wives of these assholes. Of course, that didn't stop her from taking their money. At least she was honest about what she was.

"Seventy-five an hour."

"For... anything?"

"What do you have in mind, handsome? You're gonna have to tell me at some point."

He reached over and opened the door. "Get in. It shouldn't take more than an hour."

"Okay, but you have to drive me back here."

The john nodded, and Candie held out her hand. "And you have to pay upfront."

He fished the cash out of his wallet. Candie took it and slid into the car.

Forty-five minutes later, the man dropped her off where he'd picked her up, and she continued her walk to her particular corner. She wasn't there for a half hour before another john cruised by, checking out the merchandise.

CLAY WAS ON SOLO PATROL WITH RANGER, FOLLOWING A guy in a brown, late-model 90s Ford Taurus. The car coasted at less than five miles per hour while the driver checked out the girls on the street. Five women flaunted themselves at cars and passers-by. The driver in the sedan eased by a long-legged black girl, and a sassy looking blonde with a fake fur. He said a few words to a woman with overly-teased streaked hair and then moved forward. He braked hard at the corner, surprising Clay who had to stop fast in response.

The man stretched over the seat to talk to a girl in a tight red dress with long brown curls. *She fits the target victim profile.* Clay's pulse ratcheted up a notch as he watched the woman lean into the window. He saw the silhouette of the guy handing her a wad of cash. The girl opened the door and got into the car. The warning hairs on his neck prickled, and Ranger emitted a deep, guttural growl.

"I'm on it, boy." Clay sat at the corner after the Taurus turned and drove up the block. He'd pursue them, but needed to allow for some distance. It wasn't difficult to guess where they were going. The motel these girls used was a mere two blocks away. He spun the steering wheel, and followed, keeping the sedan in sight.

The car veered into the expected parking lot. Clay pulled in as the two crossed the parking lot toward the girl's room. The man held the girl by her upper arm and it looked like he pulled her along. She slipped and fell off one towering shoe only to be yanked back up and forced to keep pace. The muscles in Clay's jaw tightened as he watched impatiently from his SUV.

The couple stopped at the room, and the girl fished in her tiny purse for the key card. She unlocked the entrance and pushed it open. In that second, the reflection of a long knife blade flashed in the light just before the door slammed shut. Clay immediately called for back-up, but he couldn't wait for them to arrive. He flung open Ranger's kennel, and the two of them sprinted across the cracked and pitted asphalt. He paused at the entrance only long enough to shout, "FBI". Then, with his SIG level and ready, he booted the flimsy door open. It flew, splintering off its hinges.

Before him, Wayne Horton stood over the girl. His pants were down around his ankles and he rammed himself into her while his hands gripped her tight around her neck. The girl's eyes bulged and gagging noises choked from her throat.

"FBI! Let her go!" Clay shouted.

Horton snatched up the hunting knife he'd placed on the bed next to the girl's head and wild-eyed, he pressed the blade into her bruised neck.

"Drop the knife." With his eye on the blade, Clay's finger hovered on the trigger of his gun, prepared to shoot at the slightest movement.

"I don't think so."

"Look, there's no way out of this, so before you add another murder to your rap sheet, put down the knife."

Tears flooded the girl's face. White with terror, she lay frozen.

"Sounds like I have nothing to lose." The blade pressed deeper until a thin crease of blood appeared at its edge. "You need to drop your gun. Drop it and kick it over here."

The seeping red line glared in stark contrast to the girl's pale skin. Clay's mouth dried up as he considered his options, his throat sticking to itself when he swallowed. If Clay rushed the guy, he'd slice the girl's throat before he got there. If he gave up his gun, he still had Ranger and his second gun strapped to his leg. As long as Horton couldn't reach Clay's SIG, it might work. Drool dripped from Ranger's bared fangs. He was raring to attack.

"Okay," Clay released the grip of his handgun and it hung upside down by his finger in the trigger housing. "Look, I'm setting this on the floor." He bent down slowly and placed his weapon in front of his boot.

"Kick it over here."

"First, it's your turn to give me something. Take the knife away from her neck." Clay forced a steadiness into his voice that he didn't feel. He held this girl's life in his hands. One wrong move on his part and she would be dead.

Horton laughed and released the blade's pressure on the girl's tender skin, but he moved the knife and pointed its tip a half-inch from the girl's eye. "Kick your gun over here. And you better keep that beast on his leash, or she's dead."

Clay nudged the gun forward to a spot between them. Horton would have to reach for it if he wanted it, but so would Clay. "Okay, put down the knife."

The laugh that spewed from the monster hovering over the girl chilled Clay's soul. "She must die." Horton's shoulder flexed as he drew his arm back to gain leverage for his thrust.

"Drz!"

Before Clay fully formed the guttural command, Ranger

sprang from the door toward the attacker. His teeth sank into the man's shoulder joint, and they both fell to the floor. Ranger, growling and twisting, subdued the killer who screamed, his voice saturated in agony.

"Call him off! Fuck! Get him off me!"

Clay retrieved his gun from the floor, kicked the knife out of Horton's fist, and ran to the girl. "Are you hurt? Do you have any injuries other than your throat?"

Huge brown eyes stared at him, and as the girl shook her head, she burst into tears. She frantically tried to pull her tight dress down over her hips while scrambling up on the bed to distance herself from her attacker and the violence of the take-down scene.

Ranger held the attacker on the ground, shaking his head back and forth, tearing muscles and ligaments, crushing bone, and causing maximum pain. Clay picked up the knife and joined Ranger. "*Pust.*"

Ranger released the man, but stood inches away, drool dripping on his face. He growled while Clay rolled the man to his stomach. Pinning him to the floor under his knee, he cuffed Horton's hands behind his back. Clay patted him down, searching for additional weapons. He found only a small knife stuffed in the man's boot before he yanked the killer to his feet and shoved him into a chair. "Stay there."

Clay returned to the terrified girl cowering on the bed, holding his hands up. He slowly and deliberately holstered his gun. "You're safe now. I'm with the FBI, and a police back-up is on its way." No sooner had he said that, sirens sounded from down the street. "Can you talk? What's your name?"

The girl raised her hand to her throat. It was already bruising and swelling. She needed the paramedics right away before she could no longer breathe. "Candie," she whispered and then tried to swallow.

"Okay, Candie. Don't talk anymore for now. Help is on the

way. I'm Clay." He gave her a reassuring smile. "This is Ranger. He hates guys who attack women."

Candie stared at the dog snarling at the killer in the chair.

Two cops burst through the door, their weapons drawn.

"Thanks guys. Everything's under control here. Where are the paramedics?"

"They're right behind us."

"Good." Clay glared at his captive. "Are you Wayne Horton?"

The attacker appeared shocked that Clay knew his name, and he dipped his head in acknowledgement.

"Wayne Horton, you are under arrest for the murder of your wife, Mindy Horton, in Salina, Kansas, and for the murder of at least two other women since then. These officers will read you your rights and accompany you to the hospital."

The cops yanked up the man's pants, took him by his arms and led him out to the ambulance. When Clay returned his attention to Candie, Ranger was already there, licking her hands and smiling up at her with his silly dog grin.

Clay brought her a blanket and sat next to her on the edge of the bed. He ruffled the fur on the top of Ranger's head. "Candie, are you willing to press charges? To testify against this guy? He's been on a killing spree, murdering prostitutes from here to Kansas City. You're lucky to be alive."

Candie focused on Ranger and kept her hands busy stroking his face. Finally, she nodded. "Yes. I'll testify," she whispered. Paramedics raced into the room and began administering medical aid. Clay and Ranger moved out of the way and waited for the crime scene investigators to take control of the room and evidence.

The medics laid Candie on their stretcher and were wheeling her out of the door when Clay reached for her hand

and gave it a gentle squeeze. "I'll see you at the hospital. You're safe now. I have a friend who can help you."

Candie's big brown eyes stayed on him until he couldn't see her anymore. He hoped she believed she could trust him. He pulled his phone from his vest and dialed El.

Chapter Thirty-One

El stopped at the reception desk in the hospital's emergency room. After showing her Social Services ID, she asked the nurse about a young woman brought in by ambulance after an attempted rape and murder. After requesting El's identification and credentials, the nurse directed her to the girl's room. Clay was already there, sitting in the corner with Ranger at his side. While the doctor examined the girl's throat, El entered and stood next to Clay, attempting to stay out of the doctor's way in the small exam room.

On the bed lay a young woman El guessed to be in her mid-teens. The nurse had wrapped her in a hospital gown but her make-up still smeared her cheeks. She had pulled her hair into a long ponytail that hung over her right shoulder and she rested her head back on the pillow while the doctor peered into her mouth. An IV dripped into the tube attached to her hand in rhythm with the beeping of the monitors.

"The x-rays don't show any serious damage, but the muscles and tissue in your throat are quite swollen and will be sore for a week or more. I'm admitting you overnight because

I'm concerned about swelling hampering your ability to breathe, and we want to be sure you have suffered no minor brain injury. You have two small, superficial cuts on the front of your neck along with the bruising, but they don't need stitches and should heal nicely on their own." The doctor acknowledged Clay and El. "I see you have some support, and that's a good thing. I hope you get all the help you need. A nurse will be here shortly to transfer you to your regular room upstairs." She patted Candie's blanketed leg and turned to go. "Ms. Clark? You're from Family Services?"

"Yes." El shook the doctor's hand.

"I'm Dr. Stavros. May I speak with you in the hall for a minute?" She gestured toward the door, and El followed her out.

"As requested, we did a rape kit, however I don't know how conclusive it will be."

"Thank you, Doctor. Otherwise, will she be okay?"

"Yes. I hope you can get her off the streets."

"Me too." They shook hands again, and El returned to the room.

"Hi Candie, my name is El Clark." El smiled at the scene she came in upon. Ranger stood on his hind legs, propped up on the edge of Candie's bed. The girl rested her hand on the back of his head. "I see you've met Ranger."

"He saved my life." The girl whispered and glanced at Clay. "Along with Agent Jennings."

"I'm so glad they got there in time." El approached the other side of the bed. "I'm a social worker with Denver County, and I'm here to help you in any and every way I can. I heard you're willing to testify against the man who attacked you tonight?"

Candie nodded. "And..." she rasped, her breath speeding up.

Alarmed, El took her hand.

She continued, "Maybe you can help a little boy I know. His name is Steven." She paused. "Actually, his real name is Tom. Jonny stole him from his family and forced him to... to..." Candie's eyes flashed with tears.

"We can help. Where is Tom now?"

"Normally he stays with me at Jonny's, but Jonny sent everyone to a week-long party at an estate in Florida. They're supposed to be home on Tuesday."

Clay stood. "Where in Florida? Do you know?"

Candie shook her head. "Only that they went to an exclusive estate somewhere near the Florida Keys."

El sat on the edge of the bed. "Is Jonny your pimp?"

Candie hesitated, and then nodded, yes.

"Why didn't Jonny send you to Florida too?"

Liquid brown eyes met Els. "Fourteen is too old."

A thick paste sloughed through El's gut. "How old is Tom?" Her voice failed her and her words came out in a rasp.

"I think he's nine." Candie dropped her gaze to her hands. "I tried to help him." Tears formed new tracks across her mascara-stained cheeks.

Clay jumped to his feet with his phone in hand. "Excuse me a minute." He took a step and then said, "*Zustan.*" Ranger settled in to stay where he was.

El rubbed her thumb over the girl's hand. "I'm sure you have helped him just by knowing he has a friend." She paused. "Is Candie your real name?"

The girl shook her head.

"Will you tell me what it is?"

She blinked up at El. "My name is Lilly."

El swallowed her own tears. "Hi, Lilly. You're safe now, and you're not alone. I promise to walk every step of the way with you. Okay?"

Lilly dropped her chin, and her chest shook with silent

sobs. El gathered the girl into her arms. "You aren't alone anymore."

"You've got to help Tom. He's just a little boy." Lilly's eyes poured out emotion. "Please."

"Yes. We'll do everything we can to find him."

A nurse pushed open the door. "They're all set for you upstairs. Are you ready to go to your room?"

Lilly nodded, and the nurse unlocked the wheels on the bed and pushed it toward the door. "I can't believe they let you bring your dog in here. It's not sanitary."

"He's an FBI K9 agent, and he might not be sanitary, but he sure helps with the healing." El motioned to Clay who was still on his phone that they were going to Lilly's room. He mouthed that he'd be right there.

"WITH HER TESTIMONY, WE HAVE ENOUGH TO ARREST Jonny Gold tonight. We've finally got that son of a bitch, and not just for prostituting children, but for kidnapping and assault."

"Good job tonight, Jennings." Sanchez sounded like he'd been asleep. "Get the girl's statement tonight, before she changes her mind."

"I will, but I think she is desperate for the kind of help El Clark can provide through social services and El's contacts with recovery groups. Lilly wants us to help the little boy Jonny abducted. If for no other reason than because of him, I doubt she'll change her mind."

"This whole thing sickens me. Makes you think twice about bringing kids into this world."

Clay had never really thought about wanting kids and wondered if Rick and Kendra considered it. "I hear you. It's hard to remember with our jobs sometimes that not everyone in the world is dark and twisted."

"No kidding," Sanchez sighed. "Kendra was just saying it's crucial for decent people to raise good kids to keep the evil out there in check."

"Sounds like her." A fleeting thought breezed through his mind about what it would be like to have his own kids. He blinked to clear the idea away.

"Yeah. So, I'll see you at the task-force meeting. Again, great job catching our killer. Be ready to present the case."

"Will do." Clay ended the call and went in search of El, who had followed Ranger and Lilly upstairs. He stopped by the reception desk on his way to get Lilly's room number and asked to borrow a pad of paper and a pen.

Lilly was not in the bed when he arrived. Instead, she sat on the guest chair with her face buried in Ranger's neck, leaning on his strong shoulders for support. Clay looked to El to see how things were going.

"These two are fast friends." A ghost of a smile breezed across El's mouth. "No surprise there. Ranger gives me the same comfort."

Clay nodded, silently wishing he was the one El felt like she could turn to. What did Ranger have that he didn't? *Christ, I am jealous of my dog!* The fact was, Ranger didn't try to say the right thing and end up sticking his paw in his mouth, and he came to both women with zero judgment and pure sympathy. He took on their pain and weakness with no expectation. Clay wanted to be like Ranger, but just being a human prevented that.

"I'm glad he's here." He squatted in front of Lilly, next to Ranger, and waited for her to look up at him. When she did, he saw that her face was clean of all the make-up. She looked young and vulnerable. "Lilly, do you think you could give me your statement? Just write, in your own words, what happened tonight?"

"Clay..." El interrupted. He understood she wanted to protect the girl from having to relive her nightmare, but it was best to get the details while they were fresh.

Clay ignored El for the moment and waited for Lilly to answer him. She nodded and reached for the paper and pen.

"Thank you. I know this is hard, but you're saving other young women from going through what you did, or worse." He said the words to Lilly, but he hoped that El heard them and understood. "When you're done, sign and date it. Then, please write down everything that you know about Jonny Gold and your friend Steven—or Tom. Anything you can remember might help us find Tom and put Jonny in jail."

Lilly nodded again, bent over the pad of paper, and began scrawling. Clay ran his hand down the length of Ranger's back. "You stay here with her, Range—good boy."

The doctor on call entered the room. "How's everyone tonight?"

Clay and El responded with grim expressions, and the doctor cleared his throat.

"Yes, understandable. Lilly's blood work has come back from the lab. However, she's a minor, and I can't discuss this information without consent."

Lilly looked up, "It's fine. These are my friends."

Deep in Clay's belly something unclasped. A warmth radiated outward. *Her friends?* Her words both pleased him and stung his heart. *Poor girl probably doesn't have any real friends. What a lonely, horrible life to face each morning.* Well, no more. Clay vowed then and there that he'd do everything in his power to change that for Lilly.

"My name is Eloise Clark. I'm from Family and Social Services. Lilly is currently a ward of the state, and I am acting as her guardian for the time being. So, you are legally safe to share her information with me, especially since Lilly agrees."

The doctor opened his chart and stared at the information before he addressed Lilly. "You have a significant level of opioid in your blood. Have you taken any drugs? Oxycodone, or... heroin?"

Lilly didn't look up from her writing, but Clay noticed her cheeks turn pink.

"We need to know what you've taken so we can make good decisions about how to best care for you. Not because you'll be in any trouble." The doctor glanced at El, unsure how to proceed.

El walked across the room and ran her hand down Lilly's back. She crouched down to look in the girl's face and drew in a deep breath. "Lilly, I've been where you are, right now." El gently lifted Lilly's chin so she could look into her eyes. "Almost exactly where you are."

Lilly's brows drew together. "You mean..."

"I was forced to work the streets too, and I get that survival depends on using drugs. You're not in any trouble at all. The doctor, Clay, and I—we all just want to help you."

Lilly's gaze slid to Clay's dog. "And Ranger."

El smiled. "Yes, and especially Ranger." She rubbed the dog's head. "So, don't be afraid to be honest. We're all on your side here—and you are safe."

Lilly's shy gaze met the doctor's. "We all take Oxy. It helps me go somewhere else. It takes the pain away."

The doctor wrote on the chart before asking, "Do you feel you need these pills, even when there isn't any pain?"

Lilly stared at him a moment before dropping her head and nodding. "I want one now, but..." She crossed her arms and held them tight across her middle. Chewed off fingernails scratched at her arm.

"Thank you for your honesty, Lilly. We are all proud of

you. I'm prescribing Lucemyra for you which will help ease your withdrawal symptoms. You are likely to experience anxiety, increased heart rate, nausea, and insomnia. These are expected, but we'll help you get through it." The doctor's eyes met El's. "She will need to be admitted into a rehab facility as soon as she leaves here."

"Yes, thank you, doctor."

"I'll have the nurse bring a sedative in right away that should help you sleep." He left the room, closing the door behind him.

When Lilly finished her statement, Clay photographed the pages with his phone, and sent the images to Sanchez.

A text buzzed back. *I'll call you as soon as we get the warrant for Jonny Gold.*

Clay thumbed his screen. *Ranger and I are ready and waiting when you do.*

Chapter Thirty-Two

It was a long but extremely gratifying night. Clay had been working on impulse engines, with little to no sleep since the team's trip over to the western slope. He and Ranger rescued Lilly, not only from a murderer, but hopefully from a life lived on the streets. Together, he and his dog put a serial killer in jail for the rest of his days. On top of that, with Lilly's statement, they received arrest and search warrants for Jonny Gold and his house.

He and Ranger were on location when police executed a no-knock warrant at Gold's residence. They watched from behind Clay's open car door as S.W.A.T. bashed the front door in and filed inside. They performed the raid without firing a single shot. When the 'All Clear' sounded, Clay and Ranger met Sanchez on the porch. They each slid on a pair of rubber gloves and entered the house.

Clay scanned the living space and kitchen before turning into the master bedroom. A skinny man sat in baggy athletic shorts on the edge of a bed propped up on one corner with a cinderblock. Ranger's guttural rumble mirrored Clay's sentiment.

To their right, a forty-inch flat-screen TV hung on the wall. Scattered on the table underneath it were a dozen or more DVDs with numbers and letters written on them in permanent marker. Clay slid a disc into the DVD player. The screen filled with a homemade video showing a naked man with two children. Red fury pressed against the back of Clay's eyes and he hit the button on the machine to turn it off. "Bag this shit."

Clay couldn't look at the man the cops arrested. His blood was like lava coursing under his skin, and he didn't trust himself not to choke the living shit out of that scum. Ranger's job was attack and apprehension, but he'd had some basic drug scent training. So when he barked and tugged against his lead, Clay followed him to the nightstand. He pulled open the drawer and found it stuffed with baggies full of pills in all colors. There were bags of white powder that Clay presumed was cocaine, and several more of weed. Another drawer revealed three handguns, all with their serial numbers scratched off. Evidence piled up.

"Sir," a uniformed officer entered the room and addressed Sanchez. "The basement floor is covered in mattresses. There are at least ten."

"Who sleeps on those, Mr. Gold?"

Jonny glared at Sanchez. "I want a lawyer."

"No doubt." Sanchez turned to the officers guarding the perp. "Get him out of here."

Clay approached Sanchez. "We've already uncovered enough evidence of human trafficking, sexual abuse of children, child pornography, drugs, and guns to put that asshole away for a very long time. If he survives." Child molesters didn't do well in prison, and that didn't bother Clay one bit.

He knew Gold would plea down some of his sentence though, because the DA wanted him to give state's evidence against Barron and his cronies. Hopefully, along with Lilly's testimony, that would put one more evil man behind bars where he couldn't hurt any more children. When Clay read Lilly's account of what happened to her and the others at the ranch house near Telluride, his skin itched as though beetles crawled all over him. He, Sanchez, and Cameron had come so close, but failed to get inside Barron's compound. All the while, kids inside suffered torture. If he'd have known the extent of what was happening inside, he would have rammed the gates—gun and badge be damned.

Exhaustion seeped from Clay's bones as the sun's smile bumped against the eastern sky, but he wanted to stop back at the hospital to check on his girls before finally heading home. *His girls? Where the hell had that come from?* He rubbed his eyes and shook his head, wondering at his delirium. He desperately needed coffee, a hot shower and shave, and a solid eight hours in bed. Coffee he could have now. Hopefully, he wasn't so stinky and scruffy that he'd scare El and Lilly. He knocked, and upon hearing "come in" called out over the sound of a TV news show, he pushed open the hospital room door.

El's hazel eyes met his expectantly. A grin spread across his face, and he nodded. "We got him. He'll be in prison till he's too old to wipe his own—"

"Clay!" El stepped between him and Lilly, taking a protective stance.

He raised a tired brow at her. "I'm fairly sure Lilly has heard the word 'ass' before, El."

The girl giggled from her perch on the side of the bed. "Is Ranger with you?"

"Not this time, sweetheart. I left him at the FBI kennel to get a bath, a good meal, and some much-deserved rest. I'm on my way home to do the same thing, but I wanted to check on you."

Lilly had dressed in a pair of jeans that were a little too

big and a rainbow tie-dyed t-shirt with a smiley-face printed on the front. She wore her long hair braided and hanging down her back.

El picked up a plastic bag holding Lilly's clothes from the night before. "You just caught us. We're on our way to the rehab center to get Lilly settled in."

"Good. That'll be good." A sharp jolt poked his sleepy brain. "Wait, can she have visitors?"

El's gaze softened as she considered him. "Not for a minimum of two weeks. After that, only if her counselors feel she is ready."

Clay didn't understand the swirl of emotions that seemed to run amuck inside. He opted for a gruff tone to cover his intense feelings. "What about testifying?"

The sweet look in El's eyes melted away, replaced by speculation. "It will have to wait. Lilly's health and wellbeing are far more important."

She may as well have punched him. "Of course, Lilly is more important. I didn't mean that." Clay ran a rough hand over his grizzled face. "Besides, the DA will file a motion for video testimony." One of El's eyebrows rose, wrinkling the skin on her forehead. He needed to go before he said anything else that came across as insensitive.

BEEP. BEEP. BEEP. A loud, urgent sounding alarm blared from the TV. The plastic-blonde news anchor sat behind her desk and leaned forward. "Breaking news. Police have found the bodies of two young boys on the coast in the Florida Keys. According to an FBI spokeswoman, both boys are believed to be children reported missing from a Denver suburb last month."

"Oh my God—No!" Lilly jumped up and stood staring at the TV. "Please, not Tom!"

El went to her and slid her arm around Lilly's shoulders

and they stared at the screen together. Clay punched his speed dial to the Denver FBI headquarters.

The newscast blared on. "The bodies were found floating up on the beach near an exclusive estate—the only structure on that side of the island. The FBI is currently investigating everyone in residence at the estate, including all guests and employees. Officials believe they know the identities of the decedents; however they won't release their names until their families are notified and give their consent." The image changed to a photographer running toward the crime scene. He caught an image of the bodies before police hustled him away.

Lilly cried out, "I know that boy!" Her hand flew to her mouth and tears pooled in her eyes.

El pulled her into an embrace. "Is that your friend?"

Lilly sobbed into El's chest. "No. He was one of the new boys. One that Jonny recently brought home. Jonny called him Thad, but he never told me his real name." Lilly raised her face and stared at El. "Do you think the other boy was Tom?"

"I don't know." El's gaze met Clay's. He was talking with Cameron—asking the same thing. He shrugged.

Lilly buried her face in El's embrace once again and sobbed. "They were at that fancy sex party. Oh, God. Poor Tommy. I promised to get him out."

"Sh, sh. We don't have the details yet. Clay's trying to find out, but they might not know anything yet." El lifted Lilly's chin and brushed tears from her cheeks. "I'm so glad you weren't there."

Sad, dripping eyes peered up at El. "I was too old."

Clay gagged and cleared his throat. A powerful shudder coursed through his shoulders and down his spine. He wanted to retch. *Fourteen is too old?* He imagined choking the life out of the scum who hurt these kids—with his own bare hands.

A new camera angle filled the screen. A group of uniformed workers stood huddled off to the side as FBI agents escorted several men in handcuffs from the elegant entrance of the mansion.

"Hey," Clay covered the mouthpiece on his phone. "I recognize a couple of those guys."

El and Lilly turned to view the screen.

Lilly gasped and placed her hand over her mouth. With her other, she pointed at the TV. "He... That man was at the mountain mansion! He..." Her eyes flooded with tears and her hand lowered to her neck. She returned to El's embrace.

"The guy with the comb-over? That's Colorado Representative Peter Spiel, and the tall man next to him is Alistair Greer. He's a goddamn US Senator!" Clay's mouth dropped open as he stared at the TV. "My God... where does this end?"

El held Lilly in one arm and reached her other hand out to him. "It never ends. The money and power wrapped up in trafficking at the highest levels worldwide is too hard to comprehend. We need to focus on the lives we're trying to change for the better here at home. Keep your mind on that."

Stunned, Clay's head floated back and forth. "I haven't changed any lives. Not really."

"What about mine?" Lilly sounded small and frightened.

"You're the brave one, sweetheart. You're changing your own life." Clay's gaze moved to El, and he searched her face. "Like you did. El, you're the perfect example for Lilly."

El reached up and placed her hands on the sides of his face. "Clay, you saved Lilly's life and helped her to find a path out." She swallowed hard and hesitated before she continued. "You've changed my life too, you know. You accepted me... wanted me, without judgement. You saw my history with sorrow for what I'd gone through, but not with pity. You've shown me you believe I have value." El rose on her toes and kissed his mouth. "You accept what I can give and don't pressure me for more. Maybe one day..."

A hot tear spilled over Clay's lower eyelid and trickled down into his morning whiskers. He touched her cheek with his fingertips. "You're incredible." Awe for the woman standing before him filled his chest like helium, causing a floating sensation.

El dropped her gaze to the floor, but not before Clay saw the beautiful smile that graced her lips.

IT WAS DIFFICULT TO LET EL AND LILLY LEAVE AND DRIVE to the rehab facility on their own, and even harder to get back to his house without falling asleep at the wheel. His footsteps echoed against the walls when he entered through the garage door. He had never liked to spend much time at home alone, but this morning, for some reason, the atmosphere was even more bereft. Clay stripped off his clothes, dropping them as he went. He cranked on the faucet and leaned against the shower wall as scalding water coursed over his sore and tired muscles. He was hungry, but too exhausted to make any food. While he blotted his skin dry, he wolfed down a protein bar, and then he collapsed naked onto his bed. He slept for nine hours straight.

The sun trimmed the edge of the mountainous horizon in gold when he blinked his eyes open and gazed at the view out his bedroom window. Final beams of light shot through periwinkle clouds. "Glory Rays," his grandma used to call them. He had to agree, and the sight of them gave him hope. El was right, the fight against human trafficking would never be over, but re-energized, he was ready to win what battles he could.

Clay stretched his body, still naked from his shower that morning. Laughing at how tired he must have been, he reached for a pair of gym shorts and padded to the kitchen. His stomach shouted for attention. An omelet would do the trick. His circadian rhythm was all screwed up after pulling such an intense all-nighter. Hopefully, he'd be able to get a little more sleep before the task-force meeting the next day. The one in which they expected him to present both the Wayne Horton, and Jonny Gold cases.

He popped the lid off a beer—*Beer and omelets? Why the hell not?*—and reached for the remote to the massive flat-screen that hung on the wall in his living room. He slid his eggs onto a plate and flopped on the couch to watch a show. As he flipped through the channels, the image of the newscaster from this morning caught his eye. He turned up the volume.

The woman's newsy tone blared from the speakers. "Apparently, the owner of the estate, whose identity remains unknown, escaped the island on his private jet moments before federal agents arrived on the scene."

Clay sat forward. "What the actual hell?" he bellowed. Jumping to his feet, he paced the floor before reaching for his phone to call Sanchez.

Kendra answered. "Rick's out back. Hold on."

Clay continued to pace, fury radiating from his skin.

"Hey, Jennings. I take it you just heard the news."

"What the hell? Why haven't they found his flight plan and followed him?"

Not only did the guy not file a flight plan, which isn't surprising, witnesses say his jet had no tail numbers. The estate is owned by several dummy corporations and the money trail is so convoluted it will take months to untangle."

"God-damn it!"

"They'll find him, Jennings."

"I doubt it. That guy's in the wind, now."

"He'll surface, and when he does, we'll be there. We got some solid information from Lilly regarding her pimp, Jonny

Gold, though. When the police brought him in last night, he asked for a plea deal. He's turned over on George Barron, the owner of the ranch we staked-out up in Telluride."

"Did we get enough to bring Barron in?"

"Yep, in fact we have a team flying up there at four this morning to apprehend him," Sanchez said. "I'd like you and Ranger to be there."

"We'll meet you at the airport."

"Good."

Silence hummed on the line.

Clay squeezed his temples between his thumb and middle finger. "Were there any more on the victims found alive in Florida?"

"In fact, there were. Agents are working to reunite the kids with their families. One is a nine-year-old boy named Thomas Ross. Gold abducted him from Kansas City."

The rage Clay had built up in his muscles drained away, and a tremulous smile curved itself on his lips. "Well, that's some good news, at least."

"It will be a long road to healing, but they have reunited him with his parents."

"Thanks, Sanchez. I needed to hear that."

"Every once in a while, good things happen too. Remember that."

"Yeah." Clay ducked his head. "I gotta go. I want to tell El so she can let Lilly know that Tom is home safe and sound with his family."

"Okay, see you in a couple of hours. And Jennings—good work, man."

Chapter Thirty-Three

Clay sat across the aisle from Cameron on the plane with Ranger at his feet. Sanchez worked from the window seat, reading from his laptop as the jet took off on the 50-minute flight to Telluride. Other members of the apprehension team sat scattered through the fuselage.

"What's the plan?" Clay accepted a cup of coffee from the single flight attendant.

Sanchez glanced up at him and closed his computer. "Local officials are banding together and will wait at the canyon road for us to join them before we move in for the raid. Aerial photos confirm there are twenty or more people on staff, but only five guards that appear to be armed—one of whom is the gate guard. There is no K9 presence."

"That's a good thing. Makes it easier." Clay reached down to stroke Ranger's head.

"There is only one road in and out of the property, so the plan is to disarm and apprehend the guards, block the road, surround the house, and arrest Barron, all hopefully without incident."

"Anyone else in the house besides staff? Any family?" Cameron asked.

Sanchez shook his head. "We don't believe so. Barron's adult children live in other states, and his wife is visiting their daughter in Texas." He passed out aerial views of the property to all the agents, with the mission details mapped out.

Clay studied the photo and memorized the part he and Ranger would play in the raid. "It'll be good to have this asshole behind bars. Maybe we can get some crucial information regarding the missing Florida estate owner from him."

"No doubt," Sanchez agreed. "Jonny Gold admitted that he supplied some kids for that event, but it was Barron who ordered them for the party. He has to know who the guy is. He probably knows more than that. I'm hoping for some solid banking information, too."

Cameron tapped keys on his laptop "Follow the money. That's always the way. I have Gold's banking records here with several large deposits made from a dummy corporation that he claims are transactions from Barron. We're working on tracking them down now, but the web Barron has spun is extremely convoluted. He's run the transactions through several proxy servers and bounced his web activity all around the world, which makes it almost impossible to track."

Clay peered over Cameron's shoulder at the spreadsheets on his screen. His throat constricted at the vast dollar amounts he saw in the various columns. Each sum represented lives exploited by sick and twisted powerful people who thought they were above the law—above humanity. The vast scope of human trafficking and the dollars that represented the problem were still incomprehensible to him. Clay ran his hand over his face and stared out the window at the clouds. He would never shake his new awareness of the countless children peddled on the streets every day—no matter how many sick bastards they caught and put in jail.

. . .

I<small>T WAS JUST BEFORE DAWN WHEN THE THREE</small> S<small>UBURBANS</small> carrying the FBI team pulled up next to four local sheriff's cars. Sanchez took command of the mission and within minutes, they were on their way to the Barron Ranch. A lone unmarked car approached the gate. Officers apprehended the guard before he had a chance to set off an alarm. They disabled the cameras and opened the gate for the rest of the raid team.

Clay road shot-gun as Cameron pressed the accelerator and their vehicle led the charge up the road toward the house. A handful of men starting their workday on the landscaped areas stopped doing their chores to watch. The agents approached the house, and when they came to a halt, Clay jumped out, positioning himself behind his open door for cover.

"*Zustan,*" Clay ordered Ranger to stay inside the Suburban.

A unit of men clad in full armor, all carrying Colt M4 Carbines, approached the front door in a solid group. As they rammed the beautifully custom-carved front doors of the ranch house, someone shouted. "FBI! We're coming in!" They rushed inside the log mansion.

Clay motioned for Ranger to join him, and the dog sprang from the vehicle. They joined Cameron and ran up the walkway to join the raid team as the team searched the sprawling residence. Clay, holding his SIG in firing position, followed his weapon inside, ready for anything. "Find 'em, Ranger."

Ranger sniffed the floor and scanned the perfectly designed rustic entry. He led Clay through a massive great-room, behind a grand stair-case into a vast kitchen. Several women in maid's uniforms huddled in tears against two sub-zero refrigerators, holding their hands in the air. Agents frisked them and shouted questions at them in English and Spanish while something burned in the oven. Ranger didn't hesitate. He moved down the hallway on the far end of the servants' galley.

Clay stopped cold when Ranger led him into a darkened room filled with racks of costumes, props, and what looked like torture devices. Stunned, he stared at a collection of studded collars, chains, and whips hanging on one wall until Ranger barked repeatedly at the adjacent wall.

"What is it, boy? What do you see?" Clay's adrenaline spiked as his heart rate surged. He ran his hands over the wood-paneled wall that Ranger fixed on. His fingers slid across a tiny indention that he would never have found by looking, and he pressed against it. The wall seemed to give slightly, but then it snapped back, springing open to a hidden passageway. Clay clicked on his mag-light and held it braced below the grip of his gun. Silently, he entered the dark space.

"*Knoze.*" Clay whispered to Ranger, who moved to his left side and remained next to him. Together, they crept toward a lit room at the end of the hall.

"Destroy all the papers, Bob," a rough voice growled. "I'll secure the videos. We will need those to stay alive." *Who the hell is Bob?* Clay slowed his breathing and took another careful step toward the detached voice.

A weaker voice answered. "What's my family going to think? My God, I can't believe this is happening."

"I don't give a flying-fuck about your family right now. We'll be lucky to come through this with our lives. Just burn those goddamn papers!"

Clay peered around the corner. Two men stood in front of a wall of monitors. Every room inside the house was shown on an active feed. He scanned the screens and saw agents and police cuffing staff workers and escorting them outside. The tall, skinny man on the right drew Clay's attention back to the room. He busily fed papers into what looked like a wood-burning stove, while a heavy man shoved what Clay assumed were external hard-drives and other electronics into a hidden safe in the floor.

"FBI," Clay called out. "Raise your hands above your heads."

Both men's heads snapped toward Clay. The tall man shot his hands toward the ceiling, but his bald partner slammed the safe shut and spun the dial before he complied.

"Don't move." Clay ordered.

With tears running down his face, the man with his hands in the air complied, but the fat man darted to his side, pulling a gun from a hip holster as he moved. Ranger sprang forward like a cougar.

For an extended second, there was no sound beyond Clay's rapid-fire pulse. "Drop your weapon!" he shouted.

The gun fired, grazing Ranger as his fangs sunk into the man's forearm. The gunman cried out. Ranger pivoted to the right, blood slick on his black coat. Clay squeezed the trigger of his pistol. The man screamed a second time. Bright red droplets and bone splattered the wall. The shot shattered Barron's fingers. His gun fell to the floor.

"Ranger, *Pust.*" Clay commanded, and Ranger released the man's wrist, though he stood guard with his teeth bared. "George Barron, you're under arrest, you sick son-of-a-bitch."

Two other agents raced into the room with their weapons drawn. Clay kicked the injured man's gun away from his reach before cuffing his sobbing partner. One agent, after checking for more weapons, called for the paramedics. The other took over the arrest for Clay.

Clay scooped Ranger up and carried him out to the sweeping front porch. Sanchez and the rest of the Denver team were there. "Clear a path," Clay shouted. The men moved and Clay laid Ranger on a sunny spot so he could assess his dog's injury.

Sanchez knelt beside them. "Will he be okay?"

Clay pushed Ranger's fur aside and inspected the wound. He let out a long sigh of relief. "Looked worse than it is. Thank God. I don't think he'll even need a stitch." Clay pressed his face into Ranger's side to hide sudden tears. Ranger licked his cheek. One of the paramedics ran over to clean and tend to the graze.

Deputies gathered all the ranch workers into groups. Translators communicated with the people who didn't speak English. They let them know that they were safe now, but that everyone had to go into the Sheriff's Office to give a statement before they received assistance.

"Good work, everyone," Sanchez spoke to the team. He nodded to Clay. "Jennings—great job in there." He looked down. "You too, Ranger."

"It was all Ranger. He found them and took down the gunman." Clay pulled Ranger's favorite chew toy from his vest and gave it to him as a reward.

The arresting agents led George Barron and Robert James out through the front door. Barron's hand was wrapped in thick gauze.

Sanchez addressed the agent that held the man's other arm. "Escort Barron to the ER. As soon as he's patched up, bring him to the jail at the Sheriff's Office. We'll meet you there."

"Yes, sir." The young agent held Barron's elbow in a tight grip as they went down the steps and walked toward the waiting ambulance.

A fine red spray exploded into the air, misting over five nearby agents. An echo from a large caliber rifle sounded seconds after Barron's head snapped to the side. Clay didn't take any time to think. Instinctively, he dove and tackled

Barron, covering the man with his own body. Another shot zipped silently through the air, finding its target in the center of James's forehead. Agents ran for cover, shooting into the forest from where the sniper shots originated. The tall man collapsed into a heap on the ground.

Ranger limped over to Clay, barking frantically. "*Lehne!*" Clay yelled and reached up to pull his dog down beside him. "I'm not hurt, boy. I'm okay." Ranger whined and licked Clay's face.

Several agents laid down cover for Clay. He pushed himself off of Barron, only to find that he'd been covering a dead man. The shot had gone all the way through, in one side of the man's head and out the other. Gore oozed from underneath Barron's head, spreading across the walkway.

Sanchez shouted orders for agents to track the shooter, but Clay knew they wouldn't get there in time. The sniper was a professional who undoubtedly was already gone by the time James's body hit the ground. Clay ground his molars in frustration, and he turned his back on the scene until he regained control.

"Damn it," Clay muttered to no one. He found Sanchez. "There's a safe hidden in the floor of the room where we found Barron and James. Barron locked what I think is video evidence in that safe. We need an armed guard covering that safe until we can get into it. We may not have the men's testimony, but I'd bet my life we have solid evidence, anyway."

"Excellent news, Jennings. Thanks." Sanchez ordered an armed unit to stay with the safe until they could get it opened.

Cameron approached Clay. "I wouldn't want to be the agent who has to watch all those videos."

"No kidding. That's some twisted shit you can never unsee."

Chapter Thirty-Four

Two days had passed since El enrolled Lilly in the Redeeming Hope Rehab Center. Lilly's parents had flown to Denver as soon as they got the news their missing daughter was alive. However, theirs would be a bittersweet reunion. Lilly was no longer the little girl they once knew. She'd seen and done things that no child should have to even be aware of, and there was no way to regain her stolen innocence. On top of that, she faced the long road to sobriety. El had met Lilly's family at Denver International Airport and drove them to their hotel, explaining the best she could during the drive.

The whole family would need to be in counseling, and healing would be a long, painful haul. Top priority was to help Lilly conquer her opioid addiction. Fortunately, the rehab center agreed to make an exception and allowed her parents to see her briefly before they set the visitation limits. After all, this was a unique situation, to be sure.

It had also been two days since El had seen or talked to Clay. He'd changed since they first met. A wistfulness breezed through her as she thought of the first night she saw him at the police station. He had been ready to arrest every prostitute and pimp in the Denver metro area, and woe to anyone driving through, hauling stolen children along I-70. He acted as though with the sheer power of his size and presence he could intimidate his suspects into giving up their pimps.

In a way, it was sad to see him come to realize the problem was bigger than he was. Clay used to be a man who believed he could fix anything. Now, El knew he'd realized that even when he helped pull someone out of a life of sex trafficking, the problems were a long way from being "fixed". *In fact, some things could never be fixed.*

But, for all his machoism and heroic ideas, Clay hadn't judged her for her past. In fact, he was the primary reason she could look at her image in the mirror with a sense of personal hope. She'd forged a life that helped others who struggled through the same hell she'd experienced, but that was always where her hopes and dreams ended. Now she dared to consider that there could be more. She dared to dream.

El turned her phone over and over in her hand, ginning up the courage to take the next step. Finally, she sucked in a great breath and held it while she found Clay's cell number and pressed the call button. The phone rang five times before her call was sent to messages. Her breath gushed out all at once and frantically, she disconnected the call. *Crap! Now he'll see I called and didn't leave a message. I'm such an idiot. Cowgirl up, Eloise!*

El forced herself to call the number again, hoping she wasn't bugging him with a ringtone during a meeting or something. She tapped a pen on the counter while she waited through the rings and message request. "Hi—uh—it's El. Eloise Clark. I guess you know that. You probably only know one El." She closed her eyes and cleared her throat. "I was wondering... since we've gone through a lot, and well, you've changed and—shit, I don't mean that I want to see you *since* you've changed, only that you have. And not that you needed to, or anything." She bit her lips together. Maybe Clay's phone had the option of erasing the message at the end. God, she hoped so. There was no making this train-wreck any better. "Sorry—I'm rambling. I thought maybe we could, you know, if you want—sometime. If after this ridiculous message, you for some crazy reason, would like to call me back, you have my number."

El's stomach flopped, and she clicked end as fast as she could, forgetting to wait and see if she could have erased her embarrassment. She covered her face with her hands and screamed her nerves out into them. *I can't believe I just did that. Oh. My. God! What a dork!*

A VIBRATION ON THE SIDE OF CLAY'S LEG ALERTED HIM TO A call coming in. He kept his phone secured in the side pocket of his training utilities. He was deep in the middle of running through an obstacle course with Ranger, so he let the call go to messaging. His partner's all black coat glistened in the sun as he sailed through the exercise giving no indication he'd been hurt. Clay had to push himself hard to keep up. He'd always found that a hard workout was the best remedy for getting through a tough case. Clay had spent the morning with Ranger, and he planned to spend the afternoon checking in on his old buddy, Gunner.

Clay had trained Gunner when the dog first arrived at the FBI K9 Unit. Another terrific Malinois, whose mission was sniffing for firearms and explosives along with apprehension and attack. Gunner currently worked with the Unit's newest recruit, Special Agent Logan Reed. They made a good pair so far. Reed graduated from the academy two months ago and applied to the FBI's Explosives Detection Team. When he got accepted, they stationed him in Denver. The guy came out of the Army which meant that in the nature of inter-service rivalry, Clay, as a former Marine, was required to give the kid unending rations of shit. He looked forward to it.

His phone buzzed again. Someone was clearly trying to reach him. He pressed his hands onto the chest-high, horizontal log in front of him, and swung his legs together to the right and over the top. At the next log, he pendulumed his legs to the left. He ran with Ranger at his side toward an eight-foot wall. Leaping at the same time as his dog, Clay grasped the top board and with a grunt, pulled himself up. Kicking his leg over the apex, he rolled over and jumped down. Ranger cleared the barricade with ease. They were almost there.

On the back side of the fence, Clay clipped Ranger's vest to a canvas rigging on his own chest. He had only to climb the rope while carrying Ranger, touch the top, and they would be done.

They had an acceptable run, but it wasn't their fastest. "You're getting lazy, old man." Clay held Ranger's favorite chew toy out for him to play with. Ranger bit down on his tug-toy and gave Clay a look as though he understood exactly what Clay had said, and that he also knew who to lay the true blame on. Clay laughed, "Yeah, yeah, I know."

Leaving Ranger to play at liberty, Clay found some shade, chugged a bottle of water, and pulled his phone out to see who had called. Two missed calls from El, and one message. A cold flush of dread for Lilly sent a wave of goose bumps across his sweat covered skin. He quickly pulled up El's message.

As he listened to her disjointed words, a smile spread across his face. El finding the courage to call him was a tremendous step for her. Someday he'd tease her about her message, but not yet. Encouragement was what she needed right now. In fact, instead of calling, Clay would take Ranger over to her house for a visit after they got off work.

Chapter Thirty-Five

Clay's Tahoe pulled up in front of El's house. *Clay's here? Holy crap!* El ran her hands over her t-shirt and cut-off jeans' shorts. She had wadded her hair up into a messy-bun and she didn't even have mascara on. She ran to the bathroom to look in the mirror, her heart clanging against her ribs. No time to fix that mess. She slapped at her cheeks to get some color in her face and bit down on her lips to do the same.

Ding-dong

Dashing out to the living room, El snatched up a dirty plate and glass from lunch. She practically threw them in the sink. On her way to answer the bell, she noticed a sweatshirt on the floor. *Damn him, why didn't he call?* El paused at the door and took a deep breath. Clay reached for the doorbell again as she opened it.

"Oh, hi." Hoping to sound casually surprised instead of full-bore panicked, her voice came out sing-songy.

Clay's head tilted, and his eyes narrowed slightly. A bemused half-smile curled the corners of his mouth. "Hi. I hope it's okay that I stopped by?"

Frozen, El stared at him with what she hoped was a welcoming expression, but the muscles in her face were stiff as she peered at him through her screen door. A low rumble sounded from Ranger's chest and grew to an all-out growl. Clay's head snapped up, and his gaze shot from El to the room behind her.

"What's up, Ranger?" El squatted down. His growl rumbled intermittently.

CLAY MOVED HIS HAND TO REST ON THE GRIP OF HIS SIG, at the ready. He took his partner's guttural warnings seriously. The growling continued, and then Ranger barked. Clay removed his gun from its holster, and without taking his eyes off the interior of El's house asked, "Is someone else here?"

"No." El sounded frightened, and she backed away from the entrance giving him room to enter. Clay quietly pulled open the screen door. He'd set one boot on the landing step when a gray shape darted across the room and flashed down the hall.

Clay glanced over at El's terrified face and laughed. "Do you have a cat?"

She nodded. "Smoke. She's new. I adopted her from the shelter last week." Slowly, the realization of what Ranger had growled at eased the tension in her body. "Ranger! You scared the crap out of me." She leveled a glare at Clay. "If you would have called to tell me you were coming, I would have locked her in my room."

THE SMART-ASS GRIN EL HAD COME TO ADORE, FLASHED across Clay's face. "I didn't want to give you a chance to say no."

"Oh, brother. Let me go shut the door so Smoke doesn't sneak out to torment Ranger." El moved to pass him, and he touched her shoulder to stop her.

"Don't worry about it. This is good training for him. He can learn to stay quietly while your cat prances around the room."

"She doesn't prance."

"Of course she does. She's a cat." Clay pointed to a spot by the couch. "*Lehne.*" Ranger immediately laid down on that spot, but he kept his ears and eyes focused toward the bedroom door. "Besides, I'm pretty sure Ranger likes cats."

"I seriously doubt that," El scoffed. "Can I get you something to drink?"

"Got any soda? I thought we could order a pizza or something."

"Oh—sure." Flustered over the idea of him staying for dinner, El started for the kitchen to get their drinks while Clay made himself comfortable on the couch next to Ranger.

She reached in the fridge for a couple of cans of Pepsi and set them on the counter. Briefly, she touched her hot cheeks with her icy fingers. Her heart danced some sort of jitter-bug, and she purposely slowed her next inhale. She held her breath for a few seconds before she let it out, hoping to bring her pulse rate down. She'd never reacted to Clay's presence like this before, but then again, she'd never called him and left an idiotic message on his phone before either. Nor had he ever shown up unexpected and taken up so much room in her little house.

Stealing one more breath of courage, she returned to the living room.

Clay pulled his phone away from his ear and asked, "What do you like on your pizza?"

Food was the last thing on her mind. "Whatever you want."

His head tilted to the side. "No. What do *you* like?"

Why that question made her nervous, she couldn't guess. She felt oddly under a micro-scope. When had someone last cared about what she liked? "Bacon, for sure, and green-pepper, onion, and mushroom?"

Clay repeated the list to the person taking his order. "It'll be here in about half an hour."

El handed him the can of soda. "Are you hungry now? Want something to snack on before it gets here?" Her mind raced to her empty refrigerator.

"No thanks, this is good." He pointed his chin at Ranger curled up at the end of the couch. "Look at those two." Smoke had nestled herself into Ranger's belly while he napped, and she licked her paws victoriously.

"That was fast. If I wasn't seeing it, I'd never believe it. Smoke has always been afraid of dogs—naturally." El took a picture with her phone. "Need this for proof." She laughed.

"Send me a copy. I can use it for blackmail with Ranger's buddies back at the K9 facility." Their laughter faltered, and an awkward silence draped over the room. Clay's cheeks deepened in color, and he stared at the can in his hands. El never noticed before how long his blond lashes were.

His gaze rose to meet hers. "So, I got your message."

Oh God, here we go. El raised her chin, ready to take what-ever teasing he would send her way. Though she wasn't sure she could deal with his laughing at her. "Yeah?"

"You never said why you called. You said, 'we could... If I wanted to,' but you never mentioned what you thought we could do?"

Heat raced up El's neck and flooded her cheeks. She

checked his eyes for laughter, or guile, but found neither. He was earnest—or at least appeared that way. "I'm sorry. I hate leaving messages. I just thought maybe we could hang out or something." She waved a hand in his general direction. "Like this. This is good." She swallowed. "Isn't it?"

A warm smile spread across his chiseled features, softening the hard angles. "It's better than good. Thanks for letting me stay for dinner. I took a chance just showing up, but I wanted to see you."

"You did?" El wished her tongue would ask before speaking—prior to blurting out desperate sounding phrases.

"I *do*. I want to see a lot of you, El. We can take this at whatever pace you want, as long as you let me spend time with you."

"Oh." El stood stock-still, afraid to move and ruin the moment. She'd never experienced a man simply wanting to be in her presence with no other expectations. She didn't know how to act.

Clay watched her for a few seconds before he eased her discomfort with a new topic. "How are Kendra's dogs working out with your recovery group?"

"They bring a level of comfort to the meetings. They're a warm, friendly distraction the girls can focus their attention on while they share their tough stories. The dogs offer such genuine acceptance requiring no explanations. It's awesome to see. I'm so grateful you connected me with Kendra."

"Good. Ken told me that Baxter seems to have his old energy back too. It's good for him to have a job and feel needed."

"He's the best."

"He's an incredible dog. He lost his leg saving Kendra's life. Did she tell you?"

El nodded. "He's very brave."

"True." Clay settled back against the cushions. "What's going on with Lilly? Did she see her parents yet?"

"Yes. It was wonderful, and awkward, and awful all at the same time. Mr. and Mrs. Simms and their son have rented a month-to-month apartment so they can be close by for visitations when Lilly's ready. They are all starting therapy right away, but their path will be difficult..."

Clay pulled a long swallow from his can. "I can't imagine what they're all going through. It never crossed my mind—the challenges everyone in the entire family will have to face. How about Tom Ross and his family?" He patted the couch next to him.

El sat down and curled her legs underneath her. Even with twelve inches between them, she felt the heat of his body warm hers. "He won't have to deal with the addiction piece, but in some ways, he seems more damaged, more fragile. My heart breaks for that little boy."

"When I think of what they did to those kids, a brutal rage flares inside me." He turned to her and took her hands in his. "Yesterday, we raided the ranch up in Telluride where Lilly and the others were."

El's heart sped. "You did?"

"We arrested the men who organized the party, but a hidden sniper killed them both when deputies escorted them out to the police cars."

"What?"

"Yeah. There are some powerful people out there who don't want their dirty secrets out in the open."

"My God. Did you catch the sniper?"

"No, he was long gone by the time agents found his firing location. Everything was gone, even the shells. All he left were some scuffs in the pine mulch."

"Who sent him, do you think?"

"No telling. There are so many tentacles wrapped around

this convoluted mess. The problem is so big—so multifaceted —it reaches into all corners of society. I feel helpless. It's hard to accept that we'll never see the end of these sick crimes."

"I know." El reached for his forearm. "But, I've found the best thing for me is to put my efforts into doing something positive for the victims. I think the energy that comes from my anger and frustration fuels all of my work—professional and volunteer. I have to do something positive with it, or I'll drown."

Clay covered her hand with his much larger one and laced his fingers with hers. He lifted them to his lips and kissed the back of her hand. "I want to help."

"You are helping." El held his hand with both of hers. "You saved Lilly's life, you've helped to get a handful of kids off the street, you put an end to Baron's operation, and you've only just started."

"When I joined the task-force, all I thought about was arresting the scumbags who traffic people, but honestly, I didn't really let myself think about the victims as actual people. People with families and lives. I never thought much about the horrors they faced, or that so many of them are children." Pain sharpened his clear blue eyes, and a muscle bunched in his jaw. Without thinking about it, El reached up to sooth the tension in his jaw. Maintaining eye contact, he pressed his cheek into her hand. "I can hardly breathe when I think of what you must have suffered through. You're the bravest person I've ever met."

"I'm not really. I'm just a survivor."

"That's what I find brave. Every day, you get up and face your demons in order to help others deal with theirs. You could walk a million other paths, but you chose the hardest one. You're making a difference—one life at a time. I admire that."

A golden, warm glow bloomed in the center of El's chest.

Its comfort stretched tendrils out through her limbs and pulsed in her veins. Was this hope? Perhaps it was something else, something she'd never felt for a man. A pure sense of love and trust. El studied the expression in Clay's eyes as she lifted her mouth to his. She brushed his lips with a gentle kiss. He held her gaze, bringing his hand up to cup her cheek.

She whispered against his mouth, "Thank you."

Epilogue

❦

Six weeks later
A knock sounded on El's front door seconds before it opened. Clay rushed in, followed by Ranger. "Hey, turn on the TV."

"Well, hello to you too." She crossed her arms in mock chagrin. El loved how comfortable they had become with each other over the last month and a half.

Clay grinned. "Sorry." He spanned the room in three strides and greeted her with an energetic kiss. "Hello." He smiled down at her and nuzzled his face in her hair. "You smell like lilacs," he whispered, sending sparks down her spine.

She squirmed. "What are you so excited about?"

"I want to watch the news. Alistair Greer faced further allegations today, and Federal Marshals escorted him to Washington to await his trial there."

El's head spun with disbelief, followed by the elated sensation of lightening bugs buzzing around inside her skull. "They must have more than enough evidence to prosecute him, then." The thought of Lilly having to testify against those monsters made her heart squeeze. The court in Denver had accepted her video testimonies regarding Wayne Horton and Jonny Gold because she was in a rehab facility at the time. Fortunately, since she was still a minor the court would protect her from having to testify in person against Peter Spiel as well. Reliving the horror story for the video was painful enough, but at least she'd never have to see that man again.

"For sure. After Greer stands trial in federal court, he'll have to face the senate and then all the individual states where he committed crimes will want to bring him up on charges too. Colorado and Florida, certainly."

El clasped her hands and held them to her chin. "I can hardly believe it."

Clay found the remote and turned on the TV. El sat next to him and curled up to his side, while Ranger claimed his spot under the end table. Clay rested his arm over El's shoulders and settled back to watch the broadcast.

The senator's disgrace was first up on the national headlines. The talking heads discussed the breaking story while wearing their stoic news expressions. "In shocking news tonight, Senator Alistair Greer has been arrested and is facing felony charges of sex trafficking, and several counts of sexual abuse of a minor. He has been formally charged with soliciting prostitution from a minor, and conspiracy to engage in the sex trafficking of minors. If convicted, the senator will face those federal charges along with a senate impeachment trial. Federal prosecutors will ask for the maximum sentence which could amount to sixty years to life, and fines upwards of $250,000."

Photos of Greer golfing with other familiar state officials and business executives played across the screen. "Allegations led to further investigations in the senator's home state of

Arkansas. Many women have come forward claiming to be victims of the senator's alleged abuse. Five of them have agreed to testify against the senator. There are also two minors, whose identity the FBI is protecting, who will testify to his most egregious, alleged assaults."

The news reporter's counterpart turned toward her. "What happens if Senator Greer gets convicted of these crimes in federal court?"

The woman nodded sagely and glanced at her teleprompter. "If they convict the senator, he will then face a senate impeachment trial, after which several states are lining up to press their own charges against him. When asked for comment, his wife of forty-two years reportedly removed her wedding ring and threw it on the ground, telling reporters, 'This is all I have to say.'"

Video footage of an elegant woman casting a diamond-encrusted ring into the dirt spanned the news reel before her two sons and a daughter surrounded her. The oldest son faced the reporters. "We have no comment at this time. As you can see, this news has come as a brutal shock to our family. Thank you ahead of time,"—his voice broke—"for respecting our privacy in this dark hour." He turned and ushered his mother and siblings into their Georgian mansion.

"My God, those poor people," El murmured.

Clay pulled her close. "Yeah. His family, hell, his entire state. It's disgusting the damage he's caused. Not to mention all the victims he's left in his wake."

The broadcast continued. "Following the news of Senator Greer's arrest, Denver Police arrested Colorado Representative Peter Spiel under similar allegations. Stay tuned for further details regarding these arrests."

"Maybe now the victims can have some closure—find some healing."

"I hope so." The news moved on to the next headline and

Clay clicked off the TV. "How's Lilly doing? Did you talk to her today?"

El's mood deflated, and she sighed. "She's making progress. Sometimes it's one step forward, three or four back."

"Did something happen?"

Her heart weighed heavy, and her chest tightened. "Lilly's family is falling apart. Her parents have taken to blaming each other for what happened, and her brother is getting into trouble with drugs and fighting."

Clay took El's hand and rubbed his thumb across her knuckles as he listened.

"Last I heard her parents were filing for a divorce. Lilly blames herself and then, of course, her recovery suffers."

"She's been through too much."

"She really has, and she's trying to be so brave." El sat up and turned to face Clay on the sofa. "Lilly won't do well if she goes back to her family only to have to deal with all of that, and they don't really want her there, anyway."

Clay cocked his head and studied her until she dropped her chin and stared into her lap.

"So..." She took a great breath. "I'm thinking of becoming her foster mom." Her words picked up speed. "She could live here, with me, until she's ready to stand on her own. She'll be eighteen in only three years and a couple of months." El returned her gaze to Clay and tried to gauge his reaction.

He pressed his lips together, but he said nothing.

El rushed on. "I've already put the idea up to Lilly's parents. They were both relieved and are willing to sign her temporary custody over to me."

"Is this a conflict of interest? I mean with your job?"

"I don't' think so. I'm only fostering. But if it is, then I'll quit."

"How does Lilly feel about it?"

"She cried, but with tears of relief. Maybe even joy, if that's possible in this situation."

Clay raised his eyebrows and rolled his lower lip between his teeth. "Sounds like you've thought a lot about this and have already made up your mind."

"I have." El lifted her chin, ready to face his arguments. She knew this wouldn't be a walk in the park. She wasn't romanticizing anything. God, she understood better than anyone how difficult the next ten years would be for Lilly. That's why she couldn't let her do it alone.

Clay took both of El's hands in his and stared at them for a long moment. His Adam's apple bobbed up and down his neck repeatedly before he swallowed hard and cleared his throat. He lifted his gaze to hers. "What would you say to the idea of us, of you and me, fostering Lilly together?"

All the defensive points El had prepared against the argument she assumed Clay would pose flew away and took her words with them. Her mouth hung open until she finally uttered, "What?"

Clay gave her a bashful smile when he answered. "I'd like us all to be a family. If that's what you want too—and of course, we'd have to ask Lilly if she'd be willing to put up with me and Ranger on a daily basis."

Her shock was so profound, her thoughts had trouble gelling. "What are you saying, Clay?"

"I'm asking you to marry me. I've known a lot of women, and you're the only one I've ever wanted to build a life with. I want to have a family with you, and we could start with Lilly."

Tears streamed down El's face. This was too much to hope for. "I feel like Cinderella."

Clay cocked his head, looking momentarily confused by her reference. Then he smiled. "Well, you're one kick-ass princess then. Didn't Cinderella only have to deal with mean in-laws and some extra chores?" He cupped her cheek and wiped at her tears with his thumb. "This isn't how I wanted to propose. I'll do a better job later, but for now, what do you think? Will you marry me?"

Her mind worked slower than her heart. A bright warmth radiated from her chest outward. Her arms flew around Clay's neck, and she threw herself into him.

He laughed as he caught her and pulled her close. "Is that a yes?"

"It's an, 'I think you're crazy, but I'm not letting you out of it now!'" El kissed him long and sweet and then pushed away, peppering his face with kisses. "Are you sure you want to do this?"

"I've never been more sure of anything in my entire life. I love you, Eloise Clark."

"I love you too." She stroked his cheeks with her fingers. "I never dreamed I'd find someone to love. Someone who could love me back after they knew about my past. It's hard to believe."

She sat back on her heels, keeping his face in her hands. "If you're sure, then yes, I will marry you, Clayton Jennings."

- The End -

THANK YOU SO MUCH FOR READING *CONCEALED CARGO*. I hope you you were moved by it as much as I was. Human trafficking is heartbreaking, but hopefully you enjoyed spending time with Clay and El—and of course, Ranger, who is one of my favorites! Find out what happens with them in the next book in the FBI-K9 Series when we meet Logan and Addison. K9 Gunner returns in the next book too!

Mile-High Mayhem

FBI Agent Logan Reed specializes in explosives. He can track and defuse almost any incendiary device...

Except for the one buried deep inside his soul.

Home from Afghanistan now for two years, Logan has secured the perfect assignment on the FBI-K9 Bomb Squad in Denver. His new partner, a Belgian Malinois named Gunner, is an expertly trained bomb-sniffing dog. He's everything a handler could hope for, except he's not Lobo.

Agent Addison Thorne, a Bomb Technician at the top of her game, doesn't trust the new guy. He's too quiet and never goes out with the crew for a beer after work. There's just something about him that makes her nervous, and nerves aren't what a bomb-tech likes to feel.

Tasked with finding a bomber on the loose in the Mile-High city, the explosives team must discover who is planting the devices and why before the civilian casualties skyrocket. Will they find all the bombs before panic ensues and they are forced to evacuate the capital?

When Reed finds himself in a situation mirroring his painful past, he freezes up. Will Thorne be able to snap him back to the present before it's too late? Can he hold it together or will he fail once again?

Either way, his own life and that of Thorne and Gunner could come to a fiery end.

I would be grateful if you took a minute to write a review for

Concealed Cargo. Reviews help readers find authors that are new to them. Thank you so much for reading!

Review Concealed Cargo

Stay up-to-date on all my new releases and other news. Join my mailing list!

or

Visit my website at Jodi-Burnett.com

Also by Jodi Burnett

Flint River Series

Run For The Hills

Hidden In The Hills

Danger In The Hills

A Flint River Christmas (Free Epilogue)

A Flint River Cookbook (Free Book)

FBI-K9 Thriller Series

Baxter K9 Hero (Free Prequel)

Avenging Adam

Body Count

Concealed Cargo

Mile High Mayhem

Tin Star K9 Series

RENEGADE

MAVERICK

CARNIVAL (Novella)

MARSHAL

JUSTICE

BLOODLINE

TRIFECTA

Acknowledgments

First and foremost, thank you to all the many people who dedicate their lives to putting a stop to this hidden and heinous crime and to all those who rescue victims of human trafficking and work to bring them healing and hope.

Next, I must thank those people who discussed this difficult subject with me, those who taught me to open my eyes, and investigate the horrific crimes involved with the trafficking of human beings—to see the vast extent of this treachery. At the time of this writing (2020), there is great strife in the world. Yet I can think of nothing worse than the wholesale marketing of people for abuse and torture. Now that I know what is going on, my heart is broken and I cannot help but to respond. Thank you especially to Lynn and Mike Russell, who work with Global Connection International to inform the public about the human trafficking and teach us all how we can recognize the problem in our own communities and offer help.

I also want to thank my incredible beta readers who struggled along with me to present to you the book you now hold. It was a difficult story to write and, I know, a tough story to read. Thank you to Chris, Emily, Sarah, Kae, Elle, Jenni, Kay, Sheila, Sheri, and Barb. Thank you for your encouragement and for your willingness to take a hard look at a very dark corner of our world.

Thank you, to you too, dear readers. I sincerely hope that this book inspires you to find ways to help in your own communities. Below, I have listed some organizations that would love to have your time and/or donations. Please take a moment to look at them and help where you can.

How can you help?

Polaris Project
https://polarisproject.org/

Global Connection International
https://www.gciworld.org/

S.A.F.E. Rockies
https://saferockies.org/

Extended Hands of Hope
https://extendedhandsofhope.org/

Restore Innocence
https://www.restoreinnocence.org/

About the Author

Jodi Burnett is a Colorado native. She loves writing Romantic Thrillers from her small ranch southeast of Denver where she also enjoys her horses, complains about her cows, and writes to create a home for her imaginings. Inspired by life in the country, Jodi fosters her creative side by writing, watercolor painting, quilting, and crafting stained-glass. She is a member of Sisters In Crime, Rocky Mountain Fiction Writers, and Novelists Inc.

Jodi-Burnett.com

 facebook.com/JodiBurnettCreations

 twitter.com/jodi_writes

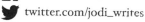 instagram.com/jodiburnettauthor

Made in the USA
Monee, IL
26 July 2023

39920788R00150